WHISPERS IN THE WALLS

A Felix Cross Casefile

E.A. Copen

Grim Cat Press

CHAPTER ONE

QUEENS, NEW YORK

The dead man's voice in my head wouldn't shut the hell up, but I knew how to silence him forever.

I threw myself against the dirty porcelain sink in an unfamiliar bathroom, abandoning the melting bodies in the front room. Liquid vomit splashed against other, older stains. It smelled of bile and rubbing alcohol, the fluid coming out of me. The world tilted as I held on, a grimy floor slipping closer.

No. I won't fall. I can't fall. I might not get back up. The words were thick, broken, slurred in my brain. I'd had too much to drink, and too many pills. Or maybe not enough of both.

"Felix, please." Sean folded his arms behind me and shook his head. I couldn't look directly at him, but I could see his face in the mirror. Sean, with his thin, angular chin, dull red hair, and judging eyes.

I spat into the sink and wiped my fist across my mouth. "Shut up." My arms trembled with the effort of holding myself up.

"Not until you listen. You've got to stop doing this to yourself."

"Fuck you," I spat and tore at the broken mirror on the medicine cabinet.

Behind my cracked reflection, there were shelves and shelves full to bursting with little orange bottles and colorful candy pills, pills that'd normally cost me twenty, thirty, fifty dollars a pop to buy on the street. But when you get the right people to invite you back to their place, sit and drink with them as they fill their veins with poison, and wait just long enough, they don't care if you go rifling through their things. They don't care about anything.

I tore the bottles out of the cabinet one by one, scanning the drug names before popping open a few childproof caps and dumping the bottle contents into my mouth. The pills might have looked like candy, but they tasted like chalk and vitamins all chewed up. Worse than the vomit taste on my tongue.

"What are you doing?" Sean's voice was desperate. He stepped closer, but he couldn't touch me. He couldn't stop me. He wasn't real. He was just some bullshit my broken brain made up to cope with the shit that'd happened to me. Jade had taught me that.

Then again, she'd also told me what wasn't real couldn't hurt me. Guess that was bullshit too.

2

My stomach revolted at swallowing so many pills with nothing to drink, especially since I'd already filled it with cheap vodka. Both tried to come up at once. I spat out what I couldn't swallow and grabbed another bottle, repeating the process. How many oxycodone tablets did it take to kill a man of a hundred and thirty pounds? Fifty? Seventy-five? Better double that to make sure.

"Think about what you're doing, Felix," Sean urged. "Suicide is a cardinal sin. You'll go to Hell."

"I'm already there," I said and swallowed more pills.

A gun would've been faster, surer, but the only gun in my dealer friend's house was tucked in his waistband, just in case someone came through the door and pointed one at him. Not that he'd stir. He was blissfully unaware of everything with heroin snaking through his veins. I could've gone out that way too. Dead and dull to the world, foaming at the mouth and choking on my vomit, but I was too afraid of needles.

Stupid. Stupid, stupid, stupid to be suicidal and too afraid to prick a little skin.

I don't know how many bottles I emptied. It didn't matter. Handful by handful, they went in my mouth. I chewed. I swallowed and tried not to vomit.

Then, out of nowhere, the memory of the

horror at a secluded house in Kentucky surfaced. It was funny. When the memories came, I didn't think about the terrifying demon, the blood spatter all over my naked body, or the people whose brains I'd just bashed out, still twitching on the floor. The things that should've terrified me faded into background noise. All I could remember from that moment was Senator John Hemlock's pleas.

"Help me," he'd screamed. "For God's sake, help me!"

I could've saved him. Instead, I left him there to die. To be ripped apart by an angry demon. To burn alive. To be crushed by the smoldering remains of the house his wife had been so proud of.

Gravity pulled me to the floor where I lay clutching my stomach as it clenched. Suicide by overdose was painful, but not as painful as the crucifixion I'd endured. Not as horrific as knowing Sean was dead and that I had killed him.

"Felix!" Sean's ghost knelt beside me, screaming. I closed my eyes, but I felt his hands on me, lifting my limp body into a lap that wasn't there. "Felix!"

Is this what it takes, I thought sleepily, *to get you to put your arms around me?*

In the next room, bass pumped away on speakers while I lay drunk, drugged, and dying.

Hands closed over mine. Cold hands. Ghost hands. "I'm here, Felix. I'm here with you."

4

WHISPERS IN THE WALLS

But he wasn't. No one was. I was alone on the cold tile of a dirty bathroom floor. Alone in the world, a predicament of my own making.

How long would it take for them to find my body? The so-called friends I'd been staying with wouldn't call the cops when they found me cold and stiff. They wouldn't want to face charges themselves for possession and intent. No, if they were smart, they'd dump my body somewhere else. With no ID, no name, no money, I would be John Doe. Nobody.

But at least it would be quiet.

As I lay on the thin line between sleep and death, a voice called out to me. A voice that wasn't Sean's. Hands gripped the side of my face and someone leaned over me. I wanted to open my eyes, to tell them to go the hell away and let me die in peace, but my eyelids were too heavy.

"He's breathing," said a voice. "Call an ambulance!"

Somewhere distant, I thought it might be Bishop Xavier, but it couldn't be. How would he have found me? I'd covered my tracks too well.

It didn't matter. I was already gone.

Finally, silence.

CHAPTER TWO

SIX WEEKS LATER...

I shuffled my slip-resistant socks against the linoleum floor and watched the second hand on the caged clock spin. Uncomfortable padded chairs squeaked as people shifted their weight. Some people in the circle were just impatient, anxious to be anywhere else. It didn't matter where. Some people found comfort in roaming aimlessly. Others rocked back and forth, constantly in motion, their bodies drawn up as if they were terrified.

But Mickey had been told to sit on his hands. It was the only way to keep him from putting them down his pants. He squirmed in the seat next to me, leaning one way and then the other, his pale, unshaven face twitching with effort.

Across the circle, Reuben told the same story he told every Tuesday at group therapy about how the angels were aliens and God was a computer that could scan our brains. I had to admit, despite being nuts, Reuben was an excellent and compelling public speaker. If he wasn't a paranoid schizophrenic, he would've made a hell of a preacher or a politician. Maybe one day he'd get out of Saint Dymphna's and go places.

And maybe God *was* a computer hive mind controlling the anti-theft scanners at the local Walmart. Anything was possible.

Sister Mary Sabina patted Reuben on the back with a warm, dimpled smile, cutting him off mid-sentence. "Thank you, Reuben. Does anyone else have anything they'd like to share?"

"Why'd you cut him off?" I said. "He was just getting to the good part."

The sister's warm smile faded as she regarded me. "What about you, Felix? Have something to share with the group?"

"Me?" I sat up straighter and shrugged. "Nah, nobody wants to hear my boring stories. I'd love to hear Reuben's theory about credit card chips again. How'd that go, Reuben?"

He opened his mouth only to have Sister Mary Sabina cut him off again by standing. She paced to the middle of our little circle and folded her hands in front of her. "Reuben's had his time. We haven't heard very much from you, Felix, since you joined us here at Saint Dymphna's. Why don't you share a little bit about yourself with the group?"

I glanced around the circle, at all the faces suddenly turned toward me. Even on my best day I wasn't the public speaker Reuben was, and no one there gave a damn about me, or why I was there. I wasn't crazy like the rest of them. I'd just had a bad day, made a bad choice. One minute, I was drinking away my sorrows and the next they were taking away my belt and shoelaces. Now, here I was, measuring the days by which therapy room they shoved me into in the afternoons.

"Felix is an exorcist," said Mickey. He freed his hands from under his ass and they immediately went down his pants, rising and falling with a rhythmic motion.

The sister frowned. "Mickey, mind your hands."

"Sorry, Sister." He pulled his hands back out and sat on them again.

"What's an exorcist?" The skinny fellow three seats away leaned forward, rubbing his bald head. I couldn't recall his name, but he didn't speak up much either.

"Someone who casts out demons, retard!" Simon shouted.

"That's not a n-nice word. Cunt! Fuck! Excuse me, my dick's on fire." George's whole face twitched and yet he still managed a click of the tongue and a whistle.

Even crazy people were too polite to point out the irony of a man with Tourette's calling out someone else's poor choice of words.

One of the rockers in the circle began to rock harder, mumbling to himself.

Sister Mary didn't seem to notice. "That's

right, George. We don't use that word, Simon."

"Demons," whispered another. He drew his fist up and knocked his knuckles repeatedly against the side of his head. "Demons, demons, demons. Whispers in the walls, demons and red eyes and hungry teeth sharp as needles."

Reuben shook his head, bloodshot eyes wide. "It's in his head. Look! The computers are in his head. They scramble your brains up like eggs."

"Demons, teeth, whispers, needles..."

George wrapped his skinny arms around his chest and huddled up as if it were cold. "Sister Mary, may I be excused? Ryan is scaring me and my dick's on fire."

"Demons, teeth, whispers, needles!" The poor man was rocking back and forth hard enough to lift the chair's legs from the floor. They rose and fell with a rhythmic clunk.

Mickey's hands were down his pants and he was going at it again, faster than normal this time.

"All right!" Sister Mary Sabina's hands went up. "Everybody just relax! Let's take a deep breath!"

Reuben surged from his seat, pointing an accusatory finger at me. "See now the prophet who heralds the coming of the damned! He who brings upon us the blood and the darkness! It is you who calls death down upon us, blasphemer! Liar! Unholy one! I cast you out!"

The double doors burst open just as Reuben's voice crescendoed; two orderlies in white pushed through the circle to grab him. Reuben spun and sent one orderly stumbling back, but the other held on long enough to force the syringe of strong sedative into his hip.

Reuben let out a scream that left the chair legs vibrating and ripped the syringe out of his side before shoving the second orderly away. "I will not be silenced! I won't!"

I stood and slid behind my chair as he reached for me, staggering forward a step.

"He comes," Reuben uttered, his voice a strained whisper. "The devil in white!"

Then the orderlies were back on him. This time, Reuben didn't fight. He went down with a knee in his back, limbs folded into a restraint I'd seen half a dozen times since my arrival at the asylum.

Sister Mary pulled several members of our group from their seats and herded us all toward the door with promises of an early snack time. That was enough to get almost everyone moving. After all, it was pudding day; nobody wanted to miss that.

In the hallway, Sister Mary pulled me out of the snack line and marched me to the table without being allowed to retrieve my pudding. "I expected better of you, Felix Cross."

"What? I didn't do anything. You act like I'm the one who got them all riled up. I didn't even want to talk." I leaned around her, counting the plastic containers of pudding on the cart. There was just enough, but there should've been one extra for Reuben. Maybe someone miscounted.

"Group is supposed to be a safe place where we can all talk about our feelings." She folded her hands on the table. "If you're not going to treat the space with some respect, I'm afraid I'll have to talk to Sister Agatha about moving you from green to yellow."

Privileges on the unit were decided according to a traffic light system. Green patients had the most freedoms, which included leaving the unit to go for supervised short walks on the grounds. Those walks were the only time anybody was allowed to smoke. I'd spent two days on yellow when I first arrived. Like hell was I going back on a yellow light.

Man, I could really use a cigarette right now. "It's like I said, Sister." I shrugged. "I didn't say anything. It was the others who brought up demons. I've always made it a point not to talk about that here. You know that."

She sighed and folded her arms. "Felix, I know you're a special case. Bishop X himself entrusted you to our care. But that doesn't mean you're above the law here. A place like Saint Dymphna's only works when everyone follows the rules. That means no talking out of turn during group. Understand?"

The main unit doors opened and buzzed closed behind the two orderlies who'd hauled Reuben away. They went immediately to the front desk, back to laughing and joking with no regard for the patients, some of whom were so traumatized by what they'd just seen, they were sobbing into their pudding.

"What's going to happen to Reuben?" I nodded to the orderlies.

Sister Mary didn't even turn around. "Reuben will be moved to a red light."

"Yeah, but what happens to *him*?"

"Reuben's care isn't your concern. You need to focus on your own mental health, Felix." She sighed and uncrossed her arms. "I'm not going to recommend you be moved to yellow this time, but if there are any further outbursts in group, I'm not going to have a choice. I am, however, going to make a note in your chart so that you and Dr. Bellamy can talk about it."

I wanted to argue with her, to insist I hadn't done anything wrong because I knew I hadn't. Maybe I'd interrupted and spoken out of turn, but I hadn't brought up demons or egged on the crazies when the situation started getting out of control. I was just as disturbed as her, maybe more so. At least Reuben hadn't singled her out in his speech about darkness, death, and the devil in white.

Arguing with Sister Mary Sabina was a pointless endeavor, though. She wasn't going to budge on her position, and I had nothing to negotiate with. She was in charge. I was just one of the crazies to her.

So, I lowered my head and said, "Yes, Sister Mary Sabina. I'm sorry. It won't happen again."

She huffed and nodded in approval. "You can go get your snack now. Then it's free time until evening meeting and devotionals. I expect to see you there tonight, Felix." Sister Mary slid out of the chair and went to the nursing station. A line of tape on the floor in front of the desk designated our space from theirs. We weren't allowed to pass it.

Not that I cared to. At the moment, all I wanted was my pudding. I retrieved it from the dining cart along with a white plastic spoon before returning to my table near the window.

The Saint Dymphna Mental Health Hospital stood on twenty acres of isolated, self-sufficient land outside the tiny town of Louisville, New York. Louisville's claim to fame was its remoteness, being six hours north of New York City. It wasn't a place where I should've been admitted after my idiotic attempt at suicide. That honor should've gone to one of the state mental institutions in the city's public health system. Lucky for me, I had connections.

Bishop X's people found me in that bathroom and took me to the hospital to have my stomach pumped. They'd been tracking my movements for days. I should've known better than to think I could walk away from him and just disappear, but I wanted to believe I was still an anonymous idiot. I didn't work for him.

Apparently, being X's bitch wasn't something you could walk away from. Not even in death.

The bishop himself sat with me in the emergency room while they waited to see if I would make a recovery or die. I had to lay motionless with tubes coming out of every orifice and listen as he read me a devotional. That alone was enough to drive someone to the madhouse.

When they were sure I wasn't going to die, the conversation shifted into what they should do with me. My body was on the mend, but my mind was still broken. I'd never wanted to die. All I wanted was some peace and quiet in my head. If the doctors at Saint Dymphna's could find me a pill that would make Sean's voice go away, then I was willing to try it. I would've tried anything.

"Hey, roomie." Mickey sat down at the table with me with his pudding cup. At least as long as he had that, his hands would be busy. "I got a letter from my sister. She's coming up to visit tomorrow."

"That's great, Mickey."

He opened the pudding and set his spoon aside, preferring to eat it with a finger. I guess that left his other hand free to slip into his pants. The orderlies had tried everything to get him to stop. Even had someone follow him around one day issuing verbal prompts. It worked pretty well, but every time he wasn't focused completely on something else, or sitting on his hands, he'd have one hand on his dick, just pumping away.

Chronic Masturbation Syndrome, they called it. He'd theorized it was everything from a specific expression of OCD to a self-soothing behavior he'd learned when he was abused as a kid. Poor Mickey had tried just about everything short of chemical castration, and the last shrink he saw seemed to think that wouldn't do him much good either. His problem had nothing to do with his sex drive, they said. Mickey was a smart guy, devout, and polite most of the time, but until he dealt with his problem, he just wasn't able to make it out in the world. There were quite a few like that in Saint Dymphna's, good men and women who just needed psychiatric care to get their heads on straight.

And then there were the rest of them. Career patients, bouncing from one inpatient ward to another when they weren't homeless, and prison if they got unlucky. The population of the male ward was about a fifty-fifty split between the two types of patients.

I rolled my eyes. "Mickey, man. Come on."

"Oh, sorry." He pulled his hand out of his pants. "You know I can't help it."

I pushed my pudding away just the same.

"I know. New medicine's not helping?"

He shook his head and leaned in. "To tell you the truth, they added this little white pill this morning. I don't know what it is, but it feels like it's making things worse. Like the whole world is more intense. Faster somehow. My chest is tight. I think it's giving me anxiety."

"Did you tell the nurse?"

He shrugged. "You know what they'll say. Side effects lessen as time goes on. I've got to give it two weeks. What about you? How're your antidepressants treating you?"

I pressed my lips together and stared at the paper lid of the pudding pack. They couldn't even give us the puddings with the foil lids for fear someone would twist it into a shank.

"That good, huh?" Mickey licked pudding from his finger. "Is it the little blue one shaped like an oval? I took that one once. Gave me horrible dry mouth."

"I'm dying for a cigarette."

"You know all the chemicals in those can affect how your antidepressants work? I saw it in a pamphlet in Dr. Bellamy's office. Say, does this pudding taste funny to you?"

"No, not really."

He kept talking, but I'd tuned him out. I was too busy watching the nursing staff. Behind their desk, they had a big dry erase chart on the wall with all our names on it. Next to each name was a colored magnet. Mine was still green, as was Mickey's. Sister Mary Sabina had said they'd be putting Reuben on a red light, but the staff hadn't bothered changing his magnet from yellow to red. Instead, they just erased his name from the board. Why would they do that?

"Say, Mickey, who's Reuben's roommate?" I asked.

"John, I think," said Mickey, swirling his finger around the plastic rim of the pudding cup. "One of the Does. The Chessman."

Great. Reuben had been rooming with one of the rockers in group. Not just that, but a John Doe. There were three no-name patients in the ward. Usually, that was because the cops brought them in off the street. They were too out of their minds to know their names, or else non-verbal. Unless a relative came forward to claim them, they'd be John Does until they were deemed safe to be in society and discharged.

"Why?" Mickey looked up from his pudding cup.

I shrugged. "No reason."

"Reuben's coming back," he said. "They just took him to the rubber room is all. He'll be back soon. Don't you worry about that."

Sean appeared off to my right and behind me, wearing his seminary clothes. He tucked his hands into his pockets. "You know something's wrong here, don't you, Felix? You can feel it. A foulness in the air."

"That's just Eustice," I said, rising and

throwing a glance in the old man's direction. He sat motionless and wide-eyed in his wheelchair in front of a puzzle he'd never finish. "He's shit himself again."

Mickey looked up. "What's that?"

"Nothing. I'm going to go see if I can have my afternoon cigarette now."

"Be back in time for devotion!" Mickey called after me. "It's a good one tonight. Daniel in the Lion's Den!"

No, thanks, I thought. *Been there, done that.*

CHAPTER THREE

There were ghosts on the grounds. Old ghosts, looming, creeping, standing, barely aware that they were there. Dead things in every sense of the word, like beings of foul rot only I could see. Most were just shadows, dark stains on the emotional fabric of Saint Dymphna's. I could make out that they were humanoid, and a rough height estimate, but it was like trying to find a shape in static air.

Before Saint Dymphna's was a medical respite for those with mental health problems, it was an institution that housed the disturbed. That might sound like the same thing, but they're about as different as black and white. It used to be unfashionable to have crazy people out among the rest of society. Wealthy people, or anyone who hoped to become wealthy, locked up their offending relatives, paying a hefty sum to keep them out of the way. No one expected depressed people to get better. The goal wasn't treatment, so much as removing them from view.

In the early nineties, Saint Dymphna's closed its doors for seven long years before reopening as a privately funded and fully accredited psychiatric inpatient facility. They catered to the faithful who struggled with emergency mental health problems, regardless of their ability to pay. For three years in a row, the facility had earned top marks from some agency or another that gave out stars.

All of this I knew from the brochure I'd been given as I went through the admissions process. The little piece of trifold laminated paper proclaimed the place had a long and glorious history of helping people. Saint Dymphna's was a pillar of the community, a place of solace, prayer, and healing.

But for the ghosts, whose bodies rested beneath numbered headstones on the hill, it was Hell on Earth.

There was another subset of patients the brochure didn't tell you about, the ones that got buried on the grounds. The poor, the homeless, the nameless.

I walked among the rows of faded sandstone slabs, my cigarette hanging loosely between two fingers. Smoke curled into the bright May day. Red-breasted robins sang in the apple trees and squirrels chattered happily in the thick forest beyond. Behind me, an orderly in white scrubs kept a polite distance, close enough to grab me if I made a run for it, but far enough back that he wasn't quite a shadow.

A plaque at the entry to the old cemetery

said it was maintained by the Friends of Saint Dymphna's, preserved in its original state for the posterity of history. I couldn't read the sign without thinking about the bodies rotting in the ground beneath my feet. How well had they been preserved, I wondered? These patients without a name. The maddening dead, and the not so very mad at all. I had to remind myself that once it was considered a madness for someone to love reading too much, or for a man to love another man, or a woman to desire independence from her husband. How many had been admitted to this place, having committed no crime other than honesty to their selves?

But things were different now. The world was a kinder place, more open and accepting of mental illness as long as they didn't have to look at it, fund it, include it, or adjust for it.

"Careful now," said Sean, walking along beside me. "You're starting to sound like Jade."

"Is that such a bad thing? I mean, she was right about you. You're dead. A figment of my mind. A coping mechanism, and an unhealthy one at that."

He shrugged. "Better a sober hallucination than a drug-induced coma. Or did you learn nothing from your experience six weeks ago?"

I put the cigarette in my mouth, inhaled. Choking smoke tickled the back of my throat, but I'd long ago become too desensitized to cough. "I learned my madness is something I have to live with. Out there, in here. Doesn't matter, does it? The whole damn world is insane. Some of us are just crazier than others."

"You're not crazy, Felix." He said it with such conviction, but what did he know? He wasn't real. If a figment tells you you're sane, it makes you insane, doesn't it?

"Easy for you to say." I paused in front of one of the numbered graves and gestured to it. "There, number 1143. What do you suppose she was like?"

"Destitute, I'd imagine," said Sean. "Saint Dymphna's ministered a lot to the poor."

"Ministered," I snorted. "More like exploited. This place wasn't self-sufficient all on its own, you know? Someone had to tend the gardens, muck the stables, and milk the cows. New York's finest certainly weren't going to. They came here on respite. The rich will always need the poor. An empire of bones is still an empire, isn't it?"

"I was wrong," said Sean, crossing his arms. "You are completely mad, Felix."

I turned and he was gone, just like always. Another ghost, only he was less real than the ones all around me. I looked to the orderly.

"Fifteen more minutes," he replied to my unasked question.

Fifteen minutes. That was enough time for a conversation with the dead.

If most of the ghosts were static on dead

television stations, then Poe was a weak signal. I had no idea if that was the man's real name, but I didn't want to call him John Doe. There were too many of those in the ward. Since he was particularly grim-looking, much like the old author himself, the name seemed fitting. Like most ghosts, he was a creature of muted grays and faded color, but his eyes looked more alive than most, even if they were sunken and dark.

Poe didn't speak. Most ghosts were just broken records anyway, replaying their deaths or other traumatic moments of their life. Stuck in perpetual motion.

That was fine with me. Finding someone who would listen without interjecting with their problems was a rare thing. Rare enough it'd become a profession. That's what people paid therapists for.

I sat in the grass next to where Poe stood, his chin pressed against his chest and tilted slightly away. The orderly following me wandered just out of earshot and leaned against the gate, crossing his arms and waiting for his assigned crazy person. In this case, me.

"Afternoon, Poe," I said.

Because Poe was a ghost, probably unaware of my presence, he didn't respond.

The first time I'd seen a ghost was shortly after Sean disappeared. I'd been lying in a hospital bed at the time and screamed until my throat was raw and the sedatives kicked in. Since

E.A. COPEN

then, they'd come and go as they pleased. Sometimes, I saw them by the dozens and for weeks at a time. Other times, I could go months without ever spotting one. I'd never figured out why I could see them, or how. Everything since the possession had been strange. I just accepted it as part of my new life.

I would've thought Sean was just another ghost except he spoke to me. Sometimes, ghosts would make sounds, but they never spoke.

I placed the notebook and pen I'd brought with me on my lap and licked my thumb, turning to the first blank page. It was one of those composition books without the metal spiral. No spiral notebooks were allowed on the unit. Too risky.

Dear Sean,

I wish I knew how many days it's been since you left, but I lost count while I was in the hospital. It's a sunny May day, exactly the sort of day you used to like. I've always been more partial to rain and storms myself.

I've checked myself into a psychiatric hospital. Well, I was referred here after doing something stupid. I know you would be furious with me, but you're not here, are you?

At any rate, I don't think medication or behavior therapy will fix what's wrong with me. I know what I need to do, but I'm not sure if I'm ready. Admitting that you're gone and never coming back feels so final. I still feel you here with me every day.

Maybe that's what it's like to lose someone. I wish I knew. I wish I was certain like you used to be. You were always so sure about the soul, God, and Heaven. I could use some of that faith right now. I want to believe you're in a better place, but I can't shake this feeling that something isn't right.

I miss you, Sean. If you were here, even for just a minute, I know I'd find the strength I needed to leave this place and face the truth beyond these walls. Alone, I don't know if I can. I've seen too much to ever sleep soundly at night again.

That's the thing everyone gets wrong about suicidal people. I didn't want to die when I took all those pills. I just wanted the pain of losing you to stop.

Something creaked behind me. I looked up to find Poe staring straight at me with bright green eyes. He hadn't moved from his usual position, but I could swear he wasn't just staring blankly. He was looking straight at me, aware of me. That'd never happened before.

I slowly lowered the notebook I'd been writing in.

His hand shot out, icy cold fingers closing around my bicep. The chill of the grave crawled into my veins, turning my blood into rapidly flowing rivers of ice. Visions flooded my brain, images throbbing like strobe lights during a migraine.

Cold cells. Darkness. Can't move my arms. Everything smells. Damp, dank, dirty. There's no light. Can't get out. Why am I here? What did I do? Footsteps shuffle over the dirty floor on the other side of a metal door. I crawl toward it, the taste of blood in my mouth. Eyes in the grate on the door. Eyes in the walls. Eyes everywhere. I look down at myself, my arms strapped into a straitjacket with rusty stains, and try to remember what I'm being punished for, but there's something wrong with my head. I can't think. I know I'm not crazy. I'm not. I'm not…

A thin strip of cloth tightens around my neck and someone's knee goes into my back. The cloth twists, growing tighter, cutting off air. I try to cry out, to scream that they're killing me, the pain is killing me, but they've taken my voice, and now they've taken my life.

One tear slides down my cheek and I wish I could see my angel one last time. If only I wasn't so ill, so sick to death…

CHAPTER FOUR

THEN

My spine required three surgeries to fix, but I was never paralyzed. Some would say I was lucky. They must never have endured spinal surgery. It left me with six titanium pins in my spine, three-quarters of an inch shorter, and reliant on pain medication just to make it through the day.

You hear all these stories about patients being told they'll never walk again, but it wasn't like that for me. The doctors came in with their stethoscopes, penlights, and white coats, standing around my bed like a trio of reapers. After the surgeon explained what they'd done, the resident physician told me I'd regain the use of my legs with intense physical therapy, but that I shouldn't expect to be in any extreme sports. He laughed and left.

I lay in my bed, breathing, pissing into a catheter tube, with my steady heart rate and only slightly elevated blood pressure. I was alive, but I wasn't living and I knew I never would again.

Barely twenty-five and doomed to walk with a cane for the rest of my life. Not only that, but alone.

I closed my eyes and tried to remember what'd happened, but everything was a blur. The last thing I remembered clearly was that night in the apartment, Sean stretched across my lap with vodka in a coffee mug. It was the last moment everything felt right. I wanted to hold it in my mind and just fade away, remembering it.

A knock on the door frame made my eyes snap open.

The woman standing in the doorway wasn't someone I'd seen before. She wore a smart white button-up shirt with the top button left undone, a blue blazer, and a matching skirt that reached the tops of her knees. Her dark hair had been pulled into a tight bun behind her head. The handle of a cloth backpack hung loosely from her free hand. "Felix Cross?"

I sighed and closed my eyes. "If you're with physical therapy, you're wasting your time. I don't want an appointment."

"Oh?" She brought the backpack in front of her, gripping it with both hands. "And why's that?"

"Because I'm fine."

"Good." She stepped into the room uninvited and stood at the end of the bed. "Then let's get you out of this bed and check you out. Go on. What are you waiting for? Stand up and walk out."

I stared at her. Who the hell was she? The most sarcastic physical therapy secretary ever, probably. "I kind of can't. I'm hooked up to all this shit. Never mind the broken back."

"Is that right? And here I thought you said you were fine." She grabbed the doctor's stool and pulled it closer to the bed. "My name is Jade Haneda, and I'm not with physical therapy, Mr. Cross. I'm a counselor. Your case was referred to me through Bishop Xavier."

I turned my head away and muttered a curse under my breath. He *would* send a shrink. That asshole just couldn't keep out of my business, could he? It wasn't enough that he'd ruined my entire life and probably killed Sean. He had to convince me I was a headcase too. "No offense, Jade, but I don't think a fucking counselor is going to fix my broken spine."

"That's not very priestly language."

"Well, I'm not a priest. I was in seminary, but I'm done with that."

"You graduated?" she bent over and rifled through the backpack.

The position gave me a prime view down her shirt. I couldn't appreciate it much, stuck in that bed, but at least I still had that. "No, I'm resigning without completing the degree."

"Why? X told me you were almost done." She pulled out a yellow legal pad and set it on the bed next to me before rifling through the backpack again.

"Have you ever met a priest in a wheelchair? Broken back kinda comes with mobility problems."

"No, but you're not paralyzed, are you? Otherwise, what's the point of staring at my breasts?" She lifted her head and smiled at me.

I turned away. "No, not paralyzed. Doesn't change the fact that my back and legs are all fucked up now. Even if I did go to physical therapy, I'll never walk without a cane again. I'm a cripple. What kind of God punishes a man whose only real ambition in life was to serve Him?"

She finally sat up, a ballpoint pen pinched between her fingers. "I don't know," Jade said with a shrug. "You're the resident theologian. You'd know better how to answer that than me. I don't even go to church. I'm an atheist myself. You probably wouldn't like my answer."

I turned my head back to look at her, appraising her again. She didn't look like the sort of counselor the diocese would employ. Too young, too attractive, too secular. "What's an atheist doing working for Bishop X?"

"That's not how this works, Mr. Cross. I told you something about me. Now, you tell me something about you." She picked up the legal pad, clicked her pen, and put the tip to paper.

"Like what? My feelings?" There was unfamiliar vitriol in my tone.

Jade shrugged. "If you want. I get paid no

matter what we talk about, so feel free to talk about whatever you want. My job is to listen, not to judge."

I hesitated. "You're not going to try to convince me to go to physical therapy?"

"Why would I do that?"

I started to shrug but stopped. Moving my arms pulled at one of the monitors uncomfortably. "I figure X didn't send you here for the hell of it. He wants me to be quiet about what happened, is that it? Bastard won't come here himself. Doesn't have the balls to threaten me outright, so he sends a snake in a sexy skirt."

She made a note. "I'm not here to threaten you, Mr. Cross."

"Stop calling me that. Felix. Just Felix. And why else would he send you?"

Jade sighed. "I don't know, Felix. Maybe he does give a damn? There are good people in the world, and some of them happen to be a part of your life. Maybe he wants you to get better and recognizes the toll recent events have had on your mental health. Then again, it is much easier to sit in a hospital bed and wallow in self-pity than it is to heal."

"I'm not wallowing." I crossed my arms and turned away.

"Honestly, I don't give a damn. Like I said, I get paid either way, so feel free to wallow or sit there and pout like a petulant child."

My head snapped back toward her. She

sounded angry, but her posture was relaxed, her expression calm. "Just what the hell kind of therapist are you?"

"One who's not going to put up with your bullshit, Felix." Jade set aside the pad of paper and her pen. "I won't bullshit you either. I've seen your chart. I might not be a medical doctor, but I know your prognosis isn't the most optimistic. Now, I can sit here and tell you how lucky you were it wasn't a worse break, that your spinal cord was intact, that there are people on this same ward who would literally give a limb to be as lucky as you. But that would be a waste of my time, wouldn't it? You're a smart guy. You've had plenty of time to stew on that. You don't care that you've been given a second chance because you're not interested in the future. You're stuck in the past, feeling guilty about having survived something you don't think you deserved to."

I turned my head away again.

"It's called survivor's guilt," she said, "and it's common in those who witness the traumatic passing of someone dear to them."

My throat was suddenly tight. Passing. She meant death. Sean was dead and gone. A good man, one of the best I'd ever known, gone from Earth forever and it was my fault. He'd died for me. Even if I couldn't remember the specific sequence of events, I knew that much.

But I didn't want to hear it, not from her.

This bitch didn't know him, didn't understand. How could she? She was just some woman with a degree. All the training in the world wouldn't be the same as having lived through what happened. The last thing I needed was sympathy.

"I'm done," I said. "You can leave."

"I need your signature first." She flipped the legal pad closed and placed a standard billing form on top, clicking the pen twice before handing both to me. "I'm still billing for the full hour. I've got student loans to repay."

"Be my guest," I mumbled, scrawling my signature across the indicated line. "Milk Bishop X and the diocese for all they're worth."

"See?" She smiled and snatched the form, pen, and paper back. "It's not so hard to agree with me on something."

Jade packed her things back into the backpack, slung it over her shoulder, and left just as a nurse came in with my afternoon pain medications.

"What a bitch," I said to the nurse about Jade.

The nurse picked up my wrist to take my pulse. "Maybe so," she said, staring at her watch, "but that's the most I've heard you talk to anyone since they brought you onto the ward."

I thought about what she said and realized she was right. Not only had I said more to Jade than I'd probably said to everyone else combined over the last two weeks, but arguing with her had made me feel *something* other than alone. I'd felt...angry. Was it possible to enjoy an argument?

"What the hell is wrong with me?" I muttered. "If she comes back..."

"You want me to stop that woman?" The nurse snorted and shook her head.

"No. I want to see her again."

The nurse raised an eyebrow and let my wrist go. "Maybe the Lord really does work in mysterious ways," she said, shaking her head again.

She moved aside to grab the little plastic cup full of pills and my heart stopped. There, standing behind her in his favorite black shirt, stood Sean. Blood dripped from his forehead in dark lines. He wiped some away and stared at it a moment before reaching for me, mouthing my name.

CHAPTER FIVE

NOW

I sat up screaming in another hospital bed, this one at Saint Dymphna's. The door burst open and light flooded under the privacy curtain a moment before one of the night-shift sisters pulled it back and shined a flashlight into my eyes.

I squinted and put up my hands.

"Is everything all right?" the sister asked.

"Fine. Just get the light out of my face!"

She finally lowered the flashlight. "You were screaming. Another nightmare?"

"I'm fine." I put my hand to my forehead. Clammy and warm. Too warm and stuffy in that room. I'd read somewhere that sleeping with the heat too high could give you nightmares. That must've been it.

But what I'd just dreamed wasn't so much a nightmare as it was a memory. That'd really happened, every last detail. It was the first time I'd seen Sean after my accident. While seeing him had initially given me nightmares for weeks, I hadn't dreamed of that moment ever before. It seemed odd to dream a memory, especially in such detail, but what about my situation wasn't odd?

The garden. The ghost...

My last memory came flooding back and I shivered. "What time is it?"

"Quarter after three in the morning," answered the sister. "Did you want to come sit in the light for a bit? I can get you a chair if you want, and pray with you."

It must've been around four in the afternoon when I sat down to talk to Poe, maybe a little earlier. I'd lost around twelve hours. Even racking my brain, I couldn't recall anything after Poe grabbed my arm, but the time had passed nonetheless. What happened? I couldn't shake the nagging feeling that I had forgotten something important.

"No." I swallowed and laid back down, pulling the blankets up to my chin. "I'm fine, Sister."

The nun stood at the end of my bed a moment longer, frowning. "If you're sure," she said and stepped back. She drew the curtain closed. "I'll be at the nurse's station if you change your mind."

I listened to her retreating footsteps, watched as the obtuse triangle of light shrank into an acute one, pooled on the right-hand wall. Once she was gone, I lay in the dark, straining my brain, searching for some shred of memory from the last twelve hours.

Mickey had said the devotional was supposed to be Daniel in the Lion's Den, but I didn't remember the reading of it. Sure, I could recall most of the passage from memory, but that was because of my seminary training, not because of the devotional. I couldn't remember who had read it, or if they'd read it well, just like I couldn't recall what I'd had for dinner. Had I taken my evening medicine? Attended evening group? What movie did they play and did I watch it or play cards with Mickey again? Had Reuben ever come back?

On the other side of the curtain, fabric rustled.

"Mickey," I hissed.

The movement stopped.

"Mickey, I know you're awake."

"Yeah," Mickey replied reluctantly. "Your screaming probably woke the whole unit up."

"Sorry about that."

"It's okay, man. I've had worse roommates."

We lay in our respective beds, silent, staring at the same ceiling. Alone, but together.

"Mickey," I whispered, "was I acting weird after I came back from my walk?"

The privacy curtain separating us moved aside. Mickey was sitting up in his bed, the safety rail on one side lowered so he could swing his legs over and face me. "This is a mental hospital, Felix. Everybody acts weird all the time."

"I know, I know." I sat up and hit the button to lower my railing. "But I mean weird for me."

He shrugged. "How should I know? I didn't see you. I had to miss devotional and dinner for some special counseling session." He cupped his hands around his mouth. "They gave me pizza and ice cream. I'm not supposed to tell anyone."

"What sort of special counseling?"

Mickey shifted his weight and glanced at the door. "I don't think I should share. It's kind of private, you know?" He leaned forward. "Why? What did I miss?"

I sighed and laid back down, folding my hands over my chest. "Nothing."

"Whatever." He drew the curtain closed.

I knew I should sleep. My aching, dry eyes and the dull throbbing in my forehead told me I hadn't had enough rest yet, but I couldn't shake the feeling that something was wrong. How did I lose twelve hours of my memory? What'd happened? Where was I?

My throat tightened as I remembered the last time I'd tried to add up missing hours of my life. Then, it'd been a possession, but that couldn't be it. Not this time. Not now. Right? I had none of the other symptoms. No strange powers or unusual knowledge. No sudden change in personality or behavior.

What had happened to me then?

I'll have to discuss it with Jade tomorrow.

She'll be happy to know I was thinking of her at least. I closed my eyes and tried to settle back into sleep.

Fabric rustled nearby.

"Come on, man," I said without opening my eyes. "I'm trying to fucking sleep!"

"What?" came Mickey's voice.

I sighed and turned over so my back was to him. "Just sleep on your hands, Mickey."

The room was silent for a while before it started up again.

"Mickey! I said quit it!"

"I'm not doing anything."

I sat up and jerked the curtain aside to find Mickey with his hands tucked under his hips, though the rhythmic rustling sound was still going. If it wasn't him, then what the hell was I hearing?

Mickey sat up, staring wide-eyed at the only exit to our room. "Do you hear that too?"

Slowly, I looked to the other end of the privacy curtain, waving in some invisible breeze. The shuffling sound was coming from the other side. The floor beneath my bare feet was cold and my legs stiff as I inched along the bed. The closer I came to the curtain, the louder the shuffling became. My fingers gathered a handful of fabric. On a three count, I pulled the curtain back only to find nothing there. The sound had stopped too. Just to make sure, I walked the perimeter of the room. There was nothing there. No one in the room but us and the shadows.

Mickey swallowed. "Do you think maybe we could sleep with the lights on for tonight, Felix?"

I'd never been one to sleep with the lights on, not even after my possession, but even I was freaked out enough by the odd events that I didn't want to sit in the dark. "Yeah," I said, and flipped the lights on.

There was no more shuffling after that, but the nurse doing rounds made us shut off the light after fifteen minutes, leaving us to fall asleep in the dark. I tossed and turned, waiting on the sound to return, on some memory of my lost twelve hours to surface, on the sun to come up. On anything, really. Ninety percent of all time spent in a psychiatric hospital is just that. Waiting.

Eventually, it was boredom rather than any false sense of security that let me drift off. Dreams descended on me like a thin fog. Barely there, a thin veil of fiction on top of reality. I knew I was dreaming, but I couldn't quite grasp what the dream was.

When I woke, it was still dark and I couldn't move. Panic closed a fist around my throat. I was paralyzed, my back broken all over again. Only this time, it was much worse.

The body of a man hung over me, his hair waving in the air like the arms of an anemone.

His face was too shrouded in shadow to make out any detail. Everything except the eyes. Poe's green, glowing eyes. Light shifted through the window, more like passing headlights than the sun. It illuminated the bottom half of his face, revealing cracked, bleeding lips moving at a breakneck pace.

His hands shot out to his sides, grubby fingers rigid. The guttural, agonized scream that came out of his dead mouth shook the bed, rattled the windows, and crawled over my skin like a colony of fire ants. It stretched on to an impossible length, longer than any human lungs might've held out, still unwavering, full of pain and anguish.

I lay under the scream, paralyzed even as my eardrums exploded and blood leaked onto my pillow. Even as the double-reinforced windows shattered and glass fell like rain. Even as Poe's hair fell out, his eyes liquified, and putrid flesh melted from his bones onto me like candle wax in a furnace.

Poe's ghost was silent only when his bones disintegrated into ash and fell over me as a fine gray powder, burying me.

"Felix?"

I blinked and it was over. The night, the ghost, the scream...all of it. I was sitting on the edge of the bed with my hands in my lap, a clear plastic cup pinched between my fingers. A medication cup. Bright sunlight slid under the drawn curtains and danced on the floor at my feet.

Sister Mary Sabina held out a paper cup of water. "Time to take your medicine."

"But this isn't my medicine." I stared down into the plastic cup where the familiar blue antidepressant waited alongside a tiny white pill I'd never seen before.

"That's your new pill," the sister explained gently. "Dr. Bellamy prescribed it for you."

"But I haven't even met with Dr. Bellamy yet." Prescribing an antidepressant to an unseen patient was one thing. I'd come in after a suicide attempt. Antidepressants were to be expected, and sooner rather than later. But this...didn't feel right. "What is it?"

"It should help with the side effects," she said.

"What side effects?"

The bed creaked as sister Mary Sabina sat down next to me. "I read in your chart this morning. The nightmares. The blank stares."

"Blank stares?"

She shrugged. "Sister Agatha said you were completely checked out last night during devotionals. Practically catatonic. You didn't have much of an appetite, either."

So, I had been acting strange the night before. A catatonic state and lost time didn't exactly add up to a possession, but it was enough to make me worry.

"Felix," Sister Mary Sabina said, taking my hand. "I don't know all of what you've been through as an exorcist—"

"I think I prefer demonologist."

"Okay," she said. "Demonologist. The point was, I know you've seen things. Awful things that would take a toll on anyone's mind. You're here to rest and recover, Felix. To find God's purpose for your life again."

"And this pill will help me do that?" I rattled the pills in my little plastic cup.

"God put Dr. Bellamy in your life for a reason. He knows what he's doing, Felix. It's just a pill. Worst case, it does nothing for you and you go right off it. Or, maybe it'll be exactly what you need. Won't know until you try it."

She sounded as if she were talking to a child rather than a full-grown man, but there was still a certain comfort in the way she spoke. It reminded me of my mother. When was the last time I'd spoken to her? She was probably worried sick about me.

I sighed, took the water, and downed both pills in a single gulp.

Sister Mary Sabina beamed. "There, you see? No harm done. Now let's go see what the others are having for breakfast."

"One second. Just need a quick pitstop." I gestured to the bathroom I shared with Mickey.

The sister rose, nodding. "I'll meet you at breakfast then."

I went to take a piss in the bathroom. For all the complaints I had about the country's mental health system—public and private —the one thing I couldn't complain about was the cleanliness of the bathrooms. They kept the toilet cleaner than most tables I'd eaten off of. It almost made me not mind the absence of a lock on the door. There weren't locks on any doors on the ward except for the one that kept us all inside. I wondered what would happen if there was a fire. We'd all be reliant on the staff to open the doors. Still, the likelihood of that was low. The ward was supposed to be a safe place. The safest place in New York for people like me.

I slid my hands under the sensor in the sink to turn on the water and squeezed foaming soap onto my palms from the dispenser on the wall. The reflection of another man stared back at me, a version of Felix Cross with a thinner face and dark circles under his eyes. He dressed in white t-shirts that were two sizes too big and gray sweats with the elastic removed. Six weeks of beard had crawled out of my face in uneven lines, steadily creeping to take over my nose and eyes. I'd been offered an electric razor when I was first admitted, told I could use it under supervision anytime I wanted, but the staff would have to stand at the door and watch me. I wasn't comfortable with that. It was easier to let it grow like everyone else in the ward.

But Jade was coming later that day, and

I looked sick. No, I looked crazy. The beard needed to go.

I finished washing my hands, dried them on a brown paper towel, and reached for the door to push it open.

Poe waited on the other side. He grabbed me by the shirt and pushed me back into the bathroom. Thoughts flashed through my mind, each moving too fast to grasp. He wasn't real. He couldn't be here. He couldn't touch me. No, don't touch!

Thin fingers curled around the fabric of my shirt. Wide green eyes darted back and forth behind limp strands of greasy black hair. "They know. Don't you hear me? They know all about you. They're fucking watching you, man. They put ants in your head when you're asleep! They're eating my brains right out of my skull!" He whispered the words so fast I could barely comprehend what he was saying.

His head jerked up, first to the right, then the left as if he were hearing other voices. His hands trembled. He let me go and backed toward the door. "They'll eat you up too. Eat you up, up, up! Then you'll see. Then you'll know. But it'll be too late for you."

I stood, plastered against the wall, frozen in shock as Poe backed out of the bathroom, but he didn't run for the door or any other rational exit. His bony, waifish body sank into the wall near the door as if the paint was liquid.

When he was gone, I pushed myself forward and fell against the wall he'd disappeared through. It was solid again. Maybe it'd always been solid.

I put a hand to my forehead. It was clammy. Was I hallucinating? And here I thought the medication they were giving me was supposed to make all my crazy symptoms go away, not make them worse.

CHAPTER SIX

At breakfast, I pushed the cold, gelatinous egg around on the tray and rolled a rubbery turkey sausage link back and forth. All around me, other patients chatted with each other in low tones or busied themselves filling out their dining preferences card for the day.

Reuben was still gone, and his name still wasn't on the board. His breakfast hadn't come either, even though he would've filled out a card the morning before.

I leaned in close to Mickey, who was checking boxes on his card with the tiny, dull pencil. "Hey, any news on Reuben?"

"Who?" Mickey said absently.

"Reuben."

He pressed his lips together and shook his head. "Don't know anyone by that name."

"Sure you do, Mickey. Big guy. Well-spoken. Hears voices. They removed him from the ward yesterday during group."

"You're the only one I know of that hears voices here, Felix." Mickey just shook his head again and checked the box for a spaghetti dinner.

I scooted away and looked for someone

else who wasn't so engrossed in their food choices. "Hey, George. Hear any updates on Reuben?"

George clicked his tongue. "I don't like sauerkraut."

"No, not the sandwich. Reuben. The patient? He was here yesterday."

George shrugged.

"Someone must know something," I said a little louder.

"Know something about what?" Sister Mary stepped out from behind the nurse's station, her hands folded neatly in front of her.

I pushed my untouched tray away and met her eyes. "Reuben. Where is he?"

"Reuben?" Her eyebrows pulled together. She'd tried to hide the hint of recognition, but it was there. She knew exactly who I was talking about.

"Don't you start that too." I rose from my seat, placing one hand about three inches over my head. "About this tall. He was a patient here yesterday and you people dragged him away."

"Felix, I'm going to have to ask you to sit down. You're upsetting some of the other patients." Sister Mary Sabina gestured to several of the rockers who'd already started swaying violently back and forth, hugging themselves tightly.

"Then just tell me what happened to Reuben. It's not that hard. Is he okay? Is he coming back? Where did you take him?" I didn't mean for it to come out as aggressive as it did, but they were pissing me off. Even if I was hearing voices and seeing things, I knew Reuben was real. I hadn't imagined what happened in afternoon group yesterday.

The two male orderlies on staff slid out from behind the nurse's station to stand on either side of the sister, just waiting for her to sic them on me. The message was clear. I should sit back down. Return to my seat and waste my time filling out the dining preferences card. Be a good psych patient like the rest of them and stop asking questions.

"Feeling a little paranoid?" asked Sean beside me.

"Shut up," I snapped. "This isn't the fucking time!"

"Control yourself," Sister Mary said sternly, "or you'll have to take a time out, Felix."

"You know it isn't paranoia if you're right," said Sean. "Something's not right here. The ghosts. The missing patient. The medication."

"It doesn't mean anything," I whispered, lowering my head.

The orderlies stepped forward.

"Hey, man. It's okay. Just sit down." Mickey grabbed my hand to pull me back into my seat.

A feeling flooded my body, an awful intense need to move, to touch myself, to feel good because that was what everyone wanted, wasn't it? Everyone else was doing it. They were just too shy to admit it.

So go on, do it. You have to do it.

It wasn't a voice, but it was a command just the same. An itch that needed scratching, that refused to be ignored. As long as I resisted, my stomach twisted in knots and this feeling crawled up my spine just under the skin, a feeling of wrongness. The only thing that would've felt right was putting my hand right down my pants the same way Mickey did whenever he was stressed. And everyone was looking at me. Staring. If they'd just stop staring at me, maybe the feeling would go away. Why wouldn't they stop staring at me?

I yanked my hand away from Mickey's, but the feeling didn't fade immediately. Anger boiled in my chest, as if my body was just a bubbling vat of lava, waiting to explode. It needed out. I needed a reset, to do something to make it all stop.

So I picked up my tray and slammed it against the table, hard enough egg and plastic silverware both struck the ceiling. The tray cracked in half. Both orderlies rushed through the eating area to grab me.

I shouldn't have resisted. I'd already seen first-hand what happened when patients resisted being taken to the time-out room. But I hadn't done anything wrong. I hadn't hurt anyone, and dammit, they were all lying!

I tried to twist away, but it was impossible once they both had me. In a flash of movement, I was on the ground, a chair was overturned, and a knee was in my back, which was screaming in pain. My lungs burned with the effort of gasping with the weight on top of me.

And everyone was still staring at me like I was the crazy one.

Fine. You want a show? I'll give you a damn show. When the orderlies lifted me and dragged me toward the time-out room, I kicked, jumped and twisted, making their jobs difficult. "I know you know who I'm talking about," I screamed at Sister Mary Sabina. "I know you remember him! Where is he, Sister Mary? Where's Reuben?"

She didn't pay any attention to me. The sister marched back behind the nurse's station to the dry erase board and picked up the eraser. She paused with the eraser next to my name and a lance of fear shot through me. It was a threat, a subtle one, but a threat nonetheless. Whatever they'd done to Reuben, they could do to me too in a heartbeat and I would be helpless to stop it.

She moved the eraser to the other side of my name and erased the big green dot, replacing it with a red one.

The orderlies dragged me to a locked door that one of them opened with their name badge on a scanner. Once we were on the other side,

I expected them to move me to another room with rubber walls and some thick observation glass or something. Instead, one of them pushed me against the wall and held me there while the other one jerked my pants down.

"What the hell, are you doing? Stop!" I tried to pull free but one of them smashed the side of my face into the brick wall and held it there.

"It's for your own good," he said. His breath smelled like day-old soda left in the sun beside a lake of rotting garbage.

The other orderly grunted. "Are all these scars in his chart?"

"How the hell should I know?" said the other. "Just dose him already."

Something pinched my hip hard, a deep muscular ache that told me I'd just been injected with something. When they pulled me away from the wall, I was already woozy. Thoughts floated in my brain like bubbles under ice, there, but impossible to hold onto. The world tilted and I found myself staring down at a rubber beige floor while the orderlies contorted my body to their will. I wasn't paralyzed, but my limbs felt like they weighed two tons each. Moving on my own was a near impossibility.

They manipulated my arms into the heavy canvas sleeves of a straitjacket. Buckles jingled as they moved them around, tightening them behind me.

"Bet you thought these were just movie props," said one.

The other laughed.

Maybe they should've been. What was the point of restraining me like that, especially drugged as I was? They could've done whatever they wanted, even without the straitjacket, and I'd be powerless to resist. That was what it was all about, though, wasn't it? The message conveyed who was in charge of my stay at Saint Dymphna's, and that certainly wasn't me.

The two propped me upright and left me in a corner, unable to move my arms and so doped up on whatever they'd injected me with, I could barely keep from drooling on myself.

The one that'd pressed my face into the bricks slapped my cheek. "This is what happens to nosy fucks. There's always one, isn't there?"

"Always one." The other hooked his thumbs into the waist of his white scrubs. "Well, better get back on the unit. You know how they get."

"Yeah," said the first, standing. "When one loses it, others follow. Gotta upstage the last guy."

I tried to shout when they opened the door, but all that came out was a weak grunt.

They shut the door behind them and locked it, leaving me alone in darkness.

CHAPTER SEVEN

Drugs weren't new to me, but whatever they'd given me was. If something like that got onto the street, no one would want it, especially if their trips were anything like mine.

At first, there was nothing. I was nothing. Unlike with normal sleep, however, I was completely aware of the onward march of time. The world moved without me, and I was dead to it. Nothingness swallowed me, cradled me in emptiness, and then spat me back into a nightmare.

I lay face-down in the same rubber room, my cheek pressed to the floor, and turned to one side. The room smelled of sweat and faintly of urine. My straitjacket was too tight, but I'd take that pain, that abuse, compared to everything else that was happening. Someone had pulled my pants down around my ankles and turned me onto my stomach.

Hands moved over my back, the insides of my legs. I tried to shift my weight forward, to get away, but those same hands touching me readjusted me however they wanted.

I felt like I was going to be sick.

"Don't squirm away, darling." Laura's

breathy whisper says in my ear, but it wasn't Laura who pushed inside me from behind, who tore my body wide open and stuck himself into the cracks. I didn't know who he was. I never saw his face, not this time or the hundreds of other times before because he never fucked me that way. Always on my belly, always on the floor. Always here, in that room, alone.

I looked at the camera in the corner, the red ready light blinking, desperate to focus on something, anything other than what was happening to my body. Somewhere, the rape was recorded, backed up on tape. Someone else knew. They had to know. How could they not? You can't record a rape and not know it, let alone dozens and dozens.

"You like that?" panted the man with Laura's voice.

I didn't. It hurt. Like being stabbed from the inside out. All I could picture was the chestburster scene from *Alien*. There was something horrible inside me and it kept poking at the tender flesh, trying to get out. Too much force, and it might come through my belly, blood and guts and all.

The man with Laura's voice told me how much I liked it and why, pointing out all the ways my body said yes even when my brain was screaming, "No, stop! Please, not again. I'll do anything if you just leave me alone."

When he was done, he zipped up his pants

and let me crawl into the corner where I curled into a ball. He gave me pills, putting them onto my tongue one by one. I swallowed them down without water, eager for the medicine to take the pain of reality away. I sat there, numb, until the drugs kicked in, my head leaned against the cool, hard surface of the rubber wall.

Whoever he was, the man with Laura's voice was long gone, the door locked behind him, but part of him will never leave me. He'd carved out a new hole in my stomach, left a void there. I was dirty, unclean, broken. No soap or shower would ever wash away what he'd done, or what he would do to me again almost every day until I died or found some way out of that horrible beige room.

I woke from the dream curled in the corner with my legs drawn up. At some point, I must've kicked enough that my socks came off because my feet were cold and bare. My head throbbed with a dull ache. How much time had passed? Ten minutes? An hour? Three days? I had no way of knowing. They could leave me in that padded room until I starved, and I'd have only hunger to mark the passage of time.

My mouth had become the Sahara, the surface dry and grainy. I had to piss like never before and my stomach...there was a new ache there as if I'd been punched a dozen times right under the belly button.

There was nothing to do by sit and try

to make sense of things. Ironic, right? A man who sees things sitting in the rubber room of a psychiatric hospital, trying to make sense of the world. If the sane people couldn't, what made me think I was so special?

"You need to find out who he was." Sean squatted next to me and then sat down, stretching out his feet. I could see his shoes. They were his favorite pair, nice black loafers. They looked ridiculous. "The ghost."

I closed my eyes against the memory, the dream, the vision...whatever I'd just been through. Even as I'd endured the whole thing, I knew it wasn't happening to me. It was him again, his memory. Poe.

I snorted. "How am I supposed to do that from inside a locked ward?"

"Maybe Jade can help." He shrugged.

"If they let me see her. You have to be on yellow to have visitors. They changed me to red, Sean."

"Then you'll just have to get back on yellow once they let you out of here."

I shook my head. "For all I know, I've already missed visiting hours." I sighed and rested the back of my head against the cool rubber wall. "I don't understand what he wants from me. If he's a ghost, he's dead, right? How the hell am I supposed to help a dead person? How am I supposed to do anything if I can't even help myself?"

Warm fingers ran over my hair, moving it

back into place. It was funny how real he felt sometimes. How alive. "What can I do to prove to you that I'm real and not some hallucination?"

"I don't know. Explain all of this? If you're real, where are you? Why do you disappear every time I look at you?"

"I don't have all the answers, Felix."

"Yes, but you must know—" I broke off abruptly because I had stupidly turned my head to face the man I was speaking with, only to find him gone. "...Something," I finished with a sigh.

The back of my head bounced gently off the rubber wall. I didn't have enough information to make sense of what was happening at Saint Dymphna's. Maybe I was just being paranoid. There were valid reasons why Reuben might leave and not come back. Maybe he'd been seriously hurt and they'd had to take him to another hospital. Maybe the sisters thought he was too much to handle and transferred him elsewhere. A family member might've even showed up to check him out. That happened sometimes, even when patients weren't well. Sometimes, the family would just come and take them home because they felt guilty. Was that so difficult to believe?

Then again, why would everyone on the ward pretend like he'd never been there in the first place? If only one of them had forgotten him, I could've accepted that. Yet the nurses and all the patients acted like there had never been a Reuben at all. It wasn't fair to Reuben to erase him from existence. He was real and I would have to prove it if I wanted to know what happened to him.

All his records will be locked behind a wall of patient-provider privilege, I thought, and closed my eyes. I couldn't access any of that, but I did know someone who could.

CHAPTER EIGHT

THEN

Jade returned that first week, this time with something for me to hold. She brought a little red foam ball and had me squeeze it whenever I got angry. By the end of the session, I'd crushed it to half its normal size, and she'd filled four pages with notes.

She closed the session, flipping her notepad closed after a heated argument over the ethics of opioid pain relievers and their availability to addicts. "Of course," she said, "you'll probably be on them for the rest of your life. You might think differently when you realize how hard it is to fill the prescription once you're discharged."

"Discharged?" I snorted. "That won't be anytime soon."

"Is Friday soon enough?"

I stared at her, mashing what was left of the little red ball in my fist. "Friday? But I'm not any better."

She stood and shrugged her purse onto her shoulder. "You're refusing treatment. If you're not going to follow the medical advice of your doctors, there's no reason for ycu to be here. You'll be released to a long-term care facility with twenty-four-hour nursing."

"A nursing home? You're advising them to send me to a nursing home?" I threw the ball at her face.

She caught it as if we were playing a game. "It's not up to me. Your doctor wanted to send you there last week. I was supposed to convince you otherwise, but...well, you're not a danger to yourself or others. You're just a stubborn ass-hole; they don't make medicine for that. If you don't want to get better, no amount of arguing with me is going to change that."

I lay in the uncomfortable bed, stewing for nearly an hour before I slammed my thumb onto the nurse call button. They sent in Dimitri, an overweight nurse with glasses who I could always count on to give it to me straight.

He poked his head through the curtains and pushed his glasses up his wide nose. "You need your bed adjusted again?"

"Is it true? I'm supposed to be discharged Friday?"

Dimitri stepped into the room. "I don't know for sure, but there's been talk. The hospital's only here to get you stabilized. You're not going to die, and your back's healed better than expected."

I tipped my head back, staring at the ceiling. "Even if I start physical therapy?"

"Probably. Like I said, you're out of the danger zone." He came over to stand beside the bed where he adjusted one of the monitors that'd been beeping a while ago. "Thing is, if you get back on your feet, the care facility doesn't have to be your last stop. Not everybody gets a second chance like you, you know."

I hated it when he said that to me, the second chance line. I didn't feel like I'd gotten a second chance at anything. The nurses had called me a survivor, lucky, even an inspiration. I hated being called those things because I still felt like a failure. Sean was gone, and Marci was dead. My broken body was just a side effect of the bad things that had happened to other people.

Jade was right about one thing, though. I wasn't going to achieve anything lying in bed for the rest of my life. Sean wouldn't want me like that, and I wouldn't want him to see me that way either. As miserable as I was, the last thing I wanted was to be helpless for the rest of my life.

"Get the chair," I said to Dimitri.

He hesitated. "You want to get out of bed?"

"I want that bitch to drop dead of surprise when she comes back on Friday." I tossed the blankets aside and looked down at my skinny legs. In the six weeks I'd been in the hospital recovering, I'd lost a lot of muscle mass, and while I could move my legs, they weren't even strong enough to hold me up.

"Hey, works for me." He finished adjusting the monitor and went to grab a wheelchair.

It took a long time for him to return with a chair and another nurse to help hold me up long enough to move to the chair. Long enough I almost lost my will to do it until I saw the crushed red ball sitting on the dresser across the room. Jade had left it there on purpose.

When they brought the chair in, I tried to sit up, but putting any pressure on my lower back was agonizing. I winced and had to lay back down a moment to work through the pain.

"Take it easy, man. We'll get you there." Dimitri's hand closed on my forearm.

In an instant, the world spun out of control. A new feeling flooded my mind and body. Fear. Betrayal. A new kind of helpless anger. My throat was suddenly raw from screams I'd never uttered, my heart broken. The ever-present dull throb in my forehead shifted, encircling my eyes in the sort of ache that only comes from prolonged crying. An emptiness settled in the pit of my chest, a void that only grew the longer the feeling went on, and something else coiled around it. A dark, bitter feeling. A wall of hate, raw and vicious, kept the void boxed in behind an impenetrable wall.

Mixed into all those feelings was such a profound feeling of loss and loneliness that I couldn't even begin to grapple with the size of it. My pain suddenly felt so small, like a pinhead next to a bowling ball.

The emotions rushed by in an instant, like wind in the window of a speeding car, and then they were gone before I even had time to process. I found myself in the front seat of a car crashing in slow motion, felt tiny pebbles of glass brush against my skin. The push-pull of gravity tugged from all the wrong directions. My arms had flown up, weightless in the death spin. Drops of crimson floated in the air above my head.

The car was all wrong. Somehow, the back seat had meshed with the front and the hood had caved in, pressing against my head. If I'd been an inch taller, my head would've been crushed.

Lucky, whispered a voice from nowhere. *So lucky*.

A tiny arm with tiny fingers and chipped red paint on the fingernails floated in the spraying glass.

Don't turn around. That voice again.

I didn't listen.

The body in the backseat belonged to a child. She wore pink jelly sandals, a yellow tank top and blue jean shorts with teardrop jewels on the pockets. Something had come through the windshield in the shape of a sword and severed her head nearly from her body. It hung on by a nothing more than a thin thread of flesh but that wouldn't be the image that would give me nightmares for years to come. That would be her eyes, the look of utter terror reflected in them. The look of betrayal. Why hadn't I saved her?

The scene lingered a second, maybe two, before it played in reverse and I was sucked back through time and space to where I lay, screaming in my hospital bed. Blood coated the front of me from the neck down. Despite the pain it caused me, I kicked like a wild man and dug my fingers like claws into the mattress.

I realized only then that I was screaming a name repeatedly. "Taylor!"

Dimitri had frozen, his eyes wide, hands hovering inches over me, shocked into inaction. Not an easy thing to do to a hospital nurse.

"Dimitri!" The other nurse rushed back to my bedside with some cloth she used to clean up some of the blood in search of the source.

Her shout shook him from his trance and he jumped into action, moving away from the bed to snap on a pair of sterile latex gloves before he returned to assess my vitals. "Felix, can you hear me?"

My breathing was fast, my chest suddenly tight. The images and the feeling had faded from my vision, but not from my memory. I reached out, clamping my hand onto his sleeve. "You couldn't have saved her."

He paused.

"Get Doctor Philips in here," said the other nurse. "I can't find the source of the bleeding."

Dimitri stared at me. "It's his nose."

The other nurse frowned. "I can see that, Dimitri, but there's no reason..."

"I broke my nose in that car accident." Dimitri lowered his hand. "But how would you know that? Nobody here knows..."

He didn't finish because my limbs stiffened, my eyes rolled back and I fell into a seizure.

***

"Do you think he could be manipulating this somehow?" The nurse's voice was the first one I heard coming back from being under sedation. I didn't know how long I'd been out, but the heavy feeling in my limbs was familiar. I'd been like that every time I came out of surgery.

"His EEG showed a slight abnormality, but it's not consistent with anything else I've ever seen." That was Doctor Philips. They stood off to my right somewhere. If I could've opened my eyes, I would've looked at them, but I still hadn't completely come around. "There's something unusual happening in Felix's brain, I just don't know what it is. Neurology will have to take this one. Get him in for the full gamut."

"You want another MRI?"

"And a CT scan at the very least."

"But he knew her name," said Dimitri. "How could he have known my daughter's name? I don't...I can't even talk about her after what happened. And that nosebleed. I had one just like it after the accident."

"I'm ruling it psychosomatic," said Doctor Philips. "His body is under a lot of stress and the machine took some elevated blood pressure readings earlier today."

Dimitri snorted. "Probably from when that counselor was in here. She's a handful all by herself, but when the two of them get to arguing...she seemed to do him good though. He wanted to get into the chair today. First time he wanted much of anything since he came to the ward."

"I'll talk to her," the doctor continued. "Prep him for more testing."

Over the next two days, the tests were nonstop. They took me for three EEGs, an MRI, a CT scan, and drew enough blood to feed a whole family of vampires. The seizure left me weak and tired for a few hours, but I made a full recovery. I was well enough to be annoyed by all the new tests, at least.

Friday morning, they came to tell me they didn't know anything useful. The only abnormalities were in my EEGs, but they weren't far enough outside the normal parameters for anyone to be concerned. Doctor Philips added an anti-seizure medication to my daily routine and kept me through the weekend for monitoring.

On Friday afternoon, Jade knocked on the door just as I was finishing my first physical therapy appointment. The therapist had put me through a lot, supporting my legs as I tried to lift them on my own, but he seemed hopeful that I'd be up and walking in no time.

As the one therapist left, my shrink folded her arms and leaned against the door frame with a big smile. "Well, look at you. I thought I was wasting my time with you, Felix Cross."

I picked up the mangled remains of the red foam ball she'd left behind and tossed it to her. "As it turns out, apparently all I need is a children's toy to destroy and a little elevated blood pressure."

She dropped the ball into the trash can and came to sit in her normal spot. "They told me what happened the other day. How are you feeling?"

"Tired of being poked and prodded. Ready to get back on my feet and get out of here. If I never have another seizure, it'll be too soon."

"I meant the other thing. The...vision, I guess you'd say." She put one knee over the other, folded her fingers overtop her leg, and quirked an eyebrow. "Really freaked Dimitri out."

I sighed and leaned back against my pillow. "Imagine how I felt."

I didn't tell her the flash I'd had with Dimitri wasn't the only one. Every time a nurse touched my skin with their bare hands, I had other, smaller flashes. Usually, it was just a feeling, whatever their prevailing emotion was. Irritation, boredom, exhaustion. Even the strongest interaction was nothing like what I'd experienced with Dimitri. It had been a vivid waking nightmare, and not one I wanted to live through again. That was why I insisted the physical therapist wear gloves. Anyone who touched me had to. I'd even made them put it in my chart.

Jade leaned forward. "Tell me about it."

"What? The vision?" I stretched out my toes. The therapist said any movement was good movement. "I'd rather not."

Jade sighed. "This might come as a surprise to you," she said, digging in her backpack, "but you're not the only one with unusual abilities in the world." She pulled a manila folder from her backpack and tossed it into my lap.

I stared at the folder without touching it. "What's this?"

"Open it."

My knee-jerk reaction was the same as it always was whenever Jade told me to do something. I resisted, glaring at her.

She folded her hands over her knee again. "You know why you hate being told what to do so much, Felix? It's fear. Fear of being out of control again. That's hyper-vigilance in action, a common symptom of post-traumatic stress disorder."

"You're not a psychiatrist. You can't diagnose me." I slid a thumb under the cover of the folder, moving it over the paper inside.

"I don't need to. You know I'm right. It's not a weakness to be affected by the things you've seen, what you've gone through. Most people don't realize how fragile a thing the human psyche is. It takes strength to accept you're not perfect."

"Fine then. You're the expert. What's the cure for PTSD?" I finally flipped open the folder. The first page inside was an incident report. It almost looked like a police report, but not quite. It detailed a date, time, and basic description of the people and injuries involved in some event. I'd have to do more than skim to pick up on what that event was.

"There's no cure," Jade continued, "but a lot of people get relief from their symptoms in a variety of ways. Counseling and medication mostly."

I grunted my response. I was too busy reading the file she'd dropped in front of me. It wasn't a single incident report, but several grouped into a single summary with the actual reports on the subsequent pages. The reports with the oldest dates were first, complaints that someone had been breaking into a home in Woodhaven belonging to James and Valarie Miller. Nothing was reported missing, but quite a few things had been moved around. The report after that said someone had broken in and stacked the kitchen chairs in a pyramid on top of the table. The police recommended they install a home security system.

The next two pages after that were time

logs from the security company, indicating that the alarm had been tripped frequently—several times a day—over two weeks. The company inspected the alarm system and found no fault, but the family asked them to remove it anyway so they could sleep through the night.

On the fifth page, a building inspection report giving the family home a clean bill of health, followed by similar reports from the gas, power, and water companies. All of them had the same complaint from the family: knocking on the walls.

My throat felt tight. Too tight. I looked up from the folder. "What is this, Jade?"

She met my eyes. It felt like a challenge. "What do you think it is?"

I didn't answer, instead turning to the next page, one of the last pages in the file. It was a hospital admissions form. Some of the information had been blacked out for privacy, but it appeared Mrs. Miller had fallen down the stairs and broken her legs. No, not fallen. She said she had been pushed, despite being alone in the house.

My heart hammered in my chest as I turned to the final page, a full-color photograph of Mrs. Valerie Miller in her hospital bed with all the tubes coming out of her. Her face was black and blue. She didn't look like she'd been pushed down the stairs. She looked like she'd been in a car accident.

She looked like I had when I arrived at the

hospital.

I closed the file quickly and pushed it away, trying to calm my breathing. "What the hell is this? Why show me all this? I don't want to see it."

"Why not?" Jade asked.

"I just don't."

"You could help them, you know. The Millers?" She picked the folder up, pushed it toward me again. "What you went through was awful, but it doesn't have to be for nothing. You can use what you know to help other people who might be facing the same thing."

"I said I don't want to see it!" I pushed the folder violently off the bed. It fell open on the floor, papers flying everywhere.

A moment later, the door opened, and a nurse stepped past the privacy curtain. "Is everything all right in here?"

"We're fine." Jade bent over to pick up the scattered pages.

The nurse frowned. "If his blood pressure spikes, Doctor Philips said—"

"I know what Doctor Philips said." Jade lifted her head to give the nurse a warning glare as sharp as needles.

The nurse backed away. She was smarter than me.

While Jade picked up the fallen pages, I crossed my arms to hide that I was hugging myself to calm down. Seeing that picture of Mrs.

Miller had brought back that feeling, that awful feeling. Helplessness, they called it, but the word failed to encompass its meaning.

When the demon had been in control of my body, I had been worse than helpless. I was powerless. People thought that meant I was out of control, but that was only part of how it'd felt. I had been terrified, constantly screaming on the inside. When it broke my back and left me temporarily paralyzed, that was only an outward manifestation of what it had been doing to me on the inside for weeks.

It hadn't happened all at once. It began with whispers in the back of my head, thoughts that weren't mine. I would be in the kitchen making a sandwich, or something equally harmless, and suddenly be overwhelmed with a morbid curiosity. How much would I bleed if I cut my finger off? Would the blood be light or dark? Would it spray or drip? How long did I think I could stay conscious after I did it? Ten seconds? Twenty? My mind would play the scenario in my head in vivid detail as if I'd already done it, except there was no pain. Only the curiosity, the fascination with self-harm.

Those fascinations grew into beliefs that came out of nowhere.

In the two years we'd lived together, I'd always been comfortable with Sean. Comfortable enough that it shouldn't have been a shock, really, all the things I'd considered in hindsight.

We were as close as—probably closer than—two friends should be, sharing everything. Sometimes, the two of us were like sisters, giggling over the stupidest things. The next minute, we'd be having a serious chat about how afraid we both were of going out into the world with only a white collar to protect us.

But as the demon grew inside me, it planted seeds of guilt, shame...things I'd never felt before when it came to him. "You're disgusting," the demon would whisper. "A slacker idiot. You really think Sean could care about someone like you? Someone who can't even pass his electives? You're worthless. Everyone hates you."

On and on in the back of my mind, he wore me down, telling me all the things that were wrong with me. I would spend hours in front of the mirror, staring at small blemishes, at parts of my body that weren't trim enough, weren't thick enough, weren't muscular enough. I was all wrong in every way. A face not even a mother could love.

The true horror of possession wasn't the helplessness, the powerlessness, or the fear of what a demon might do to my body. It had always been how easily I had let it win.

Jade was wrong. I was weak.

"I can't help anybody," I said from my hospital bed. "I don't want to help anybody."

"That's not what you said in your essay application to the New York Theological School."

I turned back to Jade. She wasn't looking at me, but tucking the folder underneath the phone, just within reach. "How do you know what I wrote?"

"Bishop X is the one who sent me, remember? He shared your school record with me. To help with treatment." She smiled. It was a fake smile, too practiced. Unnatural on her face. I was more used to the resting bitch face than the smile, and so was she.

"It doesn't matter," I said with a shrug. "I'm not the person I was back then. I'm not the man I was just a few months ago."

Jade's eyes flicked to the doorway. I couldn't see what she was looking at, but it was probably one of the nurses again, reminding her that she was supposed to leave if my blood pressure spiked high. She stood and slung the backpack over her shoulder. "Just because the demon broke you doesn't mean you have to let it win, Felix. Not everyone has a friend like Sean."

She left early that day, but her words stayed with me. I sat in bed long after she'd left, wondering what Sean would do and staring at the unopened file. It took me six hours to mutter, "Fuck it," and retrieve it from where she'd left it, but I'd always been stubborn.

CHAPTER NINE

NOW

I trembled. Whether it was from the drugs wearing off or the nonstop slew of painful visions flooding my psyche in the rubber room, I didn't know. The visions came and went, always similar. Always painful to endure, but as painful as they were to me, I knew they had to be worse for Poe.

I knew I was reliving Poe's pain because he stood in the corner the whole time, watching, his pale face sullen and covered by long, greasy strands of dark hair. Between visions, he curled up in the same corner, opposite me, and wept. I wanted to go comfort him, but after enduring the torturous visions of multiple assaults, the very idea of being close to anyone was appalling.

I felt dirty. All I wanted was a shower and to melt back into nothing.

Eventually, the door opened. Dr. Bellamy came into the rubber room, his polished shoes squeaking against the rubber floor. He was young for a psychiatrist. That was my first thought. Whenever I pictured a psychiatrist in my head, I saw an older gentleman with a neat salt and pepper beard and a quaint hat. Dr. Bellamy couldn't have been over forty-five, still young enough to be attractive to most women. That he was an impeccable dresser didn't hurt either. When he came into the rubber room, he was wearing a white dress shirt that had somehow kept from getting any wrinkles and a flawless burgundy tie.

I lifted my head from the wall, focused entirely on the tie. "Isn't it a little dangerous to wear one of those around here?"

He smiled a tight-lipped, intelligent smile and tugged on the tie. It came loose from his neck. "Magnetic. Marvelous, isn't it? I've always said, one should never sacrifice the enjoyment of fashion for the functionality of work." He reattached the tie, smoothed it over his chest and folded his hands together in front of him. "And what about you, Mr. Cross? Ready to trade out the function of the straitjacket for something more fashionable?"

"I wouldn't call sweatpants and plain shirts the height of fashion." I shifted with a grunt.

Dr. Bellamy waved two new orderlies in. There must've been a shift change while I was in there. They tugged and pulled me roughly away from the corner, positioning me so they could undo the buckles at my back. It left me nervous, especially after what I'd just spent the last few hours experiencing.

"How are your visions?" Dr. Bellamy asked.

I twisted so I could look at him over my shoulder. It was the first time anyone on the ward had called them visions instead of hallucinations. "I see dead people."

He smiled and stifled a small laugh. So, the good doctor had more of a sense of humor than everyone else. That was good to know. "And do you see any dead people right now?"

I glanced at the corner where Poe had been standing only a short while ago. He'd vanished. "No."

The orderlies finished unbuckling me and slid the straitjacket away. My shoulders ached, suddenly having nothing squeezing them tight. I rolled them one at a time and twisted my neck one way, then the other to pop it.

"We haven't spoken yet have we, Mr. Cross?"

"No. I've only been on the ward a few days, plus the weekend." Still should've seen me before you prescribed a new pill, asshole.

"Well, I'm sure you're eager to get cleaned up and put on some new clothes, but I'd like to remedy that." He held out his hand to help me up.

I stared at his bare palm and stayed where I was.

He seemed to remember a moment after. "Ah, that's right. You don't like to be touched."

"It triggers the visions." I pulled myself to my feet and leaned against the rubber wall.

"Of course." Dr. Bellamy folded his hands behind his back.

"You don't believe me, do you?"

He shrugged. "Quite simply, it's not my job to believe or disbelieve. If you say you have visions of some other time and place, then I have no doubt you're certainly experiencing something. They say Saint Joan had visions of the divine."

"Yeah, and they burned her at the stake." I pushed away from the wall toward the doctor.

To his credit, he didn't flinch. He smiled. "Humanity hasn't always been so forward-thinking. I can't discredit your visions, Mr. Cross. Only treat the illness of your mind. If the visions do not stem from the same source as your other ailment, and they aren't causing you any distress, then I see no reason to address them today. You're here for a reason, and that is because you want to be well. But you will have to do your part. You can't go around destroying breakfast trays because you're overwhelmed by the voices."

"Voice," I corrected. "There's only one."

"And what kinds of things does he say to you?"

What he meant to ask was if the voices were telling me to hurt people, myself included. I rubbed my sore shoulder. "It's not like that.

Sean wouldn't say things like that. He was a good person. It's just that…he's gone now."

"So Sean is one of these dead people you see?" His eyebrows rose expectantly.

I suppose I did sound crazy, didn't I?

"Mr. Cross, have you ever experienced a seizure?"

I blinked. Definitely not the question I expected to have thrown at me next. "Yeah. I've had enough they revoked my driver's license, but I haven't had one in years."

"And would you say your sleep is…problematic?"

"What are you getting at, Doctor?"

He smiled and stepped aside. "Nothing, nothing. Just working when I should be getting out of your way. You must be familiar with how difficult it is to leave the job behind. We can talk about it later if you'd like. After you've gotten cleaned up." He checked his watch. "Say in half an hour? That should give us time to finish so you can still make visiting hours this evening."

I frowned. "Am I allowed to have visitors? Sister Mary Sabina moved me to a red light."

"I'll have you moved to yellow after our talk." He nodded and gestured to the door. "You're free to go."

If only that were true, I thought, wrapping my arms around my middle. The thing about getting checked into a psychiatric hospital is that it's easy to get in. Getting out, however, meant getting two doctors to sign off on your chart, declaring you were no longer a danger to yourself or others. Getting tossed into the time-out room had set me back a few days. I'd be there longer now than before.

I went back to my room, avoiding the public area of the ward as much as possible. I did get a look at the clock on the wall behind its steel cage. It was three in the afternoon and everyone else was in afternoon group. I had missed lunch, but it was just as well. I didn't have much of an appetite anyway.

After a quick shower in lukewarm water, since there was never any hot water on the ward, I reported to the line of tape at the nurse's station to tell them I was ready to meet with Dr. Bellamy. Sister Mary Sabina was no longer at the desk. The afternoon nurse today was a plump, bubbly woman with glasses and rosy cheeks named Sister Glorianna. She took it upon herself to escort me from the ward to Dr. Bellamy's office.

The only way off the ward was to go with one of the sisters, each of which had been given a magnetic keycard. Before I could leave, however, I had to undergo a search to make sure I wasn't taking anything I shouldn't. Sister Glorianna led me to a small closet-sized room next to the nurse's station and stood at the door, bored, while I undressed to my underwear. She made me open my mouth, squat, bend over, and shake out the seams of my underwear too for good measure. It was beyond embarrassing. I'd passed that mile marker the moment I'd been admitted. To be embarrassed, you had to have some sense of dignity left. Dignity is the first thing the mentally ill have to leave at the door in a place like Saint Dymphna's.

Once she was satisfied, I dressed again, she slid her keycard over the lock and led me into a narrow hallway that terminated in an elevator. Instead of going to the elevator, however, we went to the door on the right. It was the first door I'd seen since my admission with a regular door handle and not a safety handle.

Beyond the door was a normal waiting room with uncomfortable chairs in a line, old magazines on an end table, and a receptionist's desk that sat empty. There was a television on the wall with an empty screen. Not a speck of dust on anything.

Dr. Bellamy was waiting for me, his hands tucked into his pockets. He'd donned a black suit jacket and buttoned it, giving his upper body a more trimmed look. He wore the suit with all the comfort most people had in jeans. "Welcome, Felix. Thank you, Sister Glorianna."

"Just page the unit when you're done with him," said the sister and she left me in the psychiatrist's care.

"You're not afraid I'll kill you or something?" I said. I don't know why I said it. It just struck me as odd that I would be left alone with someone so soon after being restrained and caged like a dangerous animal.

The room suddenly felt small, quiet. I missed the familiar buzz of many stranger's voices at once.

He smiled slightly. "I fear not death for the sooner I die, the longer I shall be immortal."

The quote sounded familiar, but I couldn't place it. "Socrates?"

"Benjamin Franklin," the doctor corrected and gestured down a short hallway to his office. "Are you a student of history, Felix Cross?"

"I've always found history boring. I like philosophy."

"Ah, they told me you liked to argue." He opened the door for me.

I hesitated at the entrance. The room on the other side looked like it was in another building. In place of the drab, white walls he had walls painted the color of oxidized copper. Like every psychiatrist, he had a stack of diplomas on the wall, but several framed paintings alongside them. He had two bookcases in the room, but only one shelf dedicated to psychology. Among the rest, I spied several biographies on Edison, Tesla, and Newton. The rest of his books were classic works of fiction, everything from *Moby Dick* to *Frankenstein*.

At the center of the room—which was much larger than I expected—was a wide desk in a modern minimalist style, all dark, polished wood. A laptop rested in the center of it, directly under an adjustable desk lamp. Everything was neat and orderly with edges sitting at ninety-degree angles.

Dr. Bellamy gestured to the comfortable-looking armchair on the far side of the desk. I took it and he slid into the wheeled computer chair on the other side. "What made such a stubborn, argumentative man as yourself want to become a priest?"

I shrugged and adjusted how I was sitting. "I guess I haven't always been this much of a bastard. It started after—"

"After your possession?" he cut in. "Bishop X filled in some blanks for me. I spoke with him this morning, actually. Apparently, a lot of your troubles began after then. It said in your medical history that you suffered a spinal fracture. Perhaps your stubbornness worked out in your favor then. Not many find themselves ambulatory after such an event. What I find interesting is that this is the only injury anyone seems to talk about in your past medical history. In many cases, demoniacs suffer multiple injuries. Did you have any others that I might've overlooked?"

I shook my head. "No, not that I can recall. The broken back was enough."

"The bishop noted that you may have taken some illicit substances in the past."

I laughed. "Of course he'd say that."

"Is he wrong?"

"No, but I'm not stupid. I didn't fuck up my brain with drugs."

"That's not what I'm saying at all." He raised his hands slightly, defensively. "I'm only trying to differentiate your condition from a host of others with similar presentations. It's entirely possible these visions you're experiencing aren't psychological phenomena at all, but rather a symptom of a complex seizure disorder. Or, we could be looking at a late-onset case of schizoaffective disorder. The two things present with nearly identical symptoms, but the treatment for each will make the other worse. Are you following me so far?"

"I guess." It was refreshing to have someone talk to me like I wasn't a complete nutcase. In fact, Dr. Bellamy spoke to me almost as if I were his equal. "I've never had a head injury."

"The reason we ask about head injuries is because of the brain." He opened his computer and pressed the power button. "But it's not the only organ that can cause neurological symptoms if damaged. The spinal cord is a sort of pre-mammalian brain all on its own. In fact, it's capable of making its own decisions and taking its own actions when certain external stimuli are introduced. It's why you jerk your hand away from a hot pan before your brain registers the pain of being burned. That's because the message only makes it as far as your spinal cord before action is taken, and the pain message takes a flash longer to get to the brain. This is a simple explanation, of course. Suffice it to say a spinal injury could be responsible for a whole host of long-term neurological symptoms. You could have some messages being scrambled when they reach the brain, sensory input. With the post-traumatic stress disorder and an extended period without any treatment, it's hard to tell. How is your sleep, by the way?"

He'd already asked me once before, hadn't he? It was getting difficult to keep track of everything he was saying. I understood the words coming out of his mouth, but there was still a slight fog in my brain from the earlier drug they'd injected into my hip. "I have a lot of nightmares," I said.

"Not surprising." He typed something into the computer. "PTSD and schizophrenia have a high co-morbidity, you know."

"Don't listen to him," said Sean beside me. "You're not schizophrenic."

"That's just what the voices in my head would say," I mumbled.

Dr. Bellamy looked up from his computer. "What's that?"

"I'm not just in your head, Felix," Sean said.

"Felix, are you hearing the voice right now? Can you tell me what it's saying to you?"

I swallowed. "Sean says not to listen to you. I'm not schizophrenic. It's not all in my head. I want to believe him but..."

Dr. Bellamy closed the laptop and slid it aside. "Who was he to you? This Sean?"

I squeezed my eyes closed. "He was everything. He died for me. Saved me."

"And you wanted to save him?"

I nodded, my throat tight.

We sat in the doctor's office in silence a long moment before he clicked his pen and pulled out a pad of prescription papers, scribbling furiously as he spoke. "I'm going to prescribe you a new medicine, Felix. Now, we're going to introduce it to your regimen slowly, but you should know that this drug, while effective, may increase your risk of having another seizure. If that happens, we can try another. There are other side effects, but we'll get you a pamphlet on them later. You'll be taking this in the evening since it has a strong sedative effect."

"Will it help?" I asked, my voice sounding too small.

He looked up from writing and smiled. "I hope so. We'll get you well, Felix. I promise."

CHAPTER TEN

I returned to the unit after my visit with Dr. Bellamy, feeling ashamed of my behavior earlier for no reason. Reuben was real. I knew it just as I knew my name. That didn't mean I had to interrogate the staff and patients the way I had. I should've kept it together better. Maybe I was losing it.

It was dinnertime on the unit. Since I hadn't filled out my dining preferences card, my tray contained a generic dinner that was supposed to be meatloaf, mashed potatoes, and mixed vegetables. Instead, I got a slab of brown, a scoop of gray, and a pile of cold lima beans. I pushed everything around on the tray without eating any of it. Strangely, my stomach didn't seem to mind not eating all day. I was more thirsty than anything, even after downing the little plastic cup of apple juice that came with dinner.

"Not hungry, Felix?" Sister Glorianna tilted her head to the side. She stood off to my left, hands folded in front of her neatly.

I shook my head and finally pushed the tray away. "Maybe it's a side effect of the new medicine, but I'm not at all hungry."

She smiled. "Well, to be honest, I don't blame you. That doesn't look at all appetizing, does it? And with the day you've had, I imagine you might not be feeling so well. Would you rather go and lie down?"

My eyes traveled to the double doors that separated the male psych ward from the hallway where Dr. Bellamy's office waited. It was the only door in and out, the same door my visitors would have to come through to see me. "No, thanks. I'm expecting visitors tonight."

"Me too!" Mickey's voice had an extra jolt of excitement in it. He spooned a heaping pile of rice into his mouth. "My sister's coming. She's really coming this time."

"That's good to hear." Sister Glorianna smiled and moved on to the next group of patients.

I tapped my fingers on the table surface, avoiding Mickey's eyes across from me. The chances that his sister would actually show up this week were slim to none and everyone knew it. Mickey had been at Saint Dymphna's for eight weeks, and every week when visiting day rolled around, he boasted his sister Julia would come for a visit. Yet she never came. There was always some excuse she left him with. Either her car broke down, or there was an accident on the freeway, or her job wouldn't give her the night off. Julia was the only family Mickey had that gave a damn according to him, but maybe he was just being hopeful. Still, it was hard to watch his excitement, knowing he was probably just going to be let down again.

"Mickey," I said gently, "if she doesn't show this week..."

He cut me off, shaking his head. "No, Julia is coming. She said so when I talked to her on the phone. She said she'd move Heaven and Earth to be here tonight and I believe her."

"I know. I'm just saying."

"She's coming," Mickey said with more force. "What would you know? You haven't even been here a week."

"You told me yourself the day I got here, Mickey."

He refused to look at me. "Yeah, well, that was before she called me. Julia's coming. You'll see."

Mickey finished his meal in silence, and I let him. Maybe he'd be right this time and she'd show up.

I took my tray back to the dining cart, slid it into the appropriate slot, and went to sit in my assigned chair for visiting hours. Strange butterflies woke in my stomach, spinning, turning, fluttering their wings against my ribcage. As I sat, I worried about what Jade would think of me. Would she yell at me? I could take that. It wouldn't be the first time she'd reprimanded me for doing something stupid, and she'd be right.

What I couldn't take would be the sympathetic looks, the careful phrasing, the worried fussing. I told myself Jade wouldn't be like that, she'd never been like that, but what if it wasn't just Jade who came to see me? X might come, and I didn't want to endure his false sympathy.

People were lining up in the hallway outside the ward behind another strip of tape on the floor. I strained my neck to try and see through the tiny windows on the safety doors, but I couldn't see anyone I recognized.

When the doors finally opened, it wasn't to let people enter. Sister Glorianna went out into the hall with a big locker on wheels and had everyone surrender their personal items. Purses, cell phones, wallets, ties, belts...They all went into the locker on shelves and then the sister locked them up tight out of our reach.

The doors opened a second time and people filed through in a neat, orderly line. Spouses, mothers, fathers, sisters, brothers all with loved ones locked up at Saint Dymphna's. They split off into little groups around the public area. Some went straight to the shelf of games and puzzles while others sat down in front of the cartoon movie playing on the television.

When I saw who had come to see me, my stomach dropped into my toes. I had expected Jade, and she was there, but she came with her arm wrapped around a thin, white-haired, and fragile-looking version of my mother.

How long had it been since I'd seen her? It must've been the week before everything went to hell with me and Sean. I'd driven across the city to help her repair a leaky pipe when the landlord didn't bother.

Ten years. I hadn't seen my mother for ten years. The realization made me want to crumble back into the nothing, to run to my room and hide. She hadn't done anything to deserve what I'd done to her, the worry I'd caused. I wanted to melt into the carpet and leak through the floor at the sight of her.

She smiled widely, let go of Jade's arm, and had pulled me into a hug before I could run. "It's so good to see you, Felix! I've missed you!"

"It's…good to see you too, Mom." I shot a glare in Jade's direction. She could've warned me she was bringing my mother.

Jade just smiled.

"Let me see you." My mother stepped back, her hands still on my arms. "Oh, you look so thin. What are they feeding you in here?"

"I'm fine, Mom."

She frowned. "Well, if you were fine, you wouldn't be here, would you?"

"Felix is here to get better." Jade placed a hand on my mother's shoulder and Mom let me go. She guided us both back to the table I'd been sitting at and we sank into the chairs.

My mother sat on the very edge of hers, leaning forward as if she might have to catch me if I fell. Pale fingertips moved thin strands of graying hair aside. I wanted to take her hand, to apologize, to tell her I hadn't meant to cut her out of my life, but I knew if I did, I would see things I shouldn't.

So, instead, I swallowed and stared at the floor between my feet. "I..." My throat was suddenly too tight to speak. I tried to clear it several times.

She shook her head. When she spoke, it sounded as if she were struggling to hold back tears. "I almost didn't come. I wasn't sure you wanted to see me."

"Of course I do. I mean, maybe not like this. I just...I didn't mean for ten years to pass. I was just *busy*."

"Now you sound like your father." A small, bitter laugh escaped. "But let's not talk about all the things that've gone wrong in the past. We're here now, together. You're just so grown up. I just can't believe it. And this beard!" She reached to put her hand on the side of my face.

I flinched away.

My mother looked like I'd slapped her.

"Remember," Jade whispered, "Felix doesn't like to be touched."

Mom nodded and folded her hands in her lap. "Jade told me about your...visions." The last word sounded strange coming from her, like her mouth didn't quite know how to form the word.

"I'm not crazy, Mom." I shook my head. "I

know that's what a crazy person would say. The visions are real. I think. No one here believes me, but I know I feel something."

Jade frowned. "I've seen you have them before, Felix. I know they're real, but maybe that's the sort of thing you shouldn't be talking about here." She glanced at Sister Glorianna standing ten paces away, supervising the visits.

"I'm not in here because I have experiences when I touch people." I rubbed the back of my head. "I overdosed on some pills."

Jade's attention snapped back to me. "You were stupid."

There it was, the venom I knew so well.

"I know." I leaned forward, gripping the back of my skull with both hands. "I know it was stupid. I just...you don't have to live with this. You don't know what it's like. He's right there, always talking to me just out of my line of sight. Every time I hear his voice, it's like losing him all over again. I couldn't take it anymore, Jade. I didn't want to die. I just wanted this to stop. I want my life back."

My mother put a hand over her mouth, saying nothing.

"I don't know if they have a pill or a therapy in here to do that," I continued, "but I'm willing to try anything. I can't be who I've been the last ten years, bouncing from place to place with no future. I can't keep living the past, hoping someday Sean is going to resurface. What the hell is the point? He's gone. He's dead. He died because of me, and I have to find a way to live with that."

"It's not your fault." Jade put a hand on my leg and squeezed. "I know you don't want to believe that."

"You've always been the self-blaming sort," said my mother, lowering her hand. "When he was younger, there was a stray cat that he liked to feed. He brought it inside one day. We weren't allowed to bring it inside because of the terms of our lease so I made him take it back out. The poor thing was hit by a car not too long after. He blamed himself."

"I blamed the landlord." I raised my head. "His precious carpet was more important than a living creature. That's when I learned capitalists were assholes."

"You can't blame him. It was his carpet, and carpet is expensive," my mother said.

"It's *carpet*. And he would've been litter-trained. I would've made sure." I threw my hands up. "Why are we even talking about this?"

My mother shrank back slightly. "I'm sorry. I didn't mean to bring up something so upsetting. Let's change the topic. Jade tells me you traveled a lot. Did you ever meet anyone in your travels?"

"Tammy..." Jade shook her head.

"What? My son is a handsome man, even if he could stand to eat a little more and shave.

I'm sure there were plenty of interesting women along the way you shared your time with. I want to hear about them."

"You really don't," I said.

My mother looked from Jade to me and back to Jade. "You two must think I'm an idiot. Please, you think a mother doesn't know her own son?" She looked straight at me, through me practically the way only an irritated mother could. "Felix, I know you like boys and girls. You always have. I knew when you were in the third grade and you had that crush on...what was his name? Devon or something."

I crossed my arms and leaned back into my chair, wishing I could sink through it into the floor again. "It was Dillon and he was my friend."

Mom rolled her eyes and smiled. "I know a crush when I see one. Your dad thought you might be gay and almost lost it, but I knew. I have a good sense about these things."

There was a long, awkward pause. During it, I glanced around at all the other groups of people talking about nothing, ignoring the elephants in their proverbial rooms. Almost everyone had someone there to see them. Everyone except for Mickey. He sat alone at his table, his hands folded on top of it and not in his pants for once. His legs bounced up and down with nervous tension, but his eyes were locked on the door as if Julia might come walking through it if he only stared hard enough.

"So?" said my mother with a sly smile. "Tell me about the boys *and* the girls."

Some of us don't deserve our mothers. I was lucky enough to be one of them. Realizing that just made me feel worse for Mickey.

I cleared my throat. "I'd rather not talk about that with you, Mom. One second." I got up out of my chair and walked over to Mickey's table. "Hey, man."

"Hey," he said, staring at the door.

"Do you want to come meet my mom?"

He swallowed and forced a polite smile. "No. I don't want to miss Julia when she comes. She said she was coming this week."

I stood at the lonely table for an extra beat in case he changed his mind before I walked back to sink slowly into the chair. "I hate this place."

"Any idea when you're getting out?" Jade shifted her weight so she could focus on me more rather than studying the other patients. She was analyzing them in her head. That's what Jade did. She couldn't help herself.

I shook my head and leaned in closer. "No, and not to sound paranoid, but something weird is going on here, Jade. There was another patient here, Reuben, who got taken away yesterday. They erased him from the board and everyone's pretending like he was never here."

Jade and my mother exchanged a glance before Jade asked, "Are you sure he was here?"

"I only see one person who isn't there,

Jade. I know Reuben was a patient here. I know they took him away and he hasn't been back, and everyone is acting weird."

"Well, it is a psych ward." Jade shrugged. "Things are always weird."

"Not like this." I bit my bottom lip, considering how to approach the subject without sounding like I'd lost my mind. Jade should've been one of the few people who would believe me no matter what. After all we'd been through, she'd never doubted me when I said I saw things. Why would that change because I was in a psych ward? Why was I so afraid she wouldn't believe me? "And there are ghosts here. I keep seeing one in particular. Not just seeing him, but hearing him. He can touch me, Jade, and ever since he has, I've been seeing the things that happened to him. Terrible things."

Jade's frowned deepened. "What medications did you say they put you on?"

"I'm *not* hallucinating this!" I curled my hands into fists until the knuckles hurt. "You know I've seen things before. You just fucking said so! Why would I make this up?"

She sighed. "I don't doubt that you believe you're seeing a ghost and experiencing his trauma. It might even be possible that it's really happening to you. But you have to realize, from where I'm sitting, hearing you say this, seeing you like this...it's hard to swallow. I have to be sure. The Church investigates possessions as psychiatric illness first, don't they? Well, I have to do the same. If we can rationally explain all of this, wouldn't that be better?"

"You're not *listening* to me, Jade! I'm telling you this is happening and asking for your help!"

She raised her hands, gesturing for me to keep it down. I'd raised my voice and attracted the attention of Sister Glorianna. She walked over, smiling. "Is everything okay here?"

Jade smiled wider. "We're fine. Just having a heated debate. You know Felix."

Sister Glorianna glanced at me. "He does like to argue," she said. "Just keep it down, please. We don't want to disturb the rest of the patients, do we?"

"No, of course not." Jade's smile lasted until Sister Glorianna was out of earshot. "God, I hate nuns."

"I thought you went to Catholic school?" I said.

Jade crossed one leg over the other. "I did. Why do you think I hate them?"

I leaned even further forward. "Jade, I want you to look into this place. Dig up what you can."

"With what to go on?" She shook her head. "Unless you've got a full name and dates, I won't be able to find anything."

"Not even about Reuben?"

Jade shook her head again. "Not without

a last name. Even then, it wouldn't be easy. I'm not connected to his case the way I am to yours. I can't just walk into the records department and demand patient documents because I want them. I have to justify that."

"What about historical records? Stuff from years ago? Before the place reopened? Can you find out what happened here?" It was a long shot, but knowing the history of the facility might come in useful, even if I couldn't find out what had happened to Poe or Reuben. "And if there are complaints about the facility, those would be in some public archive somewhere, right? You could find that."

"I could," she agreed with a sigh. "But Felix, you have to realize there are lots of reasons why a patient might leave the unit and not come back. There are even reasons why the staff wouldn't want to talk about him once he was gone. Privacy reasons."

"Why don't the patients remember him then? Something's not right here, Jade. I'm telling you." I pointed emphatically to my palm. "And don't say I'm just being paranoid. I'm always paranoid. That's how I've survived as long as I have."

"You poor thing." My mother must've forgotten Jade's warning because she wrapped her hands around mine.

Worry bled from her into me, guilt, sadness, loneliness.

Pain.

I pulled away.

She blinked. "Oh, I'm so sorry. I forgot."

I flexed my fingers. "Your arthritis. It's worse?"

Mom let out a heavy sigh and lowered her hands. "Right now, I'm more concerned about you. Do you have anywhere to go once you get out of here? Somewhere to stay? I've got a little one-bedroom off of 71st Street. It's not much, but the couch has a pull-out bed, and I could use the company."

I wanted to tell her no. The last thing I wanted to do at my age was move back in with my mother, especially since we'd been apart for ten years. It felt like we didn't know each other anymore. While my mom was one of the most wonderful people I'd ever met, she was still my mom. She didn't know how to be anything else. After holding her hand, though, and knowing how alone she felt, I couldn't find the words.

"We'll talk about it after," I said.

"You'll need a safe release plan before they'll discharge you." Jade nodded to my mother. "And they'll be much more inclined to release you into the care of local family than on your own."

"After," I insisted and let my back rest against the wooden supports of the chair. "Or later at least. I'm less worried about what I'll do when I get out of here and more about if I can get out. Please, Jade. It would make me feel a lot better if you'd find that information for me. And maybe get in touch with X. I have some questions for him."

"I can try, but no promises on either front," Jade said.

A sister at the front desk rang a bell and announced that visiting hour was ending. I glanced over at Mickey, still sitting alone at his table, and my chest ached.

"It was so good to see you," said my mother, standing.

I stood with her. She wanted to hug me as she'd done when she came in but was unsure now. She must've seen it in my face, the change when I picked up on what she was feeling. It made my chest hurt more.

I put my arms around my mother and pulled her into a loose hug, careful not to let my skin touch hers. Her shoulders jerked and I heard her sniffle in my ear, holding back tears.

She took a step back, hands gripping my shoulders again. "I love you, Felix, no matter what. Please don't ever forget that."

"I won't," I promised, and I meant it. What I couldn't tell her was that I hadn't forgotten. In the moment I tried to take my own life, I simply couldn't think through the pain.

As I watched my mother leave with Jade at her side, Sean appeared beside me, arms crossed. "She's wonderful, your mother."

I nodded. "She would've loved you."

"I don't understand." Mickey's small voice grabbed my attention. He sat at the table, staring at his hands, still folded neatly on the table. Another sister sat with him, listening. "I don't understand. Why would she lie? Why didn't she come?" He looked as if he were about to break down into tears.

The sister patted his hands. "Why don't we go for a special walk, just you and me, and we can talk about it?"

Mickey nodded and they rose. The sister gave a subtle nod to Sister Glorianna behind the desk. She picked up the black eraser and pressed it to the board next to Mickey's name, but paused when she saw me looking at her. We traded a long look, me and the sister.

She narrowed her eyes.

Go on, I thought. *Take Mickey and try to tell me he wasn't real. I fucking dare you.*

Her fingers curled around the eraser, bending it in her hand. Then, with a familiar, pleasant smile at me, she lowered it back to the tray, leaving Mickey's name untouched.

CHAPTER ELEVEN

THEN

I was on my feet within days, covering short distances helped by a walker. I thought I would be ashamed to move around the public areas of the hospital with it, scooting along as if I were a ninety-year-old and not a man in my twenties. Instead, the pain and difficulty of movement pissed me off enough that I was more determined to conquer the hallway than anything else.

Step after agonizing step, I made it across the room and then into the hall, but they wouldn't let me go further. Not until Jade came back, at least. She convinced them to let me off the ward where I was recovering for a fifteen-minute walk. She stayed beside me as I made slow, steady steps, grunting and sweating in the stale air of the hospital corridor.

"I'm supposed to ask you about your post-discharge plans," she said, shifting the folder under her arm. I'd asked her to bring it along.

I grunted and scooted the walker further ahead of me before pulling my body along after it. "Don't have any."

"What about your apartment near the theological school?" She leaned forward to watch my face.

I shook my head and kept moving. "The lease lapsed when the semester ended." I had let it. There was no reason for me to go back there. Too many memories. It wouldn't be the same without Sean.

"What about your mother? Will you move back in with her?"

I stopped to give Jade a hard look. "My mother has three jobs and can barely make rent. You think she wants to take care of her cripple son on top of that? No way in hell I'm laying my burdens on her."

"Well," said Jade without turning to look at me, "maybe you should talk to her about it. If your mother loves you—and I'm certain she does—you'll never be a burden to her."

"She'll say I'm not, but I will be. You only have to put up with me a couple of hours a week. Imagine having to live with me." I stopped in front of a set of locked glass doors, the entrance to another inpatient ward.

"So, you plan to sleep on the streets?" Jade slid her keycard over the lock and punched in a code. The doors slid open with a whisper. "You're stubborn, Felix Cross, but even you must realize that's a death sentence."

We shuffled onto the ward, crawling at a snail's pace. A bleached white hallway with white tile floors and low ceilings with fluorescent lights pressed in too tight, like a throat flexing to swallow me, funneling me toward a stomach somewhere I couldn't see.

Jade was right. I had no home, no friends, no job, and no hopes of securing one either. With my back so messed up, and my joints still healing from other trauma, it would be a long time before I could sit at a desk for eight hours, let alone stand. Without a completed college degree, I had no marketable skills either. Maybe I could get some church somewhere to feel sorry for me and put me up in a halfway house, but that was the best I could hope for. I'd let my life fall apart while I was in the hospital, and now there was no hope of putting it back together.

Jade swept up in front of me, blocking my path forward by putting a hand on my walker. "You're going to have to leave the hospital one way or another, and sooner rather than later, Felix. You can't keep running away from reality."

I leaned forward, face hovering inches from hers, and ground out, "I'm not running anywhere at this pace." With a jerk, I freed the walker from her gasp and painstakingly redirected myself so I could move around her.

Valerie Miller was in room 417, resting but awake. The television was off, and it was just after lunch. No one was with her when I knocked on the door. A woman in her forties leaned forward on the bed, her brown hair knotted into a bun atop her head. Both her legs were in casts— one bright blue plaster, the other hidden under a plastic brace. She frowned at me, but recognition touched her face when Jade appeared next to me.

"Jade, you're early," said Mrs. Miller. "I wasn't expecting you for another hour at least."

"I have someone who'd like to meet you," said Jade as she slipped into the room ahead of me. "Valerie, this is Felix Cross. Felix, Valerie Miller."

Valerie offered a nervous smile, the sort of smile everyone fakes when meeting new people. "Hello."

"You didn't fall down the stairs, did you?" I asked.

Valerie's smile faded. "How did you—?"

I pulled myself into the room. "You were pushed. Felt a hand on your back even though no one was there with you?"

"How do you know that?" She shook her head and looked to Jade for an explanation.

"What else has been going on in your house?" I stopped at the end of the bed, leaning heavily on the handle of the walker. My back was killing me, and I wasn't in the mood for stupid questions. "Is anyone in your family behaving strangely? Unusual violent fits? Withdrawn when they're usually outgoing? Saying or doing anything out of character? An unusual interest in the occult or a fascination with religious iconography?"

Valerie grabbed Jade's hand. "What is this? Who is he? You're scaring me!" Only the last line was spoken to me.

I glanced at the heart rate and blood pressure monitor next to her bed. All her vitals seemed to be okay, so I kept pushing. "Answer the questions, Mrs. Miller, or I can't help you."

She let go of Jade. "If you're going to be like this, maybe I don't want your help. I never asked for it."

I scooted even closer to the end of the bed. One of her toes protruded from the cast, pale and waiting to be touched. One touch, one vision, and maybe I could see what it was stalking the Millers. Maybe I could feel it there.

I stared at her toe, waiting for something, for some sign that this was what I was supposed to do. Was this why Jade had brought me here? Why she'd shown me that file to begin with? She'd said I could use what had happened to me to help others. That's what Sean would do, wasn't it? Help people who were suffering? He'd always been such a sacrificial lamb, and that was why he was dead and I was alive.

But what if I had another seizure? All the tests said I had mostly recovered from the last one, but the doctors seemed to think it was dangerous. It couldn't be good. Maybe the visions I was having were damaging my brain somehow.

"And what if you can save this poor

woman's life with a touch?" Sean said behind me.

I almost turned my head to look at him. He'd been coming and going, the apparition of my dead friend. It wasn't like a vision with him. He felt more real, and I had no control over when he would show up, or what he would do when he got there. Still, I felt him with me every day at all hours. Sometimes, I would wake in the night and feel him standing off to the side of my bed, but I could never see him. If I looked, he would just disappear.

"You can help her, Felix," Sean continued. "You know this thing, whatever it is, isn't going to stop. Next time, when it pushes her down the stairs, it could be her neck that breaks."

What do I care? I thought. This woman is no one to me. Nothing. A stranger. I looked up at her and found her gripping a cross hanging around her neck. "Do you believe in the Devil, Mrs. Miller?"

"I believe in God," she said.

"Without the Devil, we have no need of God." I raised a sweaty hand from the bar of my walker and closed it over her toe.

The world spun. Fear, panic, and pain took turns slapping me in the face, punching at my legs. I let them. Already, I'd had enough visions to learn that fighting them only made it worse. Once the surface emotions and feelings throbbed in my head, more came. Deeper feelings like worry and guilt. They fell like a dark curtain over a bedroom scene.

But I didn't see anything, at least not the way I had with Dimitri. Valerie's guilt and fear were too strong, practically blocking out everything else.

I let her go and fell against my walker, against the end of the bed, suddenly feeling fifty pounds heavier.

"Felix!" Jade rushed to my side and carefully helped me back up while I tried to catch my breath.

Valerie stared at me, horrified.

I steadied myself and shook my head. It was heavy with foggy thoughts and feelings that weren't my own. "If there is an entity in your home, Mrs. Miller, as I suspect there might be, then two broken legs may only be the beginning of your trouble. Whether it is some ghost, a spirit, or a demon, it means you and your family harm. I suggest, as soon as you're well, that you don't go home. Leave your belongings and flee. Move out to the country where it's quiet. Have your two and a half kids, your picket fence, and quiet, normal life. Or burn the place to the ground, but whatever you do, don't go back there. Not if you want to live."

"A demon?" Her voice shot high in disbelief.

"I can't help you." I turned the walker around as if to move toward the door but stopped.

Something else was in my way.

The black creature was bigger than any human, thicker, and devoid of humanoid shape or features. Its body was flat, like a tick, with wide shoulders and spindly, hairy arms and legs. The arms ended in hands that might've been human, if only stretched too far. A long, snake-like neck curved and drooped, dripping into a black head without lips or ears. It had eyes, though; eight, like a spider. All of its eyes were focused on Valerie as she lay in her bed, waiting patiently with mandibles twitching near a gaping hole of a mouth in the center of its face.

"What is it?" Valerie asked, her terror evident in her voice.

"It's here," I whispered. "It's here with you."

Valerie immediately began to cry.

I scooted closer to the creature, which didn't seem aware of me in the least. It didn't feel like a demon, or at least not any demonic entity I had encountered. Then again, I had only been a host to one demon. Maybe they all felt slightly different. I needed to know more about Valerie, about this creature, about everything.

"What can I do?" Valerie sobbed. "I'm so afraid!"

"Well," I said with a shrug, "I retract my earlier statement. I don't think moving will help."

CHAPTER TWELVE

NOW

Mickey came back from his walk, but he was withdrawn for the rest of the day. He didn't talk, participate in evening group, or even stay up for the evening movie. Instead, he went back to our room and turned in early.

I had to stay up to take the new medication Dr. Bellamy had prescribed. It was a little pink pill that practically dissolved on my tongue. I barely needed any water to get it down. The sisters said I might feel extra sleepy after taking it, and shuffled me off to my room.

When I came in, Mickey wasn't asleep, but sitting at the tiny desk on his side of the room, scribbling furiously on a page. His other hand was down his pants. To his credit, he pulled his hand out when I came into the room. We both pretended I didn't see him do it.

"Hey, Mickey. Feeling better?" I asked.

He shrugged and focused on his drawing.

I grabbed the chair from my side of the room and dragged it over to his, sitting at the desk next to him. "What are you drawing?"

"It's nothing." He hurried to cover up what

he'd been working on with both arms.

"Come on, Mickey. I won't judge. You should see my drawings. I can barely manage stick figures." I gestured for him to show me.

Slowly, Mickey uncurled his arms from over his drawing and leaned back in his chair. Mickey wasn't an artist. At least, his art wasn't going to win any awards anytime soon, but he was better than me. He'd drawn a portrait of a dark-skinned man with his mouth open, standing in a circle of empty chairs.

"Is that Reuben?" I asked.

Mickey glanced at the doorway then put a finger to his lips.

"You *do* remember him!" I grabbed for the page, but Mickey quickly pulled it away.

He ripped the sheet of paper into a dozen pieces and started putting the small shreds into his mouth. "They can't find it. Can't let them see or they'll take me too." He shoved another wad of paper into his mouth, chewed, and swallowed.

I leaned in closer and spoke in the lowest whisper I could manage. "Who told you not to talk about him? What did they promise you?"

He just shook his head and kept chewing.

I gripped him by the shirt. "Tell me, Mickey! Tell me what's going on!"

"Okay!" His hands shot up and he pushed me away. After, he wrapped his arms around himself and started to rock. "I don't know. They didn't tell me. I just know Reuben's not the only one. It was Sammy before that and before that Owen. They've all gone to the rubber room and not come back. When they took you this morning, I thought...I thought..." He curled his arms around his head and sniffled.

"Hey, it's okay, Mickey." I put a comforting hand on his back. "I'm not going anywhere."

"That's because you have people who would miss you. Reuben and Sammy and Owen didn't. They didn't have visitors. They watch us, the sisters. Looking for people whose family stops coming. For people who get forgotten. And when they see us, they take us to the rubber room, and we don't come back." He shook his head back and forth violently. "They take the people nobody misses, and the people who ask too many questions, and the people who keep talking about those people. I'm so scared, Felix! I'm terrified that I'm next because Julia didn't come again today. What if I'm next?"

He sounded paranoid. No, I thought, he sounds like me. He knows something's wrong here too, and Mickey's been here longer than me. I retracted my hand from his back. "I won't let them take you, Mickey."

Mickey raised wide, wet eyes. "But you can't protect me all the time. One day, you're going to get out of here. Or you'll fall asleep, or go away again. They're going to take me, Felix, and not even you can stop it."

"Then how about this?" I pulled a fresh sheet of paper from the stack on his desk and picked up one of his pencils. "My friend who came to see me today? She's a licensed counselor in New York, which means she has access to patient records. If anything happens to you, she can intervene. She can come to the hospital and demand they release you."

Mickey blinked and wiped tears away on his sleeve. "She can do that?"

I didn't know if she could help Mickey or not, but I had to do something. I couldn't just share a room with the guy and let him be taken for whatever the sisters and Dr. Bellamy were up to. "You might need to bring her on as your therapist. You have to use your phone call to talk to her tomorrow, Mickey. Tell her Felix Cross sent you, understand?" I ripped the page in half and handed one half to him along with the pencil.

"What's this for?" he asked, staring at the pencil.

"I need you to write down your name, date of birth, and any other information that can be used to locate you if you go missing. Just in case. If there's one thing I've learned, it's that if you can't stop something from happening, you need to be prepared for when it does." I pushed the pencil at him again.

This time, Mickey took it. He scribbled his information down on the blank half-sheet of paper and handed it back to me. I traded his half for mine, which contained Jade's business phone number. She wasn't a practicing counselor anymore, but she kept her credentials up just in case. If he called Jade tomorrow and dropped my name, though, she would know this was important. She would step in without question to help just like always. At least, I hoped she would. After how things had gone during visitation, I was less sure. She seemed to think I was as crazy as the rest of them.

Once I had Mickey's information, I folded it into a tiny square and went back to tuck it under my mattress where I hoped no one would find it. It wasn't the most secure spot, but it was the only place I had.

The sisters rang the bell for lights out. Mickey and I turned off our respective lights and lay in our beds, staring at a darkened ceiling in silence. I missed the buzz of a fan, or the sound of constant traffic, the sirens in the distance. The sounds of the city were a lullaby to me. Out there, far from the crowds, it was too quiet and my mind was too loud.

"I'm sorry Julia didn't come," I said to Mickey.

"It's okay," he answered. "She'll come next week."

CHAPTER THIRTEEN

I didn't have trouble falling asleep, but once I got there, I wished I'd stayed awake.

I lay on a cold, steel table, staring up at a light. Bright white rays shone through a faceted surface. It was round, hanging maybe three feet above me. Somewhere nearby, a host of hospital equipment beeped with a steady rhythm. Feet shuffled over a linoleum floor and paper gowns rustled.

Somewhere in the back of my mind, I knew what was happening. I was in a surgery room for a surgery I had no idea I needed. Maybe I didn't need one. Panic welled up in my chest. The beeping came faster. I let out two quick, fearful breaths and my vision fogged. There must have been a mask over my face.

"Doctor, he's awake." It's a woman's voice. One I recognize, but in the dream, I couldn't place it until her face was hovering on the edge of my vision. It was then I recognized the face of my mother beneath a surgical hood and a sterile mask.

"Mom?" I tried to form the word, but my voice was too thick to come out, speech too difficult with the mask on.

Jade leaned over me next. "Good. Wouldn't want him to miss this. The mirror?"

Mom reached up to adjust a mirror I hadn't seen before. It caught the light a moment, flashing it over my face. I flinched and squeezed my eyes closed. When I opened them again, the mirror gave me a perfect, close-up view of my genitalia, visible through a square cut in blue paper.

The monitor beeped faster. I tried to raise my arms, to kick my legs, but they were held fast in solid restraints. Not only that, but my whole body was heavy under the influence of sedation. "No! What are you doing?"

"Shh, don't try to talk." My mother put a gloved finger over the clear mask covering my mouth and nose. "It'll all be over soon."

But I didn't want it to be over. Whatever they were about to do, I didn't want it. I pulled my arms, twisted, and tried anything and everything to get free. The monitor behind me beeped even faster.

Something pinched the outside of my left hand. I turned my head and watched a needle slide into the tender flesh on the back of my hand. The flesh rose, forming around the shape of the small tube inserted there. Jade smiled. "Just a little something to help with the pain when you wake up."

"Why is it going to hurt? What are you doing to me? Please, Mom! Jade! Let me go!"

"It's for your own good." Jade pulled off her gloves and walked away.

"Mom, please." I blinked. A tear fell and pooled at the bottom of the plastic mask near my ear. "Just tell me what's going on."

"There, there. It's nothing to be concerned about." Dr. Bellamy stepped up to the table, his kind eyes shining above his paper face mask. "You won't feel any pain. There might be a slight ache after, but that's completely normal. No worse than say a little tummy ache after you've had too much Halloween candy."

He laughed.

Jade and Mom laughed.

I tilted my head back and tried again to pull free.

"There's no reason to be so uneasy," Dr. Bellamy said as Mom helped him tie on an apron. "We're far removed from the olden days. Modern castration is a standard medical procedure. Why, with the general anesthesia, you won't feel anything at all but a little pressure down below."

Castration? There was no way in hell I'd ever signed up for that. Why? Why would they want to mutilate me? What had I done?

I fought to lift myself off the table, but the restraints were too strong and I was too drugged. All I could do was tilt my head back and scream. "Why? Why are you doing this to me?"

Dr. Bellamy leaned over me, staring at me from behind a protective plastic screen over his eyes. It looked more like he was prepping to use a saw than a scalpel. "When basic therapies and drug therapies fail to root out the perverse, more extreme measures must be taken. You consented upon your admission to any means necessary."

"Any means necessary," Mom and Jade repeated, nodding.

I thought back over every piece of paper I had signed when I came to Saint Dymphna's. What had I signed? They'd shoved the papers at me so fast, and I had been so tired. Maybe I should have brought someone with me, someone who would've better understood all the legalese, but the transfer had happened in the middle of the night. I was all alone.

Alone and betrayed by the people who were supposed to protect me.

"Please," I repeated, because there was nothing else I knew how to say. "Please let me go. I don't consent!"

"Swab," called the doctor, and my mother gave him a sterile swab. "A little pinch and it'll all be numb. There we go. That wasn't so bad, was it?"

I turned my head away and wept onto the mask, repeating again and again, "I don't consent! I don't consent!"

Nobody listened.

With time and trauma, even emotions become numb, dead things. I sank underwater, away, trying to find some safe space in my mind, but nowhere was safe. Danger lurked everywhere, even inside.

Latex-gloved fingers poked and prodded me until they didn't anymore. It didn't feel like the pins and needles numbness I expected. It felt weightless. Dead. Everything below the middle of my spine had gone into the nothing, but my brain was still stuck in consciousness. It was wrong. I was wrong.

"Did you feel that?" asked Jade.

I had stopped crying. What was the point? All I could do was stare numbly at all the prepping they were doing in my reflection. They had shaved me, taped the offending member out of the way, and marked the rest of me with little black x's and dotted lines.

I blinked, slowly, tired. My eyes and forehead ached. "Does it matter?"

"Of course it does," Dr. Bellamy said. "We're not barbarians. Nobody wants you to be in pain."

I looked away from the mirror. "I don't feel anything."

"Good." The doctor nodded. "The procedure is quite simple and quick. I'll make two incisions. You'll feel a strong pressure on each side, and it'll all be over. Shall we do the right or the left first?"

I barely heard him. I was still trying to find some part of my mind left to sink into, some safe place. Some warm and pleasant memory. All of them seemed out of reach. Maybe they'd never been real at all.

Dr. Bellamy chose for me. "Let's start with the left."

He had described the procedure perfectly. It was simple, quick, and painless, just as he said. All I felt was a strong, downward pressure as he coaxed pieces of me out into a dish. Important pieces. Unimportant pieces. I couldn't decide.

What makes a man a man? Is it parts and pieces? Or are we more than the sum of our parts? I'd never considered the question before, and it felt as if I should have. If a man is only his parts, does the removal of those parts make him a monster? Some proto-beast that is neither man nor woman but simply...alive?

So much of my life was wrapped up in those particular parts. What I wore, the products I bought, the people I developed relationships with. Everyone wanted to know about my parts. The size, the shape, the function. Who did I let touch my parts? Do they work best with males or females? How do I know?

Without those parts, was I still me? When I stood naked in front of a mirror, would I still see me, or would something so small, so previously insignificant, make me into someone else?

Maybe they were only making me into the monster I had always been inside, and all it had taken was removing two small lumps on the outside.

Poe crept out of the darkness, hovering near the operation table. Pale, thin fingers shook as he reached out to touch me. I flinched, fearing another vision, but I wasn't assaulted by more feelings and visions. His touch was gentle, sympathetic. Without words or visions, I knew he understood. Poe understood because he had been on that very same table, undergoing the same operation.

"They'll eat you up," he said, sadly caressing my arm. "Until you're all gone and then you'll see. You'll see you were never really there to begin with. We're all just meat in the end. Meat for the hungry."

My jaw trembled. "Why did they do this to you?"

"We're alike," said Poe. "All I wanted was to live. To love. To be loved. They said it was wrong. I thought I was broken. Too broken to live." He retracted his hand and offered a sad smile. "But I wasn't broken. I was a summer fruit trying to flower in the spring. We could've been so beautiful."

"Who are you? What do you want from me?"

Poe's smile faded and his outline dimmed. "Don't forget me. Don't forget my name."

"But I don't even know your name!"

He said nothing, but stepped back into the darkness, disappearing.

Something bit into the delicate skin on the inside of my elbow.

I woke and found a hand clamped onto my outstretched left arm. The pinch I had felt in the dream followed me back into the waking world as one of the sisters held a needle in my arm, pulling blood into a tube. "Easy there," she said. "Almost done."

"What the fuck are you doing?" I tried to move my arm away, but she held tight. The woman had an iron grip.

"Taking your blood. Doctor wants some labs run."

"You could've waited until I was awake, you know."

Cold blue eyes stared at me. She pressed her thin lips into a pouty line and narrowed her eyes. "Maybe you've got all day to do nothing, but I don't. I have a schedule to keep. There. All done." She dropped the tube into the bed next to my knee and forced a cotton ball over the needle hole roughly before forcing me to bend my arm up to hold it in place. The blood-stealing sister said nothing as she collected the five vials of blood she'd taken from me, placed them in a plastic holding container, and left the room, drawing the curtain behind her.

As soon as she was gone, I pulled a Mickey and slid my hand down into my sweatpants, but just to double-check and make sure everything was where it was supposed to be. Of all the weird vision dreams I'd had, that last one was the most vivid and terrifying.

With a sigh, I sat up and held the cotton to my arm firmly. "What a bitch. They ever do that to you, Mickey?"

Mickey didn't answer.

"Mickey?" I pulled the privacy curtain separating our respective sides of the room back.

Mickey's bed was empty. Not just empty, but stripped. Someone had taken the sheet, pillow, and blanket. His papers were gone from the desk too. I hopped down from my bed and plodded over to his side to pull open the dresser drawers. Empty.

A cold chill went down my spine. Those bastards. They'd already taken him.

CHAPTER FOURTEEN

THEN

There was more talk of discharging me from the hospital once I was up and able to move around on the walker.

After my initial visit with Valerie, I didn't go back to her room, but I did spend all my free time digging around on the internet for answers. No one had any, or at least, the community was divided on what the Millers were dealing with.

Three days after I met Valerie Miller, I checked myself out of the hospital against the doctor's advice. Jade was supposed to come and talk me out of it. I didn't wait for her.

On my way out of the hospital, I stopped at the ATM in the lobby and pulled three hundred dollars from my savings account, the maximum I could from a non-network ATM. It was more than enough to get me a cab and a cheap bed for a few nights and a good cane at a big box store.

I stayed at the Apple Inn, a little family-owned motel in Queens. It was too far away from the Miller house to walk the distance, but I could jump on the subway and be there inside an hour, so it was still close enough.

I hadn't planned on going to the Miller house the same day I checked myself out of the hospital, but it was on the way. I wanted to see the place without Valerie in it.

The Miller house was average. About as average as Valerie was without whatever supernatural entity was stalking her. It was a two-story white bungalow sitting atop a slight hill with a bay window and a yard of perfect green grass. An American flag flew from the small, wooden back porch where a green garden hose had also been coiled. A charcoal grill stood vigil over a worn set of lawn furniture and a tie-out post for a small dog. A single ten-speed bicycle leaned against the back door.

I circled the house twice before I decided to tackle the steps. My back and knees were already screaming from the effort of the short walk, but I was determined to make it up the five cement stairs that stood between the street and the front door.

Someone opened the door when I reached the third step. "Can I help you?" I didn't know whether to consider him a boy or a man. He was stuck in that weird, transitional age where he was blessed and cursed with the features of both. A teenager who had yet to grow into his big feet and strong jaw.

I paused and let out a heavy breath. "Maybe. My name's Felix Cross. I met your mother in the hospital. She asked me to come take a look at the house."

That was an outright lie. Valerie hadn't mentioned anything of the sort, but the curiosity was eating away at me. What was it stalking her? What exactly was going on in that house? Besides, I had nothing better to do with my time, as Jade had pointed out.

"Why?" The kid crossed his arms.

"I'm a priest," I lied.

He looked me up and down, frowning. "If you're a priest, where's your collar?"

"I left it in my other pants." It was supposed to be a joke, but he didn't laugh. The kid just kept staring me down angrily, as if I'd eaten his dog. I sighed. "Look, kid, is your dad here?"

"No, he's at the hospital with her. He's always somewhere else." He rolled his eyes sullenly. "What's wrong with you?"

"I broke my back in two places fighting a demon. What's wrong with you?"

He blinked. "Huh?"

"For a scrawny little bastard, you've sure got an epic-sized chip on your shoulder. I was asking you why."

The kid appraised me again, giving me a full look up and down. "What kind of priest talks like that?"

I grunted and pulled myself up the last two stairs. "Kid, my back hurts. My knees are killing me. I just got out of the hospital and all

I want to do is have a look around to see if your house is haunted. I get that you're wary of letting a stranger into the house, especially since mommy and daddy aren't home, but I swear I'd rather sit on your sofa and steal your ibuprofen than nick the good china."

He snorted and uncrossed his arms. "We don't even have any good china." He searched his pockets and came up with a cell phone. "Just so you know, I'm going to record all of this. In case you decide to kill me or whatever."

"You're a cheery kid," I grunted as I took the last step up onto the porch.

He stepped aside so I could pass.

The front room of the Miller home was cozy with a sensibly thin but still stylish carpet, plush sofa, and a coffee table that might've been out of a catalog five or six years ago. Pictures and knick-knacks hung on the wall, smiling faces and family portraits. One shelf held books and a couple of basketball trophies, but the dates engraved on them were too far back for them to have belonged to the kid. His dad was a star basketball player, it looked like, or had been in his high school days.

"You play sports, kid?" I asked, scanning the room.

He gave a bitter grunt. "I don't even like sports. Jocks are assholes."

"Your dad included, huh?" I limped over to the nearest basketball trophy and picked it up, waving it at the kid before gesturing to a small divot in the plaster wall next to him. "Was he throwing it at you or your mom?" I tossed the trophy to the kid.

Raw panic touched the kid's face as he dove forward to catch it. "Are you insane, mister?"

I snorted. "Mister, huh? I can tell you're not Catholic."

"I'm not anything." He carefully placed the trophy back on the shelf I'd taken it from. "And my dad didn't throw it at anyone. He just... how'd you know, anyway?"

"I'm observant. Anyway, about the trophy..." I intentionally trailed off and gestured to the kid, so he'd give me his name.

"It's Al." He adjusted the trophy this way and that, trying to make sure no one would notice it had been moved. "He just got mad one day, okay? It happens. We were fighting. He got mad and threw it at the wall. Nobody was standing over there though, so it wasn't at anyone. You've got him all wrong. My dad may be an ass, but he doesn't hit us. Trust me, sometimes I wish he would do that instead of screaming and yelling."

I knew the sort. When I was a kid, my dad could get worked up over the stupidest things. He was never a violent man, but sometimes words could hurt far worse than a trophy thrown at the wall. Even when the words weren't directed at anyone.

I gripped the cane and scooted it along the floor, carefully looking at all the pictures and keepsakes on display. Aside from the photos, there wasn't much in the main part of the house to suggest a teenaged boy lived there, and no crosses or Bible verses hung on the wall. Maybe they weren't churchgoers, although that was difficult for me to fathom. The Church had always been a big part of my life. What would it be like to grow up without that foundation?

"You don't spend much time at home?" I looked back at the kid.

He folded his arms and shrugged. "I have school."

"And after?" I picked up one of the family photos. Valerie was holding a cat, but I hadn't seen one since coming through the door. Maybe it was just shy.

"I'm not comfortable handing out my daily schedule to a stranger. No offense," said Al.

"None taken." I put the photo back. "Where's your cat?"

Al's face paled. Bingo. I'd hit on something important. Question was, what?

His arms unfolded with jerky motions. "Butters had to be put down. The day before Mom's accident."

"What happened?"

Another shrug. "He just stopped eating. Stopped drinking. It was like he gave up. In the end, he was so weak..." Al swallowed and looked away.

I grunted and scooted my way to the sofa where I plopped down to lean forward on my cane. The position took some of the painful pressure off my spine. "What sort of invisible creature pushes a woman down the stairs and affects a cat in such a way?" I rocked the cane's three legs in a circle, thinking. "I'm missing something. Whatever it is, it isn't here. It's with her, in the hospital."

The front door banged open, startling Al. I rose to my feet as the father from the photos—a broad-shouldered man several inches taller than me—helped Valerie through the front door. Valerie was in a wheelchair, one just a hair too wide to fit through the door easily and so he had to go back and jostle it a bit. It wasn't until he had her through that anyone noticed me.

"Felix!" Valerie's eyes widened. "What are you doing here? Honey, this is Felix Cross."

"The man with the visions." He frowned deeply, regarding me with all the trust a mouse would give a snake.

Valerie barely seemed to notice. "Felix, this is Ben, my husband."

Ben held out his hand, but I didn't take it. I was too busy trying hard not to stare at the ethereal creature that had followed them through the door. It was attached to Valerie, I was sure of it now. The thing hung over her like a hungry shadow.

"The visions are triggered by touch," I explained, "so I'm going to have to pass on the handshake."

"Convenient, isn't it?" Ben grunted. "You can tell a lot about a man from a handshake, like if he's genuine or not, or if he means your family harm."

"Ben!" Valerie gave her husband's arm a swat.

"If it's money you want," Ben continued, "I don't have any to give you. After the hospital bills, anyway."

"What about the tuition?" Al asked.

"Allen, sweetie..." Valerie shook her head. "We can talk about it later."

"No reason. He's not going to that sissy school, Val. We talked about this."

"Sissy school?" I shifted my weight forward, onto my right foot. That seemed to hurt a little less.

"It's an arts school," Valerie explained. "Al is a very talented dancer."

"He doesn't want to hear about that." Ben wheeled Valerie to a spot beside the sofa. "I think he was just leaving."

"Actually, I'd love to hear about it." I gestured to Valerie. "And more about your accident, and what happened with the cat, if you don't mind. I think I might be able to help."

"What's the damn cat got to do with it?" Ben's palms twisted around the wheelchair handles the same way he might choke the life out of a person before raising his hands. "Look, this all has a perfectly rational explanation. Val fell down the stairs. The cat was old. Why does there have to be more to it than that?"

"Valerie said she was pushed, Mr. Miller." I scooted one step toward him. "Not that she fell."

"Val?" Ben leaned down toward his wife. "Tell him what happened."

She wrung her hands and shook her head, refusing to look at me. "Maybe I did just fall. I can be so clumsy sometimes."

It hurt to kneel, but I didn't want to tower over her the same way her husband did, so I went to one knee in front of her wheelchair. "Valerie, I know what I saw outside your hospital room the other day. It was real. I know you feel it too, that something else is going on here. You're not crazy." I glanced up at the creature, looming just behind Ben. "I can help you."

Ben put his hand on his wife's shoulder. "The only help she needs is help upstairs to bed so her broken bones can heal." He patted her shoulder once and left her side to go open the front door. "I'd like you to leave now."

I gave Valerie one last chance to change her story before straining to pull myself to my feet with the help of my cane. My back screamed and I fell halfway through rising. Al rushed forward to grab my arm and keep me from hitting the floor.

As his fingers closed around my forearm, I was struck by another vision, this one of an empty auditorium laid out before me. I stood on a naked stage with the taste of nervous vomit in my mouth. My heart fluttered into my throat on hummingbird wings, but I didn't let it show. My face had to be perfect. Jaw relaxed, eyebrows raised, a perfect, natural smile. You're having the time of your life, I reminded myself. This is Heaven, and you have to take the audience there with you.

And then the music played, an indie pop-rock number without vocal backings. I didn't need words because my body moved and became the message. The music became an after-thought, a simple table dressing against a feast of pirouettes, pliés, and jetés and moves I didn't have words for in my head. I danced as I had never danced before, landing every move with more grace and poise than I had ever practiced. Sweat beaded on my forehead and stung the corners of my eyes. The muscles in my calves and groin complained as they stretched, contracted, and stretched again into wide leaps and daring spins. I had practiced this routine every day for the last month, and it showed. Still, I smiled, I danced. I let the emotion of the song and story drip from my temples and burst into the air with every breath. I was alive, free, and bursting with hope and pride, despite the pain.

Al finally let me go and the vision was

gone. I was in my own body again with its aching knees and healing spine, never to dance again. I'd never wanted to dance before that moment, but now I understood why someone might.

Al raised his eyebrows. "You okay?"

I swallowed and finally remembered how to speak. "Don't stop dancing, kid. No matter what he says. If you like it, keep doing it."

He made a face, a mix of shock and confusion.

"Okay, this has gone far enough." Ben opened the door wider, more emphatically. "Leave now or I'm calling the cops."

I limped to the front porch where I paused. "If you change your mind, Mrs. Miller—"

Ben slammed the door in my face before I could say anything else.

The sky rumbled above as I made my way down the street, away from the Miller home. It wasn't far to the next subway stop, and a short ride from there to the motel. It was raining by the time I got off the subway. I shelled out the money to take a cab rather than walk the rest of the way. Fat raindrops struck the cab's windshield as we sat in traffic. They sat on the incline of safety glass, distorting the red brake lights as they crept into the darkened car.

I couldn't get the memory of Al's dance out of my head. He'd had so much passion for what he was doing that it should've been criminal to stand between him and his dream. The kid wanted to go pro. I didn't know if he was good enough—I'd never seen a ballet, so I was a shit judge—but he should've had the chance. Pity he'd been saddled with a father like that, someone so restrained by his tiny worldview he couldn't fathom his own son's love for an art. Because it didn't fit into the pre-set mold of the male world, it was impossible. It made me wish I had the money to cover the kid's tuition myself, even though I didn't know him. Al had more passion to dance than I'd ever had for anything in my life.

What do I want? I thought, staring out the window at the barred windows and the spray paint graffiti. *Who am I, now that I can't be a priest?*

I supposed I could've gone back to finish. The school would've let me take my exams, and I could always finish up the next semester if I didn't pass. But what would be the point? I hadn't gone to seminary school because I wanted to. I went because that's what I thought would make everyone around me happy. Father Felix Cross was who I always thought I should become. Maybe I'd been so busy becoming him that Felix Cross, the man didn't exist anymore. I was just an idea, the byproduct of other people's desires. I certainly didn't have any of my own.

The window fogged under my breath. I stared at it a moment before I raised my finger to draw. My fingertip squeaked across the glass in two straight lines. *Hope deferred makes the heart sick, but a longing fulfilled is the tree of life.* I recited the verse from Proverbs in my head as I drew three squat crosses on the cab window. The Bible had a lot to say about all kinds of desire, everything except this one. What does a man do if he doesn't know what to do?

"Maybe it's time to stop living as Felix Cross, the seminary school dropout," Sean said. He was sitting next to me in the back seat of the cab. I could feel the change in the air whenever he was near. Or rather, whenever his ghost was. Was he a ghost? I didn't know what else to call him. "Time to start living as Felix Cross, the man."

"Yes," I agreed without turning to look. "But what does he want?"

Sean shrugged. "Probably what any man wants. What we all want deep down in our heart of hearts. It's the same thing for every human on this planet, Felix. We all want to be loved and accepted for who we are."

"But I don't deserve that. I deserve punishment. Suffering." I swiped a hand over the image I'd just drawn, erasing it.

"What if you don't? What if, instead of punishing yourself with an itchy bed full of bugs that dozens of strangers have slept in, and junk food, you accepted the help that was offered?"

"What are you talking about?" I moved to turn but stopped when I saw the cab driver giving me a worried look.

"You okay, bud?" he asked. "You're not... uh..." He made a smoking gesture.

"I'm not high," I said, and I wasn't, though maybe that wouldn't be so bad. All my life, I'd been such a good kid. A class clown, sure, but I'd never done anything too daring. I didn't even drink except for the one time with Sean. I'd had to behave myself because that was what was expected of a priest. "Maybe that's what I should do," I mumbled. "I should go get high, get drunk, and fuck everyone between here and Tokyo. I should do whatever I feel like. Who's going to stop me?"

"The sky's the limit," Sean agreed. "Or the bottom of your wallet. That tiny sum you've got won't get you far, Felix. It won't even put you up in that shoddy motel for two weeks."

He was right. I knew it. But what other option was there?

I scanned the sidewalk and an idea came to me. Maybe the money in my pocket wasn't best spent on a crappy motel bed and cheap food. "Stop the cab."

The cab driver frowned. "You sure? This ain't exactly the best neighborhood, son."

"I'll be fine."

"Suit yourself." He pulled over as soon as there was space alongside the sidewalk.

I got out, settled my debt with a generous tip, and turned to face the rainy city. I had a cane in hand, pain in my back, and two hundred dollars burning a hole in my pocket. I couldn't buy a lot of relief for that price, but I'd take anything I could get.

CHAPTER FIFTEEN

NOW

"What exactly is the nature of your relationship with Ms. Jade Haneda?" Dr. Bellamy crossed one leg over the other and rested his arm over the clipboard in his lap full of notes. My notes. Or rather, notes about me.

I stood in his office, in front of his bookshelf, slowly reading the titles on the outward-pointing spines. He had a lot of books on dreams and the mind. I wished I could take one of them out and flip through it. Maybe the answers were there.

Instead, I'd described my dream from the night before in gruesome detail, but only because I hadn't been left with a choice. After waking to find Mickey gone, I went straight to the nurse's station to demand an explanation. People didn't just disappear overnight, especially not Mickey. This time, instead of sending me back to the rubber room, Dr. Bellamy thought it would be a good idea for us to have another chat. He promised Sister Mary Sabina he'd calm me down, and promised me he'd explain everything.

So far, he hadn't lived up to his promise.

"Complicated." I placed my finger on a book titled *A History of Dreaming* and tipped it slightly.

"Romantically complicated?"

I left my finger on the book and turned my head to look at the doctor. So relaxed. So poised. Not like a guilty man about to confess. "Now that would be unethical, wouldn't it?"

"Unethical," he agreed with a bob of his head, "but not unheard of. It's extremely common. People go to therapy and bare themselves emotionally, sharing their most intimate secrets with someone. It's difficult not to develop feelings for a person in that situation." He was silent for a moment, giving me space to speak. When I didn't, he uncrossed his leg and patted the empty chair next to him. "I'm not going to judge you or her. Judgment is not the function of a psychiatrist. However, I need to understand your past treatment in order to continue."

I sighed and sat on the edge of the chair. "It wasn't like that. By the time we were involved, she wasn't treating me anymore, at least not officially."

"And unofficially?"

I shrugged. "Unofficially, a shrink can never turn off their shrinking ability. I still don't see what that has to do with the dream or Mickey's disappearance."

"Felix, would you describe yourself as a

masochist?"

I stared at the doctor, saying nothing.

He stared back, leaving an awkward silence between us that stretched long enough to border on the ridiculous. Then he sighed and shifted back to his original position. "Castration is the ultimate act of emasculation. Men often feel emasculated by their need for treatment, by the continued presence of their mothers past a certain age, and perhaps by a former lover. To go further, the fear of emasculation is not just a fear that you will lose your perceived maleness, but a large part of your identity. Humans are social creatures, and our sexual partners and preferences define how we interact with social groups, but also how we look at the world. To feel emasculated is to feel a loss of identity, Felix. There is a part of you still searching for a means to define yourself, to leave a mark on the world. To question your identity is a common part of post-traumatic stress. However, for some individuals, the concept can be...fracturing. To cope with past trauma, these individuals will often create alternates."

"What are you saying, Doctor?" I leaned back in the chair, fingers curling into the plush arms.

He set the clipboard aside. "Are you familiar with dissociative identity disorder, more commonly called a split personality?"

I surged out of my chair. "Mickey was real!

Reuben was real!"

"But Sean is not?" Despite my outburst, the doctor remained calm, collected. "I am not questioning the realness of Mickey, Reuben, or Sean, Felix. I'm not questioning your realness. To me, you are all as real as the man sitting before me, each with distinct traits, voices, and problems."

I balled my hands into fists and turned away so I wouldn't punch him in his lying mouth. I knew Mickey was real, that he was a patient, my roommate. I had talked to him, touched him, felt his broken mind.

Hadn't I?

What if Dr. Bellamy was right? It was possible, wasn't it? I mean, I was seeing Sean everywhere and he wasn't real. Would it be so farfetched for me to invent Mickey or Reuben too? At least that would explain why no one remembered them.

The paper, I thought. Mickey had written his information on the paper I'd placed under my mattress. It was still there. All I had to do was pull it out and show them the handwriting was different. Other personalities didn't develop their own handwriting, did they? Maybe they did.

I had no way of disproving what Dr. Bellamy was telling me. Truth, reality, my identity, they were all in question. How does anyone know what's real and what's not if nobody could agree on what reality *is*?

I sank back into the chair, resting my head on my fists. "I don't know if you're lying to me, or if I'm lying to myself, or if everyone is lying to me. I don't know anything anymore. I just want it to stop."

"And what it is it you would like to stop?"

"Whatever's happening to me." I shook my head. "I'm so tired."

"It must be exhausting," he agreed, "being so afraid all the time. So confused."

I lifted my head and said quietly, "What's going to happen next?"

He folded his hands and tapped his thumbs together, considering. "That all depends on you. Your ward at Saint Dymphna's is what's called a medium-security ward. There are six different wards here ranging from maximum security to minimal. Each one houses different sorts of patients with different treatments. We can continue to treat your depression and anxiety with drugs and release you to continue any further treatments in an outpatient facility of your choosing."

"Or?"

"Or," he said with a sigh, "we could try a more intense, more experimental treatment. There is no one treatment for DID, Felix. Conventional medicine is designed only to treat the symptoms, never the root cause. I believe, however, that by addressing the root trauma through intense psychotherapy, drug therapy, and, in extreme instances, electroshock therapy, these multiple facets may rebond to one another. Alternate identities are created by the psyche to protect the mind. They are an unhealthy form of coping with trauma. If the brain can be reduced to a similar state in which the trauma occurred, then perhaps the personalities will merge and you will be cured."

What he was saying made sense, but it also sounded too simple. It was too easy to believe that Reuben and Mickey were people I made up, that my own brain was playing tricks on me. Yet that was why I was there, wasn't it? Because I was a sick man, because my mind was as broken as the rest of the patients' at Saint Dymphna's. A sane man wouldn't try to kill himself. A sane man didn't talk to ghosts or have visions. What if I could make everything go away and all it took was one of Dr. Bellamy's unconventional treatments? I could get my life back. Wasn't that what I wanted?

"Don't decide now," continued Dr. Bellamy, picking up his clipboard. "Think on it. Sleep on it. For now, I'd like to talk about your appetite. The sisters tell me you haven't been eating."

I swallowed and rubbed my sweaty palms together. "I haven't been feeling hungry. It's not like hospital food is the most appetizing anyway."

He flipped through several pages. "It looks like you've lost almost ten pounds since you were admitted, and you didn't have much to spare. It's concerning. No vomiting?"

I shook my head. "I just don't want to eat."

"You have to eat, Felix. What can I do to convince you to eat?" He folded his hands into a pleading gesture and leaned forward. "How would you like it if we had a special dinner, you and I? We can't have it on the ward, of course. It might upset the other patients. But you and I can have a special dinner here, in my office."

I frowned. "What special dinner?"

"Anything you like. Pizza, ice cream, tacos..."

"How about a good old-fashioned hot dog?" I shrugged. It'd been a long time since I'd had one, but nothing reminded me more of home than an all-beef hot dog with onions and mustard on a nice steamed bun. They sold them out of carts on the street in the city. I missed the summer days where the air smelled like car exhaust, baking asphalt, and steamed hot dogs.

Dr. Bellamy chuckled. "That's right. I forgot. You're a city boy, aren't you? Well, I can't promise I can reproduce a classic, but I can certainly try. But only if you're willing to try."

"I think I can eat a hot dog." My mouth was watering at the thought of it. It'd be better than the junk they served on hospital trays. "But I'm not ready to accept that Mickey and Reuben weren't real patients here. I'm going to keep asking around."

"By all means." He rose and went to open the door. Sister Mary Sabina was waiting on the other side to take me back to the unit. "I look forward to discussing your findings over dinner, Felix. In the meantime, I believe you're late for art therapy."

I followed the sister back to the unit where everyone else was drawing a self-portrait. I glanced over some shoulders on my way to my assigned seat and found the portraits ranged from forests full of eyes to black swirls to Picasso-esque two-dimensional representations. No one in the unit was gifted when it came to art.

As I sat and one of the sisters placed a blank sheet and some crayons in front of me, I couldn't help but think of Raina. How was she? Maybe she was as messed up as me after what'd happened to her. I hoped she was still drawing, wherever she was. While she was possessed, the demon had given her uncanny talent for it, but she'd seemed to get enjoyment out of it on another level.

Passion, I thought. That's the word. She was passionate about it.

Once, I had been passionate about things too, although maybe it had been the wrong things. I had wanted to learn everything I could about demons and the occult, which was why I had spent the better part of a decade traveling the world after I left Jade. It wasn't the learning I was so passionate about, though. It was rescuing Sean. Saving him from a punishment meant for me. Without that to drive me, what was left? I'd given up everything else.

Who was Felix Cross without the need to make things right?

"Very good, Felix." Sister Mary Sabina's hand came down on my shoulder.

I blinked and leaned back from the page, which had been blank a moment ago. An expressionless mask stared back at me, the eyes colored in to be black holes. There were no ears, no lips, no features. Just the blank outline of a face with black eyes. Anyone could take it and draw whatever they liked on the mask.

I looked up from the page to find everyone else had finished their drawings and thirty minutes had passed. Yet it had only seemed like one or two to me. Once again, I had lost some time.

My fingers closed around a blue crayon and I looked around me. Sister Mary Sabina had moved on, and all the other sisters were busy helping people get in line or collecting the pages. No one noticed as I slid the crayon into my hand and closed my palm around it.

With a sigh, I rose and went to turn my self-portrait in. Dr. Bellamy would look at each of them, the sisters promised. Somehow, that made me even more uneasy.

After art therapy, we had fifteen minutes of free time, which I used to go back to my room and pull the paper from under the mattress. Sweat beaded on my forehead as I fumbled to unfold it on my desk. I shakily put the blue crayon to the page under where Mickey had written his information and copied his name in my own hand.

The handwriting was distinctively different.

CHAPTER SIXTEEN

THEN

Oxycodone was easy to get. As long as I had that, and I had money, I had friends and a place to stay. It didn't matter that I didn't know their names half the time. Probably none of the time. Everyone used fake names or nicknames like Skinny and Twitch or Batty. Mine was Puppy. I got it from a girl who said I had sad puppy eyes. Her name was Molly because that's what she sold. I never learned her real name.

My initial two hundred dollars didn't last the week. By the end of the month, my bank account was dry.

An addict with an empty bank account is a dangerous man.

Before the withdrawal was in full force, I found myself in a living room full of bean bag chairs. The old, yellowed wallpaper was peeling in the corners, but everything around me was clean. Clean-ish. There were still empty beer bottles and old pizza boxes lying around, but that was from the party the night before. The party where I blew the last of my cash away without a care in the world.

I cradled my cell phone in my sweaty palms, bouncing my knees up and down. It hurt less when I was moving, I told myself, though everything still hurt. The only time I didn't hurt was when I was high or drunk or getting laid, the holy trinity of relief. It was all so easy. I had thought it would be more difficult to let my life spiral out of control. To become everything I thought I never wanted to be.

There were three people in the room with me. Moose—the Canadian—had passed out leaning on Harley who—you guessed it—drove a Harley around. Rooster was busy trying to light a bong. I couldn't tell you why his name was Rooster except that he was a mean son of a bitch, one I avoided when I could. My buzz was wearing off, trailing off into the nothing. All I wanted to do was go back to sleep, but my brain wouldn't shut off.

What was I going to do for money?

Once they found out I was broke, how would it go? I doubted anyone would spot me cash or pills. They weren't those kinds of friends. As long as we were having a good time, they were down to come around, to bring the beers and music and pizza and pills. Then, we shared everything, as long as everyone contributed. It was a rule. Now that I couldn't live up to it, what would happen to me? Where was my place?

I needed money, but I wasn't in any condition to get it any of the normal ways. With my messed up back and drugs still in my system, I couldn't get a job. I knew my mom didn't have any spare cash to loan me, and neither did my dad, although he might have some pills worth bringing. He was always so sick, he had to have something extra in his medicine cabinet and he was only a short subway ride away.

What the hell am I doing? I rested the cell phone against my forehead. What am I thinking? I'm not the sort of person who steals pills from his sick father. I'm a good person. Or I was. How did it all go so wrong?

"It's time to go." The cushions shifted as Sean sat down next to me. "You've had your fun, seen the world. Now that you know what it's like to be here, it's time to go get some help, Felix."

"Help where?" I snapped, lowering the phone. "I can't just show up at Mom's place like this, strung out. Fucked up. She'd never forgive me."

"She's your mother." Sean put a hand on my sore back. Somehow, that made it feel a little better. "She'll help you, Felix. But if not her, what about Jade?"

"The shrink?" I snorted.

"You have her business card in your pocket still. If you didn't think you'd need her, you would've thrown it away a long time ago."

With shaky fingers, I retrieved the card from my pocket. *She might have something*, the little voice at the back of my head said. *She might even have some blank prescription pages sitting around.*

"No." I shook my head. "Not her."

"Felix, you need help. This has gone too far."

I looked at him so he would go away. The last thing I needed was advice from a dead man on how to live.

What about the Millers? the voice urged. *You don't know them. You don't owe them. They were rude to you, those rich assholes. Bet they have something worth pawning. It's the middle of the day in the middle of the week. No one will be home.*

"Mrs. Miller might be," I mumbled. She'd still be healing from two broken legs, but that meant she wouldn't be able to walk. She'd be stuck in bed, resting.

It seemed perfect. I knew where the house was, knew they didn't have a security system, not unless they'd installed one since I left. I'd been in the house long enough to know they lived a comfortable upper-middle-class lifestyle, complete with plenty of electronics just lying around. Most of all, it felt like they deserved to be robbed, though exactly why escaped me. I could barely remember my short trip to the Millers'. It seemed a lifetime ago.

"I've never robbed anyone," I said out loud to no one.

It's not like you'll be robbing a gas station. You

won't be armed. No one will get hurt. Besides, you'll just pawn their useless junk. If they want it back that bad, they can afford to buy it back. Everybody wins. Nobody gets hurt.

That was exactly the sort of thing good people told themselves before they put themselves into a bad situation.

My body didn't care, though. All my body knew was that the pain was coming back, and I had to do something to stop it. It would be worse this time than before too.

Before I knew it, I'd left the little apartment behind and boarded the subway, heading south into Queens. It was a long ride, not because the distance was great, but because there were a million stops between one place and the other. I huddled into my seat, feeling awful. The ache that had started in my back, shoulders, and knees had slowly moved into other joints. My brain was foggy, my palms sweaty. If I took my temperature, I knew I'd have a fever. I felt like I'd come down with something. Maybe I had. The things I was putting into my body weren't going in for my health, despite what I told myself.

It was mid-afternoon and freezing when I got off the subway. I'd put on a heavy jacket —one I had borrowed from someone, though I couldn't remember who. Even with gloves and the knit cap, I was freezing. Freezing and sweating at the same time. I wandered the platform in a fever dream, trying to read the signs. The letters were jumbled, too thick to fit into my eyes. I stared at them, trying to make sense of what I knew was supposed to be English, but all I saw were bright shapes, boring into my eye sockets.

"Are you lost?"

I flinched as someone put a gentle hand on my shoulder.

She was a pretty girl, white, probably a college student. A big, knitted sweater went to her thighs. Scarf, also knitted. Winter boots, worn. No money to spare, but she had more than me.

I swallowed, my mouth suddenly full of sand. "No, I just...I get confused sometimes is all."

Ask her for some change, said the voice.

"Tell her you need help," Sean urged.

She smiled. "You getting on another train or going up to the street?"

"Street...I think."

"Me too. We can go together if you want." She gestured to some nearby stairs, the ones opposite where I had been trying to read the signs.

Without a word, I followed her, a little lost puppy. Guess I would finally earn my nickname.

I put my chin to my chest. "You shouldn't be so kind to strangers."

"We're all human," she said with a shrug. "In God's eyes, you're no different than me."

I looked at her with her good, strong back,

good legs. She was getting up the stairs easily but moved slowly to keep next to me, preventing the crowds from crashing over me. "Aren't you worried I'll hurt you? You don't know me. I could be a bad person. A killer, even."

She laughed. "Maybe, but I'd rather die being kind than live being selfish when I could've helped." Her face sobered and she waited on the next stair for me. "It's just you reminded me of my brother, standing there."

"Is he lost?" I pulled myself up using the sticky, freezing metal handrail.

"He's dead," she said simply.

"I'm sorry."

"Don't be." She smiled again. It looked natural on her, as if she didn't even know how to frown. "He's not in pain anymore. My brother wrestled with his demons for a long time until one day..." She trailed off shrugging.

It was snowing at street level. The shops across the way were all decorated with lights and holly. Christmas trees stood in the windows, flashing bright, cheery colors at the bleak, dark world. People rushed around in red coats and green scarves, donning antlers and light up red noses that made children giggle.

I blinked at the scene. "What day is it?"

"It's Christmas Eve," said the pretty girl. She turned around, folding her hands in front of her. "Do you have a place to stay? Food? My friends and me are having a big Christmas dinner party. You can come if you want."

I tried to imagine what her party would be like. There would be smiling faces and Santa hats, steaming plates of food on the counter. Paper plates piled high with Christmas ham, Deviled eggs, cranberry stuffing, and yeast rolls so warm, the air steamed when you tore them open. Laughter would permeate the air along with clinking bottles and glasses as they toasted the passing of another year, the close of a chapter, the bliss of normal life.

"No, thank you." I shook my head and hugged myself. "I'm good."

"Okay, well…" She shifted opening her purse.

"Oh, please don't."

"It's Christmas," she said and passed me twenty dollars. "Everyone should get something on Christmas."

I took the twenty and watched her walk away in the snow. What would it buy me? Enough relief to put off robbing the Millers for a day, but then what? I'd have to come on Christmas. What a Grinchy thing to do, rob a family at Christmas. No, Christmas Eve was better.

The sidewalk was slick, so it took me extra time to limp my way down it, leaning on my cane. The physical therapist had been sure if I kept up my therapy that, one day, I would walk without it. I didn't believe them. The cane was a part of me now, fused to my body like an extra limb. I didn't think I could remember how to walk without it.

Snow came down, fast and angry in needles of white streaking through the air. It was gathering on the eaves of the Miller house, tiny balls of it tumbling down the slanted roof to die in gutters. No lights were on except the lights on the Christmas tree in the window. I wondered if Al had helped decorate it as a kid the way I had helped my mom. Our tree hadn't been so big though, and we didn't put real lights on it. Real lights would run up the electric bill. I wondered what it was like to grow up in a home that put real lights on Christmas trees.

I limped up the snow-covered walk and knocked on the door to see if anyone was home. If they were, what would I say to them? I could pretend I was checking in and then hobble away empty-handed. Maybe I'd be better off going into one of the neighbor's homes. They all looked like nice, affluent houses for boring middle-class families. Whatever the Millers had, they might have also.

Nobody answered.

The door was locked, deadbolt drawn, but like most people, the Millers had big front windows. Knocking out one corner of the glass to reach through was easy enough, but they would know they'd been robbed as soon as they came home. They would call the police. I had to be careful not to leave anything behind that would implicate me.

I realized I had made a mistake when I got into the living room. There were all kinds of valuables sitting around: a television, a computer, some paintings. The problem was, I couldn't lift any of them and hold onto my cane at the same time.

Maybe the kid has a laptop. I went to the stairs and slowly hauled myself up them, my back and knees screaming. As I reached the top, my stomach twisted and bile crept up my throat to coat my tongue. I made a mad dash for what I hoped was the bathroom and threw up into the toilet. After, I thought about just laying there until someone came home. I would go to jail, but at least there they would have doctors and nurses who could give me something for the pain. I'd have a safe place to get better from the flu or whatever was making me feel so damn sick.

Sean sighed. "It's not the flu, Felix. You know that."

I rose and went to the mirror. My face was a pallid shade of gray, my eyes bloodshot and my cheeks thin. "I think I'm dying."

The front door below crashed open. Panic closed my throat and made my heart jump. I looked around for some escape, but there was none. I had only one chance to avoid detection, and that was to climb into the bathtub and pull the shower curtain closed. If I was lucky, whoever had just come home would be here and gone quickly.

"I told you you're not going," Ben's voice boomed.

"I have to go, Dad. There's going to be a talent scout there. It could be the difference between getting into a good program and giving up," Al said.

Ben grunted. "Good. About time you gave that up and left the dancing to the girls."

"Why can't you just understand?"

"They're laughing at you!" Ben shouted. "Laughing at you in church, in school, everywhere! Don't you get it?"

"I don't care."

I sank further into the corner of the tub as the stairs creaked, but Al didn't come any closer than the bottom few steps.

"That's it. I didn't want to have to do this, but you're leaving me no choice."

Al let out a muffled sound and a series of dull thumps followed, the sound of a scuffle on the stairs. The thumping got louder, closer, harder. Someone screamed, but I couldn't tell if it was Al or Ben. Then, the house was silent.

I waited, too afraid to reveal myself. Possibilities marched through my mind. They could be dead. Dying. And if someone found me in the house with a body...

I pushed aside the shower curtain and gingerly stepped out of the tub with the help of my cane. Slowly, I dragged my aching body to the top of the stairs.

Al was sitting halfway up the stairs with his back to me. I couldn't see his face, but I could see his hands. They were red as if someone had gone over his palms with a paint roller. More red fell in a narrow slash of droplets across the white wall.

Ben lay at the bottom of the stairs, a gash through his stomach so deep it had almost cut him in two. Deep crimson pooled around his body. He looked up at his son, dead eyes fixed in an expression of shock.

The creature I had seen hovering in the hospital at Valerie's bedside now leaned over Ben's body, lapping at the blood with a long, forked tongue.

I scooted my cane along the floor and it made a mild squeak. The creature looked up, hissed, and fled.

Al finally let out a shaky breath. He turned around slowly. The whole front of him was soaked in blood. "I didn't…I wasn't…"

He was in such shock, he wasn't even going to question why I was there.

"Where's your mother?" I asked.

He blinked rapidly.

"When is she due back?" I pushed harder. "Al, you've got to tell me if you want me to help you. Otherwise, you're going to go away for a long time. Do you understand? And there's no dancing on death row."

"I didn't kill my dad. That...*thing* did!"

"I know that, but the NYPD isn't going to buy the 'my imaginary friend murdered my dad' defense, so answer my question. Where is your mother?" I enunciated the syllables of the last sentence firmly, partially because I could feel myself slipping away again, back toward being too confused to keep up a conversation.

Al shook his head and swallowed. "She was doing some last-minute shopping with my aunt. They took her wheelchair. I was supposed to meet her after my recital, and we were going to finish wrapping presents tonight."

"What time is your dance recital?"

"Seven."

I looked at the clock. The clock face was blurry, but it was still bright outside. That meant there was time. I scooted my cane to the very edge of the landing and leaned heavily on it. "Okay, Al, I need you to listen very carefully. Whatever I tell you to do, you do it. Whoever I tell you to call, you call them. No questions asked, understand?"

He nodded and looked behind him at the body. "What first?"

"First," I said, my words running into each other, "I need you to raid your mom's drug cabinet for me."

CHAPTER SEVENTEEN

NOW

I watched the minutes tick by, waiting. Lost in the possibilities of what was about to happen. Dr. Bellamy was manipulating me as he had Mickey and Reuben and probably others before them. How many patients had he made disappear in his tenure at Saint Dymphna's and why?

Knowing the numbers wouldn't matter unless I could prove that the patients existed to begin with.

My dinner was scheduled for five o'clock, and I needed to have an answer for him by then. Would I consent to whatever experimental treatment he had in mind? Had he proposed the same experimental treatments to Reuben and Mickey? Only a few days before Mickey disappeared, they'd offered him ice cream and pizza. My dinner would be hot dogs and French fries, but the outcome would be the same. Dr. Bellamy was a predator, preying upon those desperate for a cure that didn't exist. I was still sane enough to know that.

It's not paranoia if you're right.

At four o'clock, I approached the nurse's station. We were allowed one phone call a day, and only to someone on a pre-determined list we created at check-in. I skimmed the list and pointed to the number I wanted to call. The nurses dialed. I had fifteen minutes.

"Hello?" Jade answered the phone herself. It must've been Sloth's day off.

I glanced at the sister behind the desk and turned my back to her. "Listen to me, Jade, because I don't have a lot of time. They're going to take me. Today or tomorrow, I can't be sure. Either way, it will be inside the next forty-eight hours."

"Jesus, Felix, slow down."

"I can't. I have to get this out before they cut me off. Did you find anything about the place's history?"

She sighed. Papers rustled as she shifted things around on her desk. The click-clack of laptop keys sounded in a pattern. "Aside from the normal stuff? Yeah, there's a lot. Without knowing what I'm looking for..."

I tugged on my hair and closed my eyes. Poe had been trying to tell me something with everything he'd shown me, but what? "It'd be a scandal. A lawsuit maybe?"

"There were dozens of those," Jade said. "And most of those cases would be closed anyway." Her fingers clicked across more keys. "Wait. There's one right at the end, right before the place closed down." She sighed. "But the plaintiff is listed as a John Doe. It's all buried. The only thing I can find is that there was a lawsuit and then the institute counter-sued."

"What about news articles? Maybe some intrepid reporter did an expose."

"I looked for that already. Best I could find were tabloids and conspiracy articles."

"What's in those?"

"Felix..." She sighed again.

"Just tell me, Jade."

"Fine." Papers rustled. "The last piece written had some first-hand accounts from former patients. They claimed the staff was abusing people, but that sort of thing was rampant in the eighties and early nineties."

"What about forced castration?"

Jade was silent on the other end.

"Jade? Hello?"

"There was one. A Mary Sines that claimed her brother, Peter, had killed himself after they'd castrated him without consent. But the guy was a schizophrenic, Felix. He didn't know reality from his paranoid fantasies."

"That doesn't make it any less true." I glanced back at the nurse. She was pretending not to listen in on my conversation, but I couldn't be sure she wasn't. "I need you to find someone for me."

"Felix, don't you think this has gone far enough? I'm worried about you."

"Worry later." I made a fist and released it. "I need you to find someone named Julia Garret. She lives in New York somewhere. Her brother was Mickey Garret. Mickey was a patient here before he disappeared. He's missing, Jade. She should know."

The phone creaked as she shifted it against her ear. "How do you know these people aren't just checking out or getting transferred?"

"I'm going to find out soon enough. Whatever they did to Mickey and Reuben, they're going to do to me next."

The sister behind the desk put down her pencil. "Time's up, Felix."

I knew it hadn't been fifteen minutes but arguing with the sister would just get me sent to the rubber room again, and then I'd have to miss my date with Dr. Bellamy. "I have to go. Please just do it, Jade. Trust me."

Before I could say goodbye, the sister pressed the button on the phone to end the call. I slowly lowered the receiver, staring her down as I did. She smiled and pulled the phone back behind the desk.

I still had plenty of time before my dinner with Dr. Bellamy to finish one final task. It was free time on the unit, and everyone had gathered in the main room, waiting for the dinner cart to arrive. Some sat mindlessly in front of the television as it played through a non-violent cartoon movie, scratching at their beards or picking at the calluses on their fingers. A few had retired to their respective corners with books or blankets, just staring at the wall.

The one I wanted sat at the table closest to the wide, panoramic window. Afternoon sun came through the double panes of extra thick safety glass, pooling on the seat opposite him while he stared at a chessboard and rocked back and forth in his chair. Every day between group therapy and dinner, that was where the Chessman sat. He never touched the pieces on the board, but the sisters seemed to believe he found rocking in front of them comforting.

I left the nurse's station behind and slowly approached the Chessman's table. He didn't look up or even slow his rocking. "Mind if I sit here?"

He said nothing, so I pulled out the chair and sat.

The board was arranged as it should've been for the start of the game with all the black pieces on his side, and all the white on mine. I wondered if this was how they set it up every day. If so, they were doing it wrong if they wanted him to play. White goes first in chess. Maybe the Chessman was just waiting for someone to sit down and make the first move.

I had never been much of a chess player, but my dad liked the game, and so I'd learned to play. He'd played in some junior level competitions when he was younger, but never advanced beyond the local level. He had, however, given me plenty of lessons. I'd only beaten him once, and that was only because he let me win.

I picked up the plastic pawn and let it rest in my palm, feeling the weight of it.

Chessman stopped rocking and looked up as if he were seeing me for the first time.

I met his eyes. "I know you can hear me. You can understand me too, even if you're not able to talk." I placed the pawn back on the board two spaces ahead of where it had been resting before. "You were Reuben's roommate."

The Chessman's chair creaked as he leaned forward, picked up his corresponding black pawn, and repeated the move on his side of the board.

I smiled a little to myself, memories of the game unfolding like a flower revitalized. "I've never been much good at chess," I said, moving the knight to f3.

He responded, again mirroring the same move on his side of the board.

I folded my hands in my lap and pretended to survey the board. With my next move, I could remove one of his pawns from the game but doing so would cost me my knight with his next move.

"I've always thought it was a game for sociopaths. It's the epitome of anti-social games. Well, maybe except for solitaire. But no one holds solitaire competitions, do they? And with chess, there's an air of superiority whereas solitaire is simply...lonely. To be good at chess is to be good at outthinking your opponent, at strategizing, planning, calculating. You have to be willing to trade a few pawns, but you also have to know that sometimes even pawns must be protected in the early game." I moved my bishop far up the board and let him rest in the white space diagonal to his knight.

It was a common series of opening moves for white to play, probably the most common in all of chess. Learning the Spanish Opening was essential for every player, and every player knew it when they saw it. While it wasn't a genius play, it was safe. Reliable.

How the game progressed from there depended entirely on black's next move. He could choose the Morphy defense, which simply meant moving the a7 pawn forward one square, threatening my bishop. This was usually what my dad did, and the move I was most familiar with. It was also the move Chessman chose.

That still left me plenty of options. I could retreat my bishop, back off, and make different plays, or I could play aggressively and take his knight. The aggressive play could cost me though, as his pawn would then take my bishop anyway. After that, it would be a simple matter for him to move his queen and put me in check. An escapable end, but an easy trap to fall into.

I would take his piece, sure, but only at the cost of sacrificing one of my own. Anyone who knows anything about chess knows the bishop is generally the more valuable piece, and there aren't many situations where I would give up my bishop to take a pawn.

I pulled my bishop back.

"Isn't it interesting," I said after finishing my move, "that in this sort of opening, it's a pawn that dictates the actions of every other piece on the board? Contrary to how it works in real life, at least in my experience. People with power get to make the rules. The nurses and the psychiatrists here tell us when to eat, when to sleep, how to live. We're pawns on their board, aren't we? I suppose that would make Dr. Bellamy the king in this analogy." I chuckled. "Maybe it's not a very good analogy after all."

He stared at the board in silence, making moves in his head. He ran simulation after simulation through his mind, living through games that would never be played. Calculating. Strategizing.

"My father taught me to play," I continued. "He used to say there were two basic rules for winning at chess. First, control the center and you control the board. Second, a pawn is never really a pawn. It's a queen waiting on the right move." I picked up a pawn from the board at random and held it in my palm. "Dr. Bellamy's mistake is in thinking I'm a pawn. I'm not. But I want him to think I am for as long as possible, until his defense plays out and I get to see what's really going on. I need more information. I need to know what I'm walking into."

The Chessman stared at me, saying nothing.

"I need your help," I said. "I believe you were a witness. You saw something, something no one else has seen. I can see what you saw, feel what you felt when Reuben was taken, but that means I have to touch you, and you can't freak out when I do. If you do, they're going to know something's wrong and I won't be able to stop whatever it is Bellamy has planned."

His face was made of stone, unmoving. I didn't even know if I was getting through to him until I saw his jaw trembling. His eyes softened. He closed them and gave a slight nod, extending his arm shakily onto the table.

I closed my palm over his bare flesh and an electric current traveled up my arm, into my shoulder, my neck, and crawled over my brain. Whispers rode on the current, a chorus of a dozen voices just out of hearing, hissing, murmuring. A few words floated out from the crowd of sound, words like *idiot, poison,* and *stupid*. The world around me flashed and spun in technicolor patterns like paint dropped into oil. Lines blurred and all the colors melted together. Faces distorted, becoming smears of pink and brown without holes for eyes or mouths.

A scream lingered deep in my gut, too deep to ever find its way out. It wasn't a fear scream though. No, those tasted different. This one was a scream to be heard, to be seen, to be acknowledged. *Know me. See me. I don't need you to understand, just look at me!* More than anything, that was what the Chessman wanted. To be seen. He was the invisible man in a room full of mirrors, a sane mind folded into a silent body.

The feeling spun by in a hurricane of desperate thought and I found myself in darkness, standing in a narrow hallway. I gripped the corner and leaned around it. I wasn't supposed to be there, but I had gotten lost from the group going from art therapy back to the unit. I'd only stopped to look at a crack in the wall shaped like Florida. Just a minute, that was all the time it took for the rest of them to leave me behind. I was quiet. They forgot about me, and so it was up to me to find my way back up to the unit by myself.

Somehow, though, I had gotten confused. I'd gone down instead of up, or was it up instead of down? Now I was so lost, I didn't even know if I was in the right building.

I dragged my palm over unfamiliar walls and shuffled my socks under strange flickering lights. Plastic hung in the doorways, flapping in the breeze coming through some unknown hole. Somewhere, a machine was beeping. Maybe I would find the elevator if I found the sound.

I followed it down the hallway, the only noise from my socks scraping over the dirty floor and the beeping growing steadily louder. Something in the back of my mind told me I should be afraid, but of what? Nothing could hurt me as long as I listened to the rules, and I hadn't broken any. It wasn't my fault I got lost.

I stopped in front of a thick piece of plastic. The beeping was on the other side.

"Go back," said one of the voices in my head. "You're not supposed to be here, idiot."

"They'll poison you," said another.

"You're so stupid," repeated the first.

"They'll get you!" The second voice was so loud it startled me. I pushed through the plastic to get away from it.

On the other side was a round room with six hospital beds. The people in them were sleeping with tubes hooked up to their mouths and flowing from under their blankets. They'd been arranged in a semi-circle around a young man in a glass case. No, not a case. A coffin.

I wandered closer, pressing my fingertips to the glass. It was cold and smooth. The man inside was so perfect, he almost didn't look real. Dark hair lay around his head like a halo. His skin was pale, almost white, his lips a strange shade like the color of old slate roof tiles. He lay with his hands folded over his chest, eyes closed. Sleeping. Maybe he wasn't real at all, but a doll. He wasn't colored right, looked too stiff. All wrong.

Something creaked. I looked away from

the glass case and my eyes fell on a familiar face, a man with dark skin and hard chiseled features. His eyes were open and bloodshot, pupils big and breathing fast. He lifted one hand, reaching for me.

Another hand came down on my shoulder and spun me around. "What are you doing down here, Chessman?" I couldn't see his face, but I knew his voice. It was Dr. Bellamy.

The Chessman suddenly pulled his arm away from me, yanking me out of the vision. The chessboard flipped as he jumped up, scattering the plastic pieces everywhere. He looked at me, horrified, and finally the scream he'd been holding in for years escaped.

CHAPTER EIGHTEEN

"What did you do?" Sister Mary Sabina nearly knocked over a chair on her way to grab the Chessman by the shoulders.

He was still screaming.

The orderlies rushed out from behind the nurse's station and hauled him away faster than I'd ever seen them take anyone, leaving me alone with the sister.

She turned on me, her face hard. "Felix, what did you do?"

I looked down at my hands. They were pale, the skin mottled, palms sweaty. What would happen if I told the sister I touched him and saw his pain? I had seen the nameless man's brilliant mind tormented by voices that weren't there. Everyone thought he was stupid because he was mute, but the Chessman wasn't stupid. He knew what he had seen in that room, even if he couldn't tell anyone about it. Now that he could scream, though, would he be able to talk?

I looked to the board and all its pieces lying on the floor, swallowing the fear suddenly flavoring my tongue. "I played chess with him. White goes first. He was just waiting for someone to play."

Sister Mary Sabina folded her arms. "You've upset him, is what you've done, and there will be consequences."

I lowered my hands. "But I'm supposed to have dinner with Dr. Bellamy."

Something changed in her face. It was small, a knee-jerk reaction in the corners of her eyes. It was barely visible, but it was there. She uncrossed her arms. "Well, far be it from me to stand between you and your treatment. As long as you're not dangerous, you'll have to go to that, but in this unit, we expect our patients to respect each other's boundaries."

"Yes, but I didn't do anything!" I leaned forward, flexing my fingers in and out of fists.

"Perhaps not intentionally." She sighed and pinched the bridge of her nose. "Of course, I can't punish you for intention. Only action, Felix. There must be consequences. That's how society works. Actions generate reactions. Understand?"

I forced my fingers to relax. "And what reaction have I earned for trying to interact with another patient?"

"I think bed without an evening snack will suffice," she said, tilting her head to the side. "So be sure to eat your fill while you're with Dr. Bellamy. And pick up this mess."

Sister Mary Sabina retreated to her fortress behind the desk.

I bent over to collect the dumped chess-board and pieces, placing them back into their box one at a time. Each piece had a slot of shaped plastic where it would fit snugly, labeled with faded black lettering. I found all the pieces except for the black king, which I couldn't find anywhere. I even checked under the nearby sofa, just to be sure.

If I were a good patient, I would've reported it missing to the nurses. Instead, I drew inspiration from the missing piece and took one of my own. The tip of the white bishop wasn't pointed enough to pierce skin, but with a little work, I could wear the plastic down to such a point. I'd never be able to get it off the unit, not with the sisters searching me every time I left to meet with Dr. Bellamy, but I could no longer sit around and wait for him to make his move, not without ensuring I had some form of protection.

I slipped the bishop carefully into my sleeve and hurried back to my room. There was no lock on the door, but I closed it just the same and slid the privacy curtain closed. Running out of time, I turned to finding something rough enough to sharpen the plastic. The only thing with any grain I could find was a rough patch on the side of my hospital bed, so I rubbed the bishop's cap furiously over it. It would never get as sharp as a knife, but that wasn't my goal. I just needed something sharp enough to do damage. Just in case.

Once I had worked the point of the bishop's cap into a smaller, finer point, I had to find a place to hide it. The sisters would search me before I left the unit, but there would be places I could secure a small piece of plastic they wouldn't be able to shake out. Inside my mouth was a good option unless I had to talk. As much as I liked to run my mouth, they'd know something was wrong if I was quiet, so that was out. I'd have to take off my shirt and sweatpants, so simply slipping into those garments wasn't enough. I had my underwear, and they wouldn't make me remove that, but they would make me shake out the edges. Short of outright keistering it, that was probably my best option, and I didn't want to have something that sharp in any tight body cavities. I'd have to secure it carefully and be careful about shaking out my underclothes, but I could make it work.

I tucked the chess piece in, secured it as best I could, and tested it by jumping up and down. It shifted, but it didn't fall out. Ladies and gents, we have a winner.

Sister Mary Sabina knocked on my door just as I finished putting the rest of my clothes back on. She opened it without waiting for me to answer and slid aside the privacy curtain. "Dr. Bellamy is ready for you," she said, folding her hands tightly in front of her.

"Good," I answered. "I was just starting to get hungry."

She walked me through the unit where everyone else was just sitting down at the dinner tables. The dining cart had come up while I was in my room and the sisters were busy pulling the plastic covering off. Each tray would have a cardboard square on it with the patient's initials so they'd know who to pass which tray to.

We passed the main area and went to the little bathroom behind the nurse's station where she instructed me to undress. I tried to act normal, to keep from moving too stiffly. If I made any weird movements or went too slow, she might think something was up. Everything would be easier if I made her just a little uncomfortable and kept her mind busy. Too busy to think about where I might've hidden contraband.

"So," I said, gripping the bottom of my shirt, "why did you decide to become a nun?" I pulled the shirt over my head and tossed it lazily to the chair.

"What made you want to be a priest?" she countered.

"A fair question. One with a complicated answer."

"Then why should my answer be any less complicated?" She forced a smile and nodded for me to continue.

I hooked my thumbs on the waist of my sweatpants. "I suppose, for me, it was about the power. You put on that collar and everyone respects you. Everyone sees you."

"They see God in the collar," she corrected. "And in the habit."

"Do they?" I shrugged. "That sounds awfully egotistical; as if some item of clothing makes you holier."

"Prayer, fasting, and forgiveness cleanse the body. Repentance the mind." She crossed her arms. "Whether I wear the habit or nothing at all, I'm still a nun. I am a bride of Christ and a servant to the needy. It was my calling."

"Assisting Dr. Bellamy was your calling?" I met her gaze and held it.

She didn't show it with anything more than a slight crease between her eyebrows, but I had struck a chord. Sister Mary Sabina had her doubts that what she was doing was right. That meant she had some inkling of what the doctor was up to and wasn't fully on board.

"Assisting the sick was my calling," the sister said firmly.

"Am I sick, Sister?"

"Men who are well don't attempt to take their lives, Felix. If you were well and truly right with God, you would know it was never your life to begin with. Suicide is a cardinal sin not because you kill yourself, but because it is robbing God. It is a perversion for us to believe our lives are our own. They belong to Him. All lives do."

"Fair again." I stepped out of my sweatpants and spread my arms for her to do her quick check. "Sister, one more question, if I may. Let's say I suspect my friend of murder and I say nothing. I do nothing. I don't lie when he asks me to, but I don't report him either. I simply look the other way and choose not to see what's right in front of me. I deny what I know because it makes me feel better about myself. Is that a sin?"

She set her jaw squarely. "You can get dressed now."

"But you didn't answer my question. Would I go to Hell if I don't stop my friend?"

She picked up my shirt and tossed it to me. "The law says you would be an accessory to murder whether you confess or not. The law doesn't forgive, Felix. It punishes. God alone can absolve the sins of man. You should know better than most that absolution is deeply personal. As someone who trained as a priest, what would you advise yourself?"

"Penance," I replied, pulling my pants back up. "I would advise someone with such a problem do all they can to make it right. They should go to their friend and encourage them to come forward."

"Wouldn't that be dangerous? Your friend is a killer." She shrugged. "You could be next."

"Fear doesn't absolve me from the responsibility to act." I tugged my shirt over my head and adjusted the hem of it. "And I didn't say I would go alone or unarmed."

"You would kill a killer?" She shook her head.

The memory of Laura being ripped apart by the demon surfaced briefly. Her screams rang in my ears, fresh as the day I'd first heard them. "If he attacked me? Yes."

"If you kill a killer, then you assume his burden. You become him and we are right back where we started."

I stepped forward, closing the space between us. The room was small, too small for us to be standing this close together. "If you're going to get your hands dirty, Sister, you might as well take all the bastards down that you can."

Sister Mary Sabina didn't back down. "I'm not a vigilante."

I sighed and took a half-step back. "No, you're a nun. I guess you get to decide for yourself what that means, whether you're drawn to the power it gives you over others, the respect, the simplicity...or if it's something more. The one thing you don't get to do is take the moral high ground while you ignore the suffering of those under your care."

"I'll keep that in mind." She jerked open the door. "Let's not keep Dr. Bellamy waiting."

CHAPTER NINETEEN

I had to hand it to the doctor. He went all out to get the hot dogs right.

I had expected him to order in some fast food and be done with it. Instead, he'd brought in a small countertop grill and a hot plate where he boiled water and steamed the buns. An array of condiments lay spread over his desk on a checkered tablecloth, everything from standard toppings like mustard and relish to jalapeño and avocado. Hot dogs had never looked so good.

Yet I knew I would barely finish one. It wasn't that I wasn't hungry; I was. I was just uninterested in eating.

Dr. Bellamy ushered me to the chair on the far side of his office, which had been rearranged to accommodate the hot dog event. "Please, sit. What would you like on your first hot dog of the evening?"

"Can't beat a good old-fashioned mustard and relish dog." I shifted my weight. Sitting was uncomfortable with a chess piece shoved places sharp objects should never be. The promise of sweat prickled the back of my neck at the hairline. If Dr. Bellamy noticed and I got caught, the consequences could be worse than just being sent to the rubber room. He might accelerate his plan, whatever that plan was.

He gave no indication that he suspected anything was amiss, smiling gracefully. "Very well," he said, turning his back to prepare my hot dog.

As quietly as I could, I pulled open the waistband of my sweats and underwear to retrieve the piece I'd carefully hidden. I had to rush to tuck it into my palm before he turned around. At least I knew I could hold the hot dog with one hand. When Dr. Bellamy turned back, a paper plate in hand, I had the bishop palmed expertly in my left hand.

I took the plate with my right. "Thanks."

The doctor fixed himself a plate. I waited for him to finish and sit down in the newly added chair across from me. Anything less would be rude.

"Should we say grace?" he asked, settling in.

I shrugged. "Why? Nobody really believes God's going to bless a hot dog."

"The sisters tell me you no longer observe prayer in general, Felix. Why is that?"

"Because God doesn't talk back." I took a bite and it prompted a walk down Memory Lane where street carts stood on corners, steam rising into the hot summer sky. Asphalt baked, sending wavy lines up over tires. The air smelled of car exhaust, old newspaper, and simmering meat. Brakes that needed changing squeaked in stop and go traffic while buskers on the opposite corner sang for their supper. Crowds ebbed and flowed like water, alive and vibrant and real.

Cities spoke when you knew how to listen, and no city sounded quite like New York. I missed it. It was the first hint of feeling I'd felt deeply in a long time.

"Perhaps He does and you're simply not hearing Him." Dr. Bellamy took a dainty bite of the hot dog.

It was all wrong, the way he ate it. Hot dogs weren't steak. You didn't savor them. You wolfed them down and ran about after feeling guilty about it and wishing you'd spent your five bucks on real food. They were the official food of family reunions, firework shows, and monster truck rallies all over America, regret and all.

"If God wanted me to hear what He was saying, He should speak up. You can't whisper a secret and then get mad when someone in the next room doesn't hear you." I finished my hot dog and set the paper plate aside. "I'm not here because I don't pray enough, Doctor. I learned the hard way that prayer doesn't exist to appeal to God. It's there to make us feel better. Humans are ants and God's a kid with a magnifying glass on a sunny day."

"That's certainly a bleak way to look at the world." He took another bird-sized bite and chewed it for far too long. "You know, the mind is incredibly elastic. Whatever you put into it, it will reproduce. We are what we consume, Felix. If you live on a steady diet of self-doubt and loathing, the only possible outcome is self-hatred. Depression. Anxiety. Neuroses."

"So, I should pretend to be happy? Ignore all the wrong in the world and smile like an idiot? That'll cure my brain."

"Not likely." He put the hot dog aside, barely touched. "Medication can only mask the symptoms, however. We treat these illnesses as if they have no possible cure, problems without a solution. Symptom management is supposed to be the best we can offer. I don't believe that, Felix, and neither do you. Have you given any more thought to my earlier proposal?"

"Your experimental treatment for dissociative identity disorder?" I tightened my fist around the bishop. The plastic was smooth against my palm. "How do you know that's what I have?"

He leaned his elbows on the chair arms and steepled his fingers. "Psychiatry isn't like other forms of medicine. There are no scans or tests that will definitively tell you your patient has this or that. Instead, you look for symptoms. A group of symptoms presenting together creates a possible diagnosis, but that diagnosis is fluid and can change at any time, especially if the treatment doesn't work. You have presented with many of the classic hallmarks of DID, Felix. I believe the DID has manifested as a coping mechanism to trauma, or untreated PTSD. That makes your case complex and unlikely to respond to traditional methods."

"That doesn't explain how you know."

The plastic coating on the chair seat creaked slightly as he leaned forward. "I know because I have the experience and training to know. Beyond that, you will have to trust me, Felix. You do trust me, don't you?"

I stared at the doctor, my heart beating up into my throat. I didn't trust him to do anything but lie to me. The question was, why lie? What was he up to? What did he get out of gaslighting me and purposefully misdiagnosing me? This therapy he wanted to try had to be it, but what was it?

I swallowed my heart and let it fall hard back into my chest. "Yes, Dr. Bellamy. Of course I do."

"Then if I say this is what's best for you, you must believe me. I can't force your hand, Felix. You have to consent to treatment."

I glanced around the room. Nothing had changed. Whatever the treatment was, he probably wanted to move me somewhere else to perform it. "Can't you tell me more about the treatment?"

"All I can say is that it involves altered states of consciousness and is completely painless. I haven't had one complaint from any of my patients." He smiled warmly.

The dead don't complain, I thought. Corpses made for pleasant patients.

If I refused, though, and brought our interactions to an end, what would he do? It could provoke an equally negative reaction from the doctor. He said he wouldn't force me against my will, but he had all the power to do that if he wanted. He controlled my medication, my schedule, my diet, my freedom. Everything about my life was in his hands. With the stroke of his pen and his special prescription paper, he could turn me into someone else entirely and there would be nothing I could do about it. No one would believe me, and no one was coming to save me.

There was only one choice: risk everything and continue, or risk everything and reveal what I knew. The latter hadn't been going so well for me. It'd landed me in the rubber room, a fate I had no desire to repeat.

"Okay," I said reluctantly. "Let's do it."

"Excellent!" Dr. Bellamy rose and went to retrieve a few items from behind his desk.

The first thing he retrieved was a pack of cigarettes. No, not just any pack of cigarettes, but my cigarettes from my personal belongings. As soon as I saw them, I wanted one, even knowing he was manipulating me by presenting them.

"If I recall all the information in your file

correctly, you have experimented with illicit substances before." He placed a lighter flat on his desk next to the cigarettes. My lighter.

I shifted my weight. "I didn't start out trying to be an addict. You try breaking your back in two places and then go out on the street with no insurance. It's cheaper to buy a handful of oxy or a week's supply of Percocet from a dealer than the pharmacy."

"I'm not judging you." He met my eyes and shook his head slightly. "Opioids are for the body what antidepressants are for the mind. They only mask the pain. They don't treat the root cause." He shook out a cigarette and held it with the filter pinched between two fingers. "To address the cause, you must first bring it to the surface. Traditional medicine has yet to acknowledge what our ancestors knew, that altered states provide a window to the mind. Not only that, but they put our pain under a microscope, often letting that which is buried surface. The conscious mind represses pain as a protective measure, and so that conscious mind must be turned off if progress is to be made. Like you crave these cigarettes, your mind is craving release from the burden of reality." He gestured for me to take one.

I stared at the cigarettes, my brain crawling with the need to grab one, light it, smoke it. But to do that, I would have to let go of the bishop I had gone through great pains to bring with me. "Nicotine isn't really an illicit sub-stance, is it?"

"A socially acceptable one," he said with a nod. "What's the matter, Felix? Don't you want one?"

"I do but...won't it set off the smoke alarms or something?"

His expression remained flat. "Is that what you're afraid of? Or are you more worried I'll notice the plastic weapon you have palmed in your left hand when you put it down?"

My heart jumped back into my throat. I squeezed the bishop tighter.

"Don't worry, Felix. I won't punish you for feeling the need to protect yourself." He shook a cigarette out and held it pinched between two fingers, pointing up. Completely wrong, just like with the hot dog.

A fly suddenly buzzed into the room through a vent and flew to the wall where it hung, upside down, rubbing its little fly hands together. I stared at it and found myself wonder-ing what it was like to be the fly. Did he have any concept of how short and meaningless his life was? Did I have a grasp on that either? As I con-templated my insignificance, comparing it to that of the fly, I had the distinct feeling that I was moving, shifting behind myself. My normal first-person perspective of the world changed, and I found I was looking over my shoulder, watching myself watching the fly on the wall.

Dr. Bellamy stepped around his desk and held out his hand. "Give me the weapon, Felix."

I lifted my arm limply, uncurling the fingers one by one to free the bishop. I didn't want to give up my only weapon, but I was helpless to stop myself. My body breathed and moved and spoke all on its own with no input from me.

Dr. Bellamy caught the bishop before it could fall to the floor. "Very good, Felix."

"What's happening to me?" my body asked.

I moved around to stand in front of myself. "You're drugged. He drugged your food, you idiot."

He sat on his desk next to my cigarettes, one leg crossed limply over the other. "I imagine you're feeling the effects of the phencyclidine I put on your hot dog bun. You might know it by its more common street name: angel dust."

I should have been enraged, shocked, offended. Something. Instead, I just sat there, caring more about the fly than myself. There was a part of me that felt all those things, but it was locked away. It was enough of a task to process seeing myself and seeing the fly simultaneously.

"It's a remarkable drug." He sighed and crossed his arms. "A particularly good anesthetic. You should be completely pain-free, actually."

He was right. The nagging ache that had always plagued my back and knees was absent, as was the gnawing want for a cigarette. Yet I wasn't just free of pain. I was free of everything because I felt nothing. My body contained all of those pains, and I was no longer in my body.

"Of course," he continued, "it would've been more effective to inject you with it or perhaps dip your cigarettes into it, which I certainly considered, but, given your medical history, I thought a slower onset would be optimal. You're at risk for seizures and...well... sometimes this drug brings out the violent tendencies in otherwise calm patients."

I watched my body swallow. My face twitched as if I were holding in a laugh. "I'm not crazy, am I?"

He smiled. "Have you ever read Alice in Wonderland, Felix?"

I couldn't remember if I had, but my body burst into laughter at the very idea.

"Alice asks the Cheshire Cat how he knows she's mad and he replies, 'You must be, or you wouldn't have come here.' Sane people don't try to kill themselves. They don't become priests or exorcists or travel the world. Sane people live ordinary, unremarkable lives, Felix. That's why all the best people are mad." He threw his arms wide. "We are all mad here!"

My body doubled over laughing and nearly fell out of the chair.

Dr. Bellamy let out a slight chuckle. "It is really amusing when you get the joke, isn't it?

Life is madness, and there is only one cure. The great cure."

My laughter cut off abruptly. "But I already tried that, Doctor. That's how I got here. I tried to die but no one will let me."

"I can help you, Felix." He picked up a clipboard and placed a pen at the top. "I can take away all the pain forever. All you have to do is sign the consent form." He held the clipboard out to my body.

"Don't!" I shouted. "Come on, I'm not that stupid!"

My body stared at the extended clipboard with pinprick pupils, the black edges of my vision pulsing to a silent beat.

I tried to push the clipboard away, but I couldn't grasp it. All I could do was stand by and watch as Dr. Bellamy put the pen in my hand, placed my hand on the clipboard, and guided my fingers as I signed away my life.

A small sound made me turn around—the me that was no longer in my body.

Poe stood in the corner, his dark hair dripping from his scalp like wet, rotten seaweed on a corpse. All the color had gone out of his flesh, leaving it a strange off-white. Bloodshot eyes danced over the room before settling on me, his pupils pinpricks like mine. Dry lips parted. The cold hands of death wrapped around my throat and squeezed.

CHAPTER TWENTY

THEN

Al's hands shook as he ran them under the tap. I sat on the edge of the tub, trying to keep from melting into it. I'd swallowed just enough pills to take the edge off the withdrawal, but it would be coming back. When it did, what then?

I watched the kid wash his father's blood off his hands. I'd come here to rob the place. How far would I have gone if he and his dad had discovered me? Would it be me washing blood off my hands in that sink? The idea made my stomach turn. I wasn't a murderer and yet...

"What am I going to do?" His Adam's apple bobbed as he swallowed.

I could taste his anxiety in my mouth, or maybe that was just the powdery aftertaste of the pills. The body wasn't going to be a problem. We were very careful not to touch it and leave his father where he fell. Disposing of the kid's bloody clothes would be easy enough, and staging the crime scene was already half-done thanks to my earlier break-in. I intended to frame the scene as a robbery gone wrong. Maybe they'd find some trace evidence to link things back to me, but chances were they wouldn't. There were dozens of robberies a day in New York, and the cops couldn't give due diligence to each one. I just had to make sure they had no reason to dig too deep into this one.

The blood he was spreading all over the sink was our biggest problem. Luminol would light that sink up like a Christmas tree, high-lighting all the blood. Even if we cleaned it with bleach, it'd show. Our best efforts wouldn't be enough to catch everything. As long as they couldn't tie it back to him or me, it wouldn't matter if they detected the dead father's blood in the sink.

I closed my eyes and tilted my head to the ceiling. "Nothing. You're going to go to your room, get dressed, and go to your dance recital. You're going to dance your heart out."

"My dad is dead! I can't dance knowing his body is cooling on the floor in a congealing pud-dle of his blood and...and it's my fault!"

The world yo-yoed around me as I pushed up from the tub. I gripped Al by the shirt and shook him. "Do you want to go to prison for your father's murder?"

He stared at me, blinking. "No."

"Then quit saying shit like that!"

"But it is. I didn't kill him, but...that thing wouldn't have attacked him if not for me. I think it was defending me." He looked down at his hands a long moment before plunging them back into the steaming water.

The world swayed too much to the left. So I wouldn't fall, I closed the toilet lid and plopped down hard on top of it. "What is it?"

"I don't know." Al shook his head. "I thought it was my friend. I've seen it around ever since I was little. I used to be scared, but it never hurt me. It was just…there. I thought maybe once we moved to the city, I'd never see it again, but it followed me here."

"You moved?"

"A lot," Al answered. "We rented a lot when I was younger, before Dad got his job here. We weren't always so well off, you know. We used to be broke all the time. Always moving to a new city, always a new school."

"Always the new kid." I sighed, remembering my own experience growing up. We had moved houses a lot too, but Mom always did her best to keep us in the same general area. It didn't matter. Even moving one street over meant I had to make new friends, adjust to new schedules, and sometimes even new schools. When Mom and Dad split up, it was even worse. I had two lives, one I lived on the weekends with my dad, and the other was a lonelier life at Mom's punctuated by microwave dinners and school bullies. That was until I met Sean in high school, and we stuck together like peanut butter and bread. I thought I'd never feel lonely again.

I shook my head clear, or tried to. "We

have to get a story straight. There's going to be an investigation into your father's death. They're going to think it was a robbery gone wrong and you need to invent an alibi for yourself. You weren't here this afternoon, but you couldn't have been on your own either. Is there someone you trust that will lie for you?"

He turned off the water and stared at his blurry reflection in the foggy mirror. "You could be my alibi."

"I don't think that's a good idea."

"Why not?" he turned to face me. "No one is going to lie for me, Felix. I don't have a lot of friends, and if I say I was somewhere alone it's going to sound worse. You were a priest."

"I was a seminary student, not a priest."

"So?" Al shrugged. "They'll still respect that more than anything I say."

I looked away, studying the shampoo bottles. "Because I'm not the sort of person a kid like you should be hanging around, okay? It'll make you look like you're in with the wrong crowd, which isn't going to help you get where you want to be." Al had his whole future ahead of him and I didn't want to ruin that by associating him with what I'd been up to for the last month, or the death of his father.

An idea occurred to me, a little white lie we could tell that would fix everything. It was unfortunate, but a lie was the best way to protect Al from himself.

"If and when the police question where you were, you need to tell them you were in therapy with Doctor Jade Haneda," I said. Jade would be angry, but she'd cover for the kid. At least, I hoped she would.

"I don't know any Jade Haneda." Al shook his head.

"You do now, and you see her every week on…What day is it?"

"Thursday."

"Every week on Thursday at exactly this time. Your parents didn't know because you didn't want them to know. Don't worry about Jade. I'll convince her. You just keep telling the same story and don't say anything else."

He turned his head, looking at himself in the mirror as tiny droplets raced down over the surface of the glass, streaking across his reflection. "I still don't know how I'm supposed to dance tonight. But if I don't, I could lose my last chance. There's supposed to be a talent scout there. It's my last chance to get into Walden— the dance school. I could get a scholarship offer."

So there was more than just a dance on the line. If Al didn't show up and nail his performance, he might have to give up his dream of becoming a dancer, or at least delay it. If the police suspected he was involved in his father's death, it would destroy that dream forever. I had to make sure that didn't happen.

"You have to dance," I said. "And you have

to make it the best dance you've ever done. Not just because you want to get into this school, Al. Because you want everyone looking at you, because you deserve it. Because your father didn't want you to have it. He doesn't understand. He never did. Men like your father live average lives. Well, you're not average. You're special. You deserve to succeed. Understand?"

He swallowed. "I think so."

I wasn't sure he was getting it. "When you're up there on stage with the lights on you and the quiet faces sitting in the darkness, you're a god. Gods don't trouble themselves with the passing of small-minded men. You have to dance despite your father. Because of your father. For your father and for every kid, every man young and old sitting in that audience who wishes they could be where you are. For people like me who will never dance."

"You could dance. With practice, anyone can."

"Not like you," I said, shaking my head. "Maybe anyone can learn the moves, the jumps, the spins, but you have the spark of passion. There's a quiet fury that burns in passionate people, and when they find their spark, they have to burn bright. Most of us, we go our entire lives and never find that spark. You did. You're on fire when you dance, Al, and this isn't going to be the thing that puts out your fire. This moment, it's your gasoline."

He turned back to the mirror, gripping the sides of the sink and staring at himself. I wondered if he could see his soul on fire the way I could. He was almost too bright to look at.

"Here." I picked up the plastic bag we'd brought into the bathroom with us. "Put your bloody clothes in here and I'll get rid of them. Then you keep to your story, Al. Promise me."

He stared hard into the mirror. "I promise."

I wasn't sure anything I had said got through to the kid, but he did what I asked and put on some loose-fitting clothes that he'd change out of for his recital later. Al helped me down the stairs because I was too dizzy to go by myself, and because his father's body was still in the way. We navigated carefully around it.

I saw the creature waiting in the kitchen doorway as we came to the bottom of the stairs. It watched us silently, glued in place except for the way its head followed me, tracking my movements like a cat watches a fly. In hindsight, it should've been obvious to the kid that the creature—whatever it was—was a predator. Predators could kill. He wouldn't be the first human to befriend a predatory creature. Some people kept housecats and found comfort in the way they purred. It was easy to forget that even a small cat could kill a human if it was so inclined.

"How do you know I'm a good dancer?" Al asked as we approached the front door.

"Because I saw you dance."

He frowned. "When?"

I smiled and adjusted my coat. "Some things are probably best left a mystery. You should leave out the back door just in case."

"What about you?"

"It's no great loss if someone sees me coming and going, or even if they try to pin his death on me. I'm just a man. My fire burned out a long time ago, kid."

For the first time, Al looked like he wanted to smile. "I don't think so. I think there's still a spark in there somewhere. One day, you'll find it. You don't strike me as the sort of person who does normal."

On my way to the closest subway station, I chucked the kid's bloody clothes into the first open sewer drain I found. The rats would tear it up and turn it into nests. It was the circle of life in action.

CHAPTER
TWENTY-ONE

NOW

I woke up on the floor in my room on the unit, lying on my side and hot as hell. My breathing was ragged and irregular coming through my nose in hard, short bursts. Everything hurt, but especially the muscles in my arm. After a second, I realized there was a sharp pain on the inside of my right cheek too. The coppery taste of blood filled my mouth. All of these things, I knew upon waking, but everything else felt out of reach.

I tried to move but I could barely get my arm to respond. When I tried to speak, it came out as an inhuman groan.

An unfamiliar face in a dark hood leaned over me. "Don't try to move, Felix. You're safe."

I didn't *feel* safe. Panic made my heart beat faster. My wrists and head throbbed. God, I wished someone would get me some water or a fan, or just an ice cube to hold in my hands. It would've melted in an instant.

It took me three tries to get out one

slurred word. "What?"

"You've had a seizure." Cool hands moved over my forehead, moving hair out of my eyes.

I blinked. Involuntary tears fell and my vision cleared. One of the sisters was with me, though I couldn't remember her name. The face was familiar, even if it was anything but comforting.

I don't know how long I laid on the floor, trying to get my body to cooperate, to respond. To pull myself together and regain some ounce of dignity. I hadn't had a seizure in a long time, and it'd been even longer since I'd hurt myself during one. Most of the time, they were small, and I had a few seconds of warning.

The longer I lay there, the more came back to me. I remembered where I was—Saint Dymphna's—why I was there—I'd attempted suicide—and who was leaning over me—Sister Mary Sabina. I wanted her to go away, but she stayed with me the whole time, kneeling on the floor next to me at first, then pulling my head into her lap.

One of the last things to come back to me was what had happened at Dr. Bellamy's special dinner. At first, I doubted my own memory. Maybe I'd imagined or dreamed the whole thing. Why would Dr. Bellamy drug me and then dump me back in my room?

"Time," I muttered. "What time?"

"It's six in the morning." Sister Mary Sabina patted my chest the way I'd seen mothers pat their babies to comfort them.

I was finally able to roll my eyes and focus on her. "You're still here." She shouldn't have been. She'd come in at three the afternoon before. All the nurses worked twelve-hour shifts, which meant she should've left hours ago.

Her lips pulled back into a tight smile. "This is your fourth seizure since you've been back from Dr. Bellamy's visit. I suppose I could've left you and gone to get some sleep, but it didn't seem right. Besides, I would've had to leave you in the care of Sister Wilhelmina and she's about as comforting as a brick wall. Imagine waking up and seeing that face after what you've been through."

I wanted to laugh. I couldn't, but I mimicked a weak version of the sound. "I bit myself."

She nodded. "During the one before this. I'm afraid you ruined your shirt. I'll do my best to get the bloodstains out, but no promises. Don't you worry yourself. You should rest. I have a feeling you're not quite out of the woods yet."

I didn't want to rest, not with my head in her lap. I wanted to tell her everything that had happened, everything I knew about Dr. Bellamy. Someone needed to. He needed to be stopped. But what did I really know? Yes, he'd drugged me without my consent, but to what end? If we stopped him now, I'd never know. No one would. He'd run and get away with whatever he was doing.

Besides, I was too tired, too weak. All I could do was sleep. I was already hovering on the edge of exhaustion. When she hummed and rocked, I nearly fell asleep. I didn't open my eyes, but I did smile when I recognized the song. "That's an odd choice."

She let out a small chuckle that shook her body. "What? No appreciation for Simon and Garfunkel?"

"I always found 'The Sound of Silence' depressing."

"It is in a way," she said, resuming her rocking. "It's a lamentation about our inability to effectively communicate with each other on an emotional level. About social isolation and the pain it causes. It's strange, isn't it? The strongest instinct when we experience the pain of loss is to withdraw, yet withdrawal creates the perfect environment for pain to fester and grow. It's precisely when we need to surround ourselves with the love and compassion of others that we deny it most."

I opened my eyes. "Who did you lose, Sister?"

She stared straight ahead, the small but sad smile of a happy memory long gone playing on her pale lips. "I lost a son. He would be about your age, I think. In another life, you and I were not so different, except my drug of choice was heroin." Tears glistened in her eyes, but they never fell. Her smile faded as she looked down at me, stern again. "He didn't survive my demons, Felix. But you're going to survive yours if it kills me. And it might yet at this rate. You're very good at wearing an old nun out."

My throat was suddenly tight, and I didn't think it had anything to do with the seizure. I let my eyelids fall closed again. "Dr. Bellamy is drugging his patients. He gave me a PCP-laced hot dog. I don't remember what he did to me after that."

"I know," she said quietly. "I think I've known for a while. But I told myself it didn't matter. The people he took, they didn't have anyone who would miss them. They were problematic. Troublesome. Incurable. I convinced myself that whatever he was doing to them, it was a mercy. More merciful than that horrible ache of loneliness."

I swallowed the dryness and the bloody taste on my tongue. "What changed your mind?"

"Someone reminded me why I was here." She patted my chest. "I came to Saint Dymphna's to heal, to help God mend broken and troubled hearts. Healing is my passion, or it was. Somewhere, I lost sight of that. It became easier to hurt than to heal." The sister paused for a long time, rocking me in silence. "I'm going to make some calls. Whatever it is Dr. Bellamy is doing, it has to stop. Don't you worry about it, though, Felix. You're here to get better, and that all begins with a proper sleep."

As soon as I was able, she helped me into bed and brought me a sip of water. For all my previous contemptuous thoughts about Sister Mary Sabina, I felt guilty. There was a side to her I would never get to know. Somewhere in her was a good woman who would've been a good mother in another life. We'd both wrestled our demons alone for too long, and paid the price.

"It's not too late," I said. "You've found your spark again, Sister. There's still time to get the fire going. To heal and help. This doesn't have to be your end. Don't let yourself go down with Dr. Bellamy. It's not your fault."

She hesitated, pausing while tucking me in. The sad smile returned. She gripped my hand with both of hers and squeezed, then left without another word, holding back tears.

CHAPTER TWENTY-TWO

    I slept. If I had more seizures, I didn't remember them, and I didn't wake before or after them.

    When I woke to an unusually quiet ward, a strange foreboding feeling uncoiled in my stomach. Something was wrong, though what it was wasn't readily apparent.

    I checked myself first. Everything was where it was supposed to be. No new scars, incisions, or cuts. There were bruises from where I must've struck things while I was seizing, and my cheek still ached from where I'd bitten it. Aside from the expected aches and pains after a night of drug-induced seizures, I was fine. A thin fog still dampened my brain, but that too was normal after the night I'd had. It'd be a day or two before I was completely back to normal.

    I pushed aside the thin sheet and blanket covering me. The protective rails on both sides of the bed were up, so I couldn't just get out of bed. I had to scoot to the end and climb out that way. The plastic hangers rattled as I slid the privacy curtain aside. Mickey's side of the room was still empty. So, I hadn't dreamed it all.

My ears homed in on a female voice I hadn't heard before, the tone distressed. Not one of the sisters then. Maybe that was the reason the unit was so quiet. Usually, the constant murmur of voices clogged the air along with the constant drone of the television. Chairs scooted across the floor. Footsteps marked movement from one place to another. All of those were absent. Only the voice remained. The voice that shouldn't be there.

Slowly, on awkward legs that didn't quite cooperate, I wandered out of my room into the residential hallway. Doors lined either side, each leading to a patient room. These doors were never closed because that was against the rules. Patient doors had to be open at all times for the safety of the patients. Yet closed they were.

I limped down the hall. My back was sore, more sore than usual, but it would do me no good to complain. The only pain medication they allowed on the unit was the boring over-the-counter stuff. I'd learned long ago that wouldn't touch the sort of pain I had to live with. Everything that would help me had to be beyond reach. Dangerous. Locked away.

Like me, I thought. *Am I dangerous?*

A door that had been cracked open quickly shut as I approached. I paused and considered trying to open it to see who was on the other side. A patient, but who? Whose room was it? Why had everyone retreated and closed their doors? And why weren't the sisters disciplining them for breaking the rules?

I walked to the end of the hallway where I found another set of doors that were never supposed to be closed, the kind with the push bar and magnetic locks found in emergency rooms. The doors were closed, but the lock wasn't engaged. I pushed the door open and shuffled onto the main part of the unit.

"Get your hands off me!" A dark-haired woman in a raincoat spun away from the nurse's station pointing a tiny black bottle of pepper spray at an orderly. She had a small red purse slung over her shoulder. An umbrella leaned against the nurse's station. "Touch me again and not only will I pepper spray you, but I'll sue you out of existence. All of you!"

The orderly raised his hands and backed away.

She turned her anger back on Sister Meredith behind the desk. "Now I'll ask you again. Where is my brother?"

Sister Meredith rolled her shoulders back as if that would somehow give her the two inches she needed to be as tall as the other woman. "As I've already told you, Ms. Garrett, he isn't here, and I can't tell you where he is. It would be a violation of his privacy."

Garrett? I knew that name. "Julia?" I

stepped out of my hiding place near the door. "Mickey's sister?"

Some of the tension left her face, replaced by worry. She cast one more look at Sister Meredith before marching up to me, being sure to stop out of my reach. "Where is he?"

Sister Meredith crossed her arms and stared at me, waiting.

I shook my head. "I don't know, but he was here until a few nights ago. He was gone overnight."

"Ms. Garrett, I'm going to have to ask you to leave," Sister Meredith said.

Julia slid her thumb under her purse strap, adjusting how the purse sat on her shoulder. "Mickey shouldn't be out on his own. He'll get himself hurt. If you know anything…"

The main door to the unit opened and Dr. Bellamy strode in. At his back were three men in matching black suits. All four paused near the nurse's station as the door swung shut behind them and locked.

Dr. Bellamy looked from me to the woman to Sister Meredith. "Is there a problem here?"

"Damn right there's a problem." Julia stormed away from me to stop in front of the doctor and cross her arms. "Where's my brother, asshole?"

An orderly started to step between her and Dr. Bellamy, but Bellamy waved him off. "Who is your brother?"

"Mickey Garrett."

"Excuse me, gentlemen," Dr. Bellamy said to the men who had followed him onto the unit. He stepped forward and led Julia away with a hand on her lower back. "I'd be happy to tell you what little I can, Ms. Garrett, but I'm sure you're familiar with doctor-patient confidentiality. Mickey is a grown adult and responsible for his own care. Unless there are signed releases, there's simply very little information I can give." He cast a glance back at the three men in suits, a careful, quick look.

He doesn't want them to know what he's up to. I studied the men, none of which were wearing nametags or visitors passes. And here I thought everyone had to have a pass. Lots of rules being broken today.

Whoever they were, they had to be important. People in suits didn't just walk onto the unit with Dr. Bellamy because they wanted a tour of the place. No, if they were getting his attention, and making him so nervous, they had to have the power to shut him down, or at least punish him.

Dr. Bellamy and Julia sat.

"I just want to know if he's okay," Julia said. "He hasn't called."

"He isn't here." Dr. Bellamy patted her hand. "Mickey's been discharged on his own recognizance. Against my advice."

"What?" Julia shot to her feet and left Dr.

Bellamy's hand dangling. "How could you just let him walk out of here?"

"He's not a danger to himself or others," Bellamy explained. "So long as that's the case, he can only be held voluntarily. The patients on this unit are generally free to leave anytime they wish."

I didn't miss how he glanced over at me. That was a lie. If I tried to check myself out, they'd never let me go. He and the sisters would use every excuse they had to argue that I was a danger to society, and they'd keep me locked up as long as possible.

Or however long it took for Bellamy to do his work. Whatever that work was.

Julia's shoulders slumped. She looked at me too, as if there was something I could do about her brother's being gone. What was I supposed to do? I had nothing to tell her, no proof that Mickey was even real except for what I'd just heard.

Now Bellamy can't deny that Mickey is real. A feverish chill ran through me. He can no longer argue that Mickey and Reuben are manifestations of my own dissociative identity disorder. I didn't make them up and now I know it. Worse, he knows I know it.

I met Dr. Bellamy's eyes and we spent a long moment staring each other down, weighing options. Julia's umbrella was right next to me. It would be nothing for me to grab it, use it as an improvised weapon to defend myself. It was made if metal and cloth. Under the right circumstances, both could be deadly.

Slowly, Julia ran her thumb under her purse strap. It could be a weapon too. Dr. Bellamy could grab it, pull, twist, and wrap. In an instant, he would have a hostage in Julia, or he could erase one nosy girl from existence, to keep her from exposing him.

There were other weapons, too. Just on the other side of the nurse's station, there was a ceramic coffee cup someone had been careless enough to bring in. In my mind's eye, I watched myself dive over the top of the nurse's station, grab the cup by the handle, and smash it against the wall. The nuns panicked and backed away, but the orderlies charged forward. They were armed with hypodermic needles. One pinch of flesh and I would be helpless again, but I wasn't helpless yet. I would go for the eyes, the tender flesh of their faces, the exposed skin on their arms. Anywhere I knew it would hurt and bleed.

But then what? A standoff? I could take a hostage too and demand someone open the doors to let me out. I could be free.

The standoff I imagined droned on with Dr. Bellamy tightening the red leather strap of Julia's purse around her neck. Her face turned blue. She made desperate choking sounds, but she wasn't fighting anymore. She was dying. All I had to do to save her was drop my weapon.

Let the ceramic makeshift blade fall to the floor and everything would be all right. An innocent woman would live, but I would die. Dr. Bellamy would take me away to the room where his former patients lay half-dead in a semi-circle around a glass coffin. I would die with Mickey and Reuben. Or worse, I would become half-dead like them.

Even if I got free, what then? We were miles from the nearest town. I had nothing, not even shoes. Memories of the last time I had gotten lost in the woods came rushing back. He would hunt me, find me, and then finish the job Laura Hemlock had started all those months ago.

But that was all just a fantasy, a what-if. In reality, Dr. Bellamy and I were still trapped on the unit, staring at each other with twitching fingers and impotent, knowing looks.

For a fleeting moment, his eyes left mine and took in the postures of the three men left standing near the door. Their faces were blank, motives and purpose unclear. What would they do if either of us showed our true colors in their presence? Would they come to my aid or his? Maybe they would stand still, silent observers as blood and death collected on the ground like autumn leaves.

Reality held its breath while two madmen decided what shape it would take.

Dr. Bellamy stood. Reality exhaled, the inside of it deflating, aching like empty lungs. He gestured to the exit. "Let me walk you out, Ms. Garrett."

She turned her back to the doctor, facing the door.

He struck with practiced precision. I didn't see the hypodermic needle fall from his sleeve, didn't see him discard the protective plastic cap or hear it drop. But as he jabbed it into Julia Garrett's neck and pressed the plunger down with his thumb, I heard the small sound of surprise she made. It was the same sound I'd once heard a rabbit make in a pet store when a child grabbed it too roughly. Her eyelids fluttered and she crumpled into his arms.

On the other side of the nurse's station, the two orderlies sprang into action brandishing syringes of their own. They attacked the three men in suits, subduing two easily. The third ran for the door, but it was locked. They took their time getting to him.

I threw myself at the desk, reaching for the mug. Cold, stagnant coffee splashed out everywhere as I grabbed it awkwardly. The sisters were clamoring away from the desk in shock and awe, eyes wide. I swung the cup and smashed it against the wall, but it didn't shatter on the first strike, so I pulled it back to try again.

Dr. Bellamy's hand closed over mine and twisted away my only weapon. I felt the sting of a needle as it broke through the flesh in my neck. A nauseating rush flooded my brain and I lost all coordination. I went to the floor, groggy and clumsy. The weight of anxiety settled on my chest, increasing with every panicked beat of my heart. Blackness hovered.

No, no, no! I can't pass out. I can't lose consciousness, or I'll never wake up again!

"I'll call security." Sister Meredith reached for the phone.

Dr. Bellamy's left hand slammed down overtop hers. He backhanded her with his right. "I think the sisters have made enough calls for one day," he growled and jerked his head. "Restrain them. If they fight, you know what to do."

The two orderlies stepped over me to get to the sisters.

"You," I managed in a wheezing, breathy voice. It was all I could get out because of how tight my chest had become.

"Yes, me." Dr. Bellamy squatted in front of me, listening to me wheeze. He reached to adjust the collar of my shirt. "This isn't how I planned on doing this, but I'm afraid the poor execution can't be helped. I've waited too long for those suited idiots to ruin everything. Not when I've finally found the catalyst I've been waiting for."

I felt myself sliding to one side. Darkness closed in. There was nothing I could do to stop it.

CHAPTER TWENTY-THREE

THEN

I went to the library to do some research and get warm. I was surprised to find it open on Christmas Eve, but the New York Library System never seemed to fully shut down. There was always a branch open somewhere for people like me. People without a warm place to go. Always, except for maybe on Christmas. I tried not to think about where I would go tomorrow.

The line of computers on the ground floor was mostly empty. A middle-aged woman in thick reading glasses sat behind a desk overseeing the area. She glanced up only once as I sat down at the computer and then quickly away. I fit right in with the few other men sitting around, waiting for the library to close. Dirty, broke, hungry for something I could neither name nor attain. Whatever it was, I'd have to settle for a little research on Al's situation.

When I had seen the creature in the hospital, I thought at first it might be a poltergeist. The signs and symptoms were similar. The chair stacking, random things out of place, a gradual escalation toward violence. They had an adolescent child, too, which was common in those situations. No one truly knew what poltergeists looked like, but they tended to resolve on their own.

The thing is, poltergeists were mischievous, not malevolent. They caused annoyance, mild injury at worst. All the research I did said it was unheard of for them to kill.

Whatever was happening to Allen Miller, it wasn't a poltergeist. That didn't feel right either. This thing was like a manifestation of sorts. An imaginary friend gone bad. But I couldn't find any information on the internet about what that might be.

With no luck on the computer, I left the internet behind and went up into the stacks. The library I was in wasn't the largest in the city, and yet it felt too big to be real. There were floors and floors of books, everything from old dusty tomes and dissertations, to bright and colorful picture books. Just finding a place to begin felt daunting.

Tucked into a corner on the third floor, I found the world mythologies and religions section. Once, I would've come straight there probably to research a paper I was working on for one of my courses. I paced slowly down one of the darkened rows running my fingers over the bindings of books on theology, ministry, and history of evangelism. At the far end of the row stood a small section on demons and devils.

I stopped to select a book at random and flipped it open to an arbitrary page. The author filled that page and the one that followed with advice on how to arm oneself for spiritual battle. Useless lies. Prayer, fasting, faith...none of it had helped me. Demons took who they wanted, and no amount of belief in God would keep them at bay. What had happened to me was no battle. It was a battering of the mind, soul, and body, one for which there was no defense.

Every book on the shelf was some variation of the same. Guides on how to defeat evil, how to prepare for evil, how to confront it when it appeared. They were lies to make the helpless feel as if they had some control over their situation.

Where were the books on naming the damned? On recovering from what they did inside of you? There were no books that told the truth of the matter.

"You were hoping to find a copy of *What to Expect When You're Possessed*?" Sean leaned against the shelf on the other side and laughed. "Or did you just want a guidebook on how to survive what comes after?"

I slid the book back into its place. "Every year, thousands of people are touched by true evil. We tell stories about it. About how the light beats back the darkness, how good always triumphs. But I don't feel triumphant. I feel... empty. Like it stole a part of me. I've lost an integral part of my being, and no matter what sort of prosthetic I try, I can't find another that will fit. I'm not whole."

"A priest would say what you are missing is God." Shadows of fingers moved across book spines. "And when we're missing God, what we're truly lacking is love. Love is the antithesis of pain. But instead of seeking the real thing, you've been taking a synthetic version, something that mimics the cure, but is so far from it."

"I know that." I moved to another section of shelves, this one containing primers on world religions. "But what am I supposed to do now? Run back to my mother? She's got enough on her plate without having to take care of me again. I can't go to church. All I feel when I try to pray is bitterness where that comfort should be."

"You feel betrayed by God," said Sean.

"Yes." I turned to the opposite shelf and found a book on new age spiritual beliefs. Closer, but not what I was looking for.

"You know what I have to say on the matter is controversial." His shadow shifted on the other side of the shelves. "It's selfish of us to assume God would intervene for good or bad. We don't pray for help expecting he'll swoop down from Heaven and rescue us. We pray for it because we want to be shown another path, one we didn't think of before. We want to rescue ourselves but feel we lack the power. By placing belief in a higher power, we absolve ourselves of responsibility and He maintains His illusion of free will."

I snorted. "That doesn't sound like something they taught at seminary."

"It isn't," Sean continued. "I don't believe God is capable of betrayal. He is an inert and terrible force of creation. Birth is bloody and painful, dangerous and beautiful. Nothing new can be born without the destruction of the old. That doesn't make it evil. It's not betrayal when we are pulled from the safety and comfort of our mothers to experience the cold danger of the world. It's simply a thing that happens, Felix. It must happen so that we can grow."

I shoved a book too hard and several came toppling out of the shelf. "Do you expect me to believe what happened to me was so I could grow? Don't feed me that line, Sean! Bad things don't always happen for a reason, and I can blame God for what happened to me all I want. Fuck you, and fuck Him."

"Excuse me!"

I turned my head to the end of the row.

The librarian stood there with a pile of books in her hand, a stern expression on her face. "The library is closed. You shouldn't be here. I'm going to have to ask you to leave."

The librarian escorted me to the front door and held it open while I walked out into

E.A. COPEN

the cold. I wanted to argue with her, but it was a fight I knew I couldn't win. This was her place, her palace, and she could kick me out if she wanted.

Outside, soft snowflakes floated down from a sky blanketed in gray. Cars and taxis slid through the slushy beginnings of a white Christmas. Bundled New Yorkers trundled by, heads down in the biting wind, bags and packages tucked under each arm.

I had nowhere to go, and no money. There was still a credit card in my wallet, the one my mother had given me for emergencies. It wasn't maxed out yet, but it was close. Maybe I could get a hotel room for the night and ride out the withdrawal. A shower and a long sleep would do me some good. Surely I could get that far on sixty bucks and a dream. I'd just have to walk it.

The cold made my joints ache worse, and sidewalks were difficult to navigate with a cane. Slippery spots could mean a fall, and another fall might mean another broken back, one I wouldn't recover from this time. There was more traction in the thin layer of snow gathering on grassy lawns and dirt patches just to the right of the sidewalks, so I walked there, drawing curious looks from those who sped on by.

As I walked, I thought about all the Christmas movies set in New York. They always had a scene like this, snow falling on Christmas Eve while the busy and world-weary protagonist wandered lost through crowds. Eventually, such stories always ended with him learning the true meaning of Christmas. It was always family, togetherness, belief, hope, love…some intangible thing. A lie. The true meaning of Christmas wasn't a feeling. It wasn't to celebrate the birth of Christ either, since the date had been selected purely to appropriate existing pagan solstice festivals. While it was tempting to say the meaning was consumerism and spending money on gifts, that wasn't true either. That purpose was a modern perversion of an old tradition that used to mean more. Christmas was just another day. It meant nothing.

I stopped at the first motel that looked cheap enough I could afford it. The sign outside advertised rooms at less than forty dollars a night and access to paid television channels. A small bell jingled above the door as I pushed it open.

Every time a bell rings, an angel gets his wings, I thought.

A tired-looking old man approached the counter, peering at me from behind a quarter-inch of safety glass. There was a small slot at the bottom to pass keys and payment, but he was otherwise cut off from anyone out in the lobby. "Can I help you, son?" He had the lingering hint of a Texas drawl, the kind that must've been strong before the city watered it down.

"Just looking for a place to stay." I reached

for my wallet.

"Sorry, son, but we're full up," said the inn-keeper.

How ironic. No room at the inn on Christmas Eve. "Don't suppose you've got a stable out back?"

The man's lip twitched. "Huh?"

"Nothing. It was a joke. Have a good night."

He nodded slowly and called as I pushed open the door a second time, "Happy holidays!"

I used the credit card to buy a pack of cigarettes at a convenience store. I tried to buy two, but the card was declined until I had the cashier put one back. Guess I was closer to my limit than I thought, which meant it was just as well that the hotel was full. I couldn't have afforded it anyway.

The sky had darkened by the time I found myself in the convenience store parking lot. As the temperature plummeted and my back ached, I wondered if it would be cold enough for me to freeze to death if I slept outside. It happened every year, or so the newspaper headlines said, but not to everyone. How did the homeless survive New York winters? There were thousands of them, so there must've been a way.

Homeless, I thought, hugging myself. *Is that what I am now? A homeless addict? A would-be thief?* How had I fallen so far? It wasn't so long ago that I had been the one dropping change into open guitar cases and empty plastic cups when

I could. How many people had I passed without giving a second thought? People like me whose lives had taken a turn for the worst because of one bad day? One poor, stupid decision led to a cascade of more of the same.

What about Jade? I still had her card in my pocket. She'd written her home address on the back for me. I brought it out and stared at it resting in the palm of my chilled hand. Would she take me in if I went there? Maybe I should have just swallowed my pride and went home to my mother, but she wouldn't be there either. She'd be working at one of her jobs. At Mom's, I was just another mouth to feed. I didn't know if I could look her in the eye after everything that had happened, after everything I'd done. But Jade was a licensed therapist. She'd know what to do. If anyone knew how to help me through the next few days of hellish comedown, it would be her.

Before I knew it, I was standing in front of a small house in a row of other, similar-looking houses. A simple wreath with black and red ribbon hung on the door. I almost didn't knock, but after walking the whole way, climbing those last three steps hurt so bad I knew I couldn't go any further. I raised my fist to rap on the storm door, secretly hoping no one was home.

Those hopes were dashed when the door opened. On the other side, Jade was wearing a very comfortable set of fleece pajamas in green and red. She held a nearly empty wine glass in one hand. "Felix!" She immediately pushed open the storm door. After one look, she said, "Get in here out of the cold."

She practically had to pull me over the threshold into the narrow hallway on the other side. I had been so cold I'd forgotten what it felt like to be warm. As soon as I was through the door into the blasting heat, I wanted to melt into a puddle.

Jade ushered me to a worn sofa the color of apple butter and draped a knitted blanket over me. "God, you look terrible. What happened to you? Felix, are you high? What are you on?"

It was all I could do to keep up with her barrage of questions. "Vicodin, I think. That was all they had."

"Who?" The sofa cushion I was on shifted as she sat down next to me.

"The Millers." I explained everything to her, as much as I could remember. I told her how I had squandered all my money on pills that never made the pain completely go away. I confessed my intent to rob the Millers, only to get lucky and be there to witness a murder.

In the minutes that followed, I described everything that had happened since I left the hospital in enough detail for her to take notes. I expected her to be angry with me, but her face didn't betray anger. She seemed worried.

After I told her where I had been and what I had been doing, she asked me more questions.

How many pills did I normally take? How often? How long ago? What dosages? When I couldn't remember, I had to describe colors and shapes. It should have been more difficult to talk about. I should have felt ashamed of what I'd done, but I didn't. It all felt as if I were completing a grocery order.

When I was finished, she brought me a cup of hot tea and left me sitting alone in the living room. I could hear her securing the locks on her medicine cabinets from where I sat. That's when the shame hit me. Guilt gnawed at my insides. No one would ever trust me again. What had I done?

Jade returned with a pair of pills she told me to take.

I stared at the small, round white balls of medicine. "What are they?"

"Does it matter?" she asked.

"It should. But it doesn't." I took the pills and swallowed them with the too-hot tea.

Jade sat down next to me again, folding her hands. "You can't just quit. It's dangerous. If I were any good at my job, I would load you into a car right now and drop you off at the closest drug treatment program I could find. But I know you. I know you won't stay. No twelve-step program is going to get through to you, is it, Felix Cross?"

I shook my head, staring straight forward.

She sighed. "I'll help you, but you have to

promise me you'll accept the help. The minute you give me pushback, I'm done. You have to want this, Felix. I can't help someone who doesn't want to be helped."

A thought suddenly occurred to me. What if Al and I were in the same boat? We were both suffering because we'd made a poor choice. We had fed negative instincts, trying to make up for something else lacking in our lives. I had lost a friend. He'd never bothered to make them. Why should he if he had that thing around to talk to? What if he didn't want to get rid of it and that was why it was still hanging around?

I set my tea on the coffee table. "Jade, what do you know about dangerous imaginary friends?"

She frowned. "I know if it really is an imaginary friend, it's not going to kill people. It sounds like Al Miller has something else entirely going on."

"Whatever it is, it killed his father and attacked his mother. It's going after the people around him, and that's not random. Al said he thought it was protecting him. It's somehow attuned to how he's feeling and it's misinterpreting things that aren't dangerous as life-threatening."

"Like a deadly manifestation of anxiety." She turned and retrieved her laptop from where she'd placed it on the chair. "You want to stop it, you're going to need to find out what it is first."

"I tried that." I sighed. "It's not a polter-geist, and I don't think it's demonic. It doesn't feel like a demon."

"And what does a demon feel like?" She glanced up from her screen.

"Malevolent," I said. "They delight in misery and cause disturbance for the hell of it. This thing is like a twisted guardian angel, but one the kid created himself."

"You can't conjure a creature from nothing." Jade's fingers moved furiously over the keyboard. Her eyes widened. "I stand corrected. Apparently, you can." She passed the computer to me.

On the screen was a thread from a text-based forum with a dated layout. The threads were organized by topic along the side of the screen. The one she'd pulled up was a sub-topic of a sub-topic of a sub-topic. "Tulpamancy?"

"A tulpa is a sort of autonomous manifested creature. An imaginary friend with free will. I had a patient once who believed in them. There are whole pockets of people who try to create these things. Usually, it's because they're lonely creative types who have no one else to share their passion with."

"Kids exactly like Al." I scrolled through the thread, skimming for information. "Does he know he created this thing?"

Jade shrugged. "You know him better than me."

I thought about everything he had told me. The constant moving, always being the new kid, his love for dance, his isolation...he was the perfect example of the type of person who would create one of these things. Jade had found it after a quick search on the internet, and Al was younger, far more tech-savvy than either of us. If we knew about it, he certainly did. He might have an account on the very website I was scrolling through, though it was impossible to know.

I went to the search bar in the sub-thread and typed in "how to get rid of a tulpa". Several threads on the topic had been created, but the answers weren't encouraging. Most of the responders were aghast that anyone would want to destroy a sentient being and equated the act to murder. Only one thread had any useful information, and it had been created by someone else who had a negative and frightening experience with their tulpa. Just as I had first thought, destroying the tulpa wouldn't be easy for Al. It would mean facing the pain of the world without the anesthetic he had spent his life leaning on so heavily.

"The tulpa is his drug." I set the computer aside and stood. My legs moved on their own, carrying me around the room. I couldn't sit still any longer, not even if I wanted. "He can't cope without it, and there's no step down for him, Jade. He has to sever that connection and he has to do it tonight."

"Why?"

I lowered my hand from my chin and turned around. "Rejection. The kid is a ballet dancer. He's good, but he's not pro good, and he can't make pro unless he first learns to take criticism. That thing isn't going to let him. There's supposed to be a recruiter at his recital tonight. What if he doesn't make it? The tulpa will kill the recruiter, Jade. It will think it's protecting him as it strings an innocent dance critic's guts all through the auditorium, along with anyone else who wants to judge the kid. All his father did was yell at him and it killed him. Imagine what it will do to the crowd if he misses a step or doesn't land every jump." I shook my head and charged for the door.

"Felix!" Jade called.

I paused and almost fell over as my knees reminded me I had been walking in the cold all night.

She pushed off the sofa. "You'll need a ride." She looked me up and down, one eyebrow raised. "And a suit."

CHAPTER TWENTY-FOUR

NOW

I came in and out of consciousness. Each time I woke with a foggy sense that I was moving, floating along in a straight line, my limbs heavy and strapped down. I remember distinctly the image of lights sliding along above me, one after another, each identical.

Despite being unconscious, I still retained some sense of awareness. Part of me knew that I was strapped securely to a gurney, moving through narrow hallways into another portion of Saint Dymphna's where I wasn't supposed to go.

I dreamed of the vision I'd had when I touched the Chessman, the round basement room with its semi-circle of patients and the glass coffin at the center. In the dream, however, it wasn't a perfectly preserved young man lying inside, but Sean. Shadows moved as days marched by in a time-lapse. Days became weeks, and weeks became months. I watched helplessly as Sean's body changed colors, bloated, as the insides leaked out and dried on the sides of the case in a putrid crust of red and green. His structure collapsed in on itself and skin melted away, leaving behind ragged bone and stubborn strings of muscle.

When I woke from the nightmare, it was only because the steady beeping off to my left had changed its rhythm. Long before I could open my eyes, I was aware of the coppery smell of blood in the room. Beneath that, my nose itched with the sting of hospital grade sanitizer. Steady pressure held my arms to my sides. A bright light shone green behind my eyelids. My eyes fluttered open and I squinted at the blinding light.

As my eyes slowly adjusted, I relied on my ears to tell me where I was. To my left, several people shuffled around with different distinct footfalls. Monitors beeped. Dr. Bellamy occasionally mumbled something I couldn't quite grasp.

Finally, I had enough sense to turn my head for a look. There was another patient next to me with blue paper draped over his torso. An orderly in scrubs blocked my view of what was happening. When he moved out of the way, I recognized Reuben. One of the other orderlies had a manual oxygen pump over his face, squeezing the pump to keep him breathing. Dr. Bellamy was elbow deep in Reuben's chest cavity with streaks of crimson running up the long-sleeved surgical gown and spattering his face mask.

I strained my neck to lift my head and look around the room. I had indeed been brought to the room with the glass coffin, but the body was in the coffin no more. Instead, it had been brought out and placed on a surgical table of its own, the long black hair of the corpse tucked under a cap that looked suspiciously like a shower cap. He'd been dressed in a nice shirt and slacks in the Chessman's vision, but now he lay there naked but for a paper blanket draped over his hips. Someone had drawn lines over various parts of his body in black ink.

Next to me, the monitor measuring Reuben's heart rate suddenly halted, the wavy lines growing straight. An alarm went off. One of the orderlies tapped a button on the screen, silencing the alarm.

Slowly, carefully, Dr. Bellamy lifted his hands from inside Reuben's chest. Clutched delicately in his blue gloved hands was a perfect human heart. With all the care he'd pay to a newborn, he placed the heart he'd extracted in an ice-filled container held out to him by yet another orderly.

"I see you're awake," said the doctor without looking at me. He stripped his gloves and moved to the far wall where a sink waited. I couldn't see him washing his hands with his back to me, but I heard the water running. "That's unfortunate. I never planned for you to see this. However, it isn't unexpected given your history with pharmaceutical abuse. I had to estimate your tolerance to the sedative I gave you. Apparently, I was mistaken."

I swallowed. "What kind of doctor murders his patients?"

"What sort of seminary student gets possessed?" He turned around, patting his hands dry on a disposable towel. "Thousands of patients die every year due to medical negligence or mistakes made on the operating table. It's likely one of the leading causes of death, though one can't be sure. No one tracks that statistic accurately because if they did, physicians everywhere would have to be held liable for their actions. Nobody wants to admit that doctors are killers, not healers. What kind of doctor murders his patients, Felix? Every doctor has killed someone, even if he chooses not to acknowledge that fact."

"Not every doctor removes his patient's heart and puts it on ice."

"No, I suppose not." His face was still, his voice calm. If anything he'd said or done bothered him, it didn't show.

My eyes shifted lower to where another body lay, wrapped in plastic and moved out of the way. Julia's glassy eyes stared at me through the plastic. Apparently, Bellamy was killing more than his patients now. He had to make sure there were no witnesses.

Bellamy followed my gaze and spared

Julia barely a glance before turning back to me. "You're judging me. You believe yourself on some sort of moral high ground, that you are somehow better than me."

I tried to shake my head. It left me feeling dizzy. "I've killed people, Dr. Bellamy. By my action or inaction, people have died. I admit that. But never with malicious intent."

"You believe my intent to be malicious?" He grabbed a stool from the edge of the room and rolled it over next to my bed. "What if I told you that I was on the verge of a medical breakthrough that would change the way we think about death?"

"I would tell you you're crazy."

"I imagine they said the same to Peter Safar." The stool creaked. "He invented CPR, which is widely used today. But he was accused in his lifetime of playing God and cheating death. Giordano Bruno—a sixteenth-century Italian priest-turned-philosopher—had his tongue bound and was burned at the stake for daring to posit other solar systems existed. Now, we teach it as fact to schoolchildren. To dream of a better world, a bigger world, may seem like madness to some, but science isn't beholden to the laws of man. If we are given the power to create life from death, we must pursue it."

I met his eyes. "What about ethical science, Doctor?"

He smiled. "There is no such thing. Ethics is something we humans impose on a neutral world around us. What is and is not ethical varies from society to society, year to year, place to place. Like science, ethics is evolutionary. He who takes the first step must always be willing to move beyond the acceptable. But if it's easier for you to think of it in terms of ethics…" He pushed a button.

With a mechanical whirr, my bed rose and tilted to mimic a standing position.

Dr. Bellamy stood next to me and pointed to the dead man on the operating table. "Imagine a world where death is reversible. Where it is something we need not fear. In such a world, we could pick and choose the time of our passing. No more regret. No more tearful goodbyes after the fact. Death can become a positive experience for those that wish it. For those that don't want to embrace the option, no one will force them. But just having the option…could change lives for the better."

"You can't reverse death, Doctor. No one can."

"No one has yet." He held up a finger. "But there is a first time for everything, isn't there? No one before me has known what I know, has dared to push the limits of science as far as I have. This is the future in progress, and I am giving you a front-row seat."

"Even if this works, it won't be worth it.

One life at the cost of..." I counted the beds in the room. "Six others? No one will want that."

Dr. Bellamy tilted his head to the side. "Who have you buried? You seem so young, so naïve of the pain of death. You say you lost your friend, but did you hold his lifeless body in your arms and weep into a cold, still chest? Do you know the weight of death? Of profound loneliness? Of words unsaid?" He leaned in. "If you did, you wouldn't hesitate to sacrifice a hundred lives to bring back the one you love. Whatever you feel for Sean Yeats, it isn't love or loyalty. It's guilt." He hit the button again and the bed I was on lowered back into its original position.

My tongue was suddenly too big to swallow any more air. What if he was right? What if I was wrong about everything? I remembered the day I woke up in the hospital and heard that Sean was gone without a trace. It had been agony. Silent agony since I still had tubes in my throat helping me breathe with regularity. I couldn't even grieve properly. And when I could, I had already gone numb to the idea of it.

I'd never thought to sort out my feelings for Sean, believing that was something I could do after I had brought him back. But what if I couldn't? If I was seeing his ghost, then he was gone forever. Though if Sean was dead, did it matter how I felt?

I had loved him. At first, I thought it was the same love anyone would have for a brother or a best friend, but that love had grown into something else. That wasn't imagined. I had felt my heart race whenever he put a hand on my shoulder or leaned in close. I knew the feeling of forbidden desire churning in my chest as intimately as I knew the fear I would fail. But since he was the only man I had ever loved, I didn't know if the empty, black hole in my soul feeling of loss was because I had loved him, or because I was responsible for that loss. Guilt, love, lust, loss...it was all balled into one horrible emotion. I could no sooner separate the threads of that feeling than I could free myself from that bed.

I tried to swallow, but it felt like I had a walnut caught in my throat. "I know the difference between love and guilt."

"Do you?" His eyes bored a hole right through me, cutting sharper than the bloody scalpel he'd laid aside only moments ago. "Love is patient. Love is kind. It does not envy, does not boast."

"It doesn't dishonor others," I added. "Nor is it self-serving." I nodded to the corpse on the operating table. "Who is he to you? Someone you claim to love? It isn't love, Doctor, if bringing him back means ripping out the heart of an innocent man."

Dr. Bellamy turned his head. Sadness touched his hardened features as he took in the body on display. "I would have given him my heart if I could. But, sadly, I'm not a match. You see, Connor had a fairly rare blood type. Not many A negatives in the world. Less than seven percent of the population. Imagine my surprise to find not one, but three men in one ward with the same rare blood type. Of course, I already had a few volunteers." He gestured to the other three bodies.

They hadn't been dead for long, but each of them had undergone recent surgery. He hadn't even bothered to stitch some of them closed.

"They don't look like volunteers to me."

"Of course not, but all the paperwork will say they were. And you too. You've already signed the consent forms." He smiled.

I thought I was going to be sick. "You kept them alive."

"Necessary. Harvested organs can only survive so long out of the body."

My stomach churned. I wasn't sure I wanted to know, but I had to ask just the same. "What are you going to take from me?"

"Only what you've asked me to take." He set aside the towel he'd used earlier to dry his hands and approached my bedside. His hands settled on my chest, too heavy. "My suicidal patients often express deep regret after they've made an attempt on their lives. Not a regret that they failed, or even that they made the attempt. Do you know what they regret most of all, Felix?"

I settled into the gurney and stared at the

white ceiling until it was out of focus, nothing but a blurry wall of white and shadow. "Their failure to cope with the pain of living."

Dr. Bellamy gave a subtle nod. "There is a general misconception that those who suffer from suicidal depression are weak. But they aren't. You aren't. Most are like you, gifted with creative, passionate minds. They are poets, dancers, artists. Only some of them have forgotten. They suffer because the world is too harsh a place for gentle hearts. This is why you wish to forget. It is why your guilt over whatever small part you played in your friend's death overwhelms you. The source of your pain is your ability to feel. This is what I will take from you. Numbness is the gift I will give you."

I lowered my eyes from the ceiling to meet his again. "I don't understand."

He placed a hand on the side of my face, an almost comforting gesture. "Do you know what a transorbital lobotomy is?"

I surged forward in the gurney, hoping I could latch onto his face with my teeth. It wouldn't free me, but I wasn't going to go out without a fight. Unfortunately, they had me strapped too tight to the table. I couldn't get close enough.

Dr. Bellamy gave me a smug smile and withdrew his hand. "You see, unlike the others, I need you alive. Once I complete the final transplant and turn on the machine, I will need your power to draw Connor back to his body."

"And if I refuse?"

He tilted his head and looked at me with confusion. "You can't refuse, Felix. You're already a beacon to spirits, ghosts, and demons. Why do you think you can see them so clearly? Why did you think you could detect their presence? Just being here will be enough. I wouldn't be surprised to find out he's already been in touch with you."

I twisted my neck and shifted my head to look at the body on the operating table again. It did seem oddly familiar. Poe stepped out from the shadows of the room and stood over the body, frowning at it. He looked at me and I knew...Poe was Connor. The ghost was thinner, leaner, paler even than the dead man. His eyes were more sunken and dark, the bones of his wrists and fingers more delicate and child-like, and the hair on the corpse neater, but with only a few slight adjustments, they could be one and the same. Death had not been kind to Connor, perhaps even crueler than life.

"And what if Connor refuses?" I asked the doctor.

He laughed and shook his head as if my suggestion were so outrageous it didn't even bear consideration. "Why would anyone who is dead want to stay that way? Now, I'll need you to be quiet for a while. The transplant will take some time." He gestured to the orderlies.

Two of them stepped forward and lowered a mask onto my face. Air hissed up through a small tube and clouded the air. Another drug to knock me out.

"No, wait!" I cried, but no one did.

Bellamy leaned over me, a finger to his lips. "Don't stress yourself, Felix. If all goes well, when you wake, you'll be a new man and I will have my Connor back."

CHAPTER TWENTY-FIVE

THEN

When I thought about Christmas ballet, the only thing that came to mind was The Nutcracker. It seemed like there were always signs up for that sort of thing during the holidays. I don't know what I expected, going to a novice-level dance recital, but it wasn't a stifling, packed auditorium. Not everyone occupying a seat was a parent either. There were people with press tags on, and a few local television personalities tucked in among the seats. It was quickly apparent that the event wasn't just some high school talent show. The people gathered in the auditorium that night were serious about the world of dance.

I tugged at the choking collar as we slid into what looked like the only empty pair of seats in the house. It was in the back row, or rather, the added back row. Someone had placed three additional rows of folding chairs behind the auditorium's normal padded seats. Everyone else had been clapping while we slipped in, which meant we'd missed a few of the opening acts. I hoped Al wasn't one of them.

The auditorium quieted as the lights went down. When they came back up, they were focused on the couple on stage. After a beat of silence, the recognizable thrum of some Spanish guitar number started and they began a strange sort of tango mixed with more modern moves.

I turned away from the performance on stage and opened up the paper program. The first page was a general welcome and an explanation of the event. This was a capstone performance for all the students in the private course. Each student had been tasked with choosing their music, choreographing their dance, and, of course, the performance. The students ranged in age from thirteen to seventeen and came from all backgrounds and walks of life. All of them were kids the instructor claimed showed a passion for dance.

I looked up from the program, watching the couple on stage. Maybe the passion was there, but the chemistry wasn't. While I wasn't a dance expert, I'd heard of the tango. It was supposed to be as close as two dancers could get to sex on stage. Those two kids, however, were stiff with each other, their movements almost too practiced. They had the technical aspects of it down, but it was creatively stunted.

Christ, I thought and shifted in my seat. *Listen to me. These are kids. Children.* Yet there

I was expecting them to perform like the few dancers I'd seen on talent shows on TV. They must've felt some pressure to do the same. It wasn't right. Kids that age should have been proud of the very fact they could dance better than most adults. Hell, I didn't even know if I could jump after I'd broken my back, let alone twirl at that speed without throwing up.

For a moment, I tried to imagine what it must have been like to have that pressure heaped on you at such a young age. Al was sixteen and believed if he didn't get his shot tonight, his dance career would be over. Sixteen. Far too young to put your entire future on the line in a single dance. It must have been petrifying.

I turned the page and scanned the list of names and songs, searching for Allen Miller. I found him about three-quarters of the way down the second page and followed the dotted line across the paper. When I saw his song selection, I had to raise an eyebrow. An ambitious tune with a deep emotional history, at least for people as old as me. I wondered if he understood the significance of the song in the same way I did. Only the dance interpretation would tell.

"I thought there would be more Christmas tunes." Jade folded her program in half and tucked it into her purse.

"Glad I'm not the only one."

The tango ended and the couple took their

bows to applause that could've been more en-thusiastic. They must've known the perform-ance wasn't their best because the girl's mascara was running with tears, despite the smile. They rushed from the stage, dreams shattered. She must've felt like her life was over. I could only hope there was someone backstage to tell her that wasn't the case.

The next dance was a group of eight per-forming quick and acrobatic movements. They nailed every landing, every lift, every move. Still, it felt like I was sitting in a circus act and not a dance. Nothing about the performance was moving. It was good, and showed an incredible amount of skill, but it was still too stiff. Emo-tionless. If I had to sit through too many more acts like it, I'd fall asleep, despite the pounding music.

After the group came a pair of twin baller-inas who did a number out of Swan Lake. One of them missed a jump, landing awkwardly. She didn't fall, and made an expert recovery, but everyone in the audience saw the misstep.

It isn't easy, I told myself. They're up there under the scrutinizing eyes of hundreds, dressed in costume, under the intensely bright lights. They're doing well, considering.

But *considering* wasn't good enough, not when some harbored dreams of Juilliard. Perfect wasn't even good enough. They had to do better than master the technical aspects of dance. They had to live it, breathe it, make the dance a part of who they were and translate it for an audience that didn't speak their language.

Al can do that. The thought led me to the edge of my seat as one act ended and his was announced. My heart jumped into my throat and hammered there harder and faster than any of the dance music that had played in the auditorium that night. What if he landed awkwardly? What if something went wrong? I knew what he could do, but that didn't matter. Tonight, he had to show the recruiter sitting somewhere in the audience. He had to be better than perfect. And if he wasn't, people could die.

Part of me wanted to leap out of my seat and rush backstage to stop him. I knew the danger of his performance, but still, I couldn't bring myself to stand between a kid and his dreams of greatness. *Maybe nothing will go wrong. Al might be better than perfect.*

The curtain opened in silence. Al lay at center stage, curled into a fetal position. We waited a long moment, anxiety building as the only thing to fill the silence were errant coughs and the shifting of clothing as everyone leaned forward at once.

Then, as the opening bars of "Mad World" gave birth to a song, Al too was born. He uncurled and sat up, rolling over the stage, and dancing without finding his legs at first. It wasn't the original arrangement of the song, but a slower, more melancholic version by some obscure singer I didn't know. I liked it much better, especially watching Al.

While the lyrics narrated the mundanity of life, Al danced. While he danced, a video played behind him, personal footage from shaky and grainy cameras common in the nineties. Al danced through footage of him learning to walk. On the stage, he took a few wobbly steps before breaking into a run that ended in a delicate jump. I didn't know the names for the moves he was doing, but I understood the story they told, even without the background footage.

Here is the story of a not so very average boy born to an average family. They asked him to walk, but he wanted to fly. They bought him a football. He wanted ballet slippers. And one day, someone sat him down, tried to explain carefully all the problems with boys who wanted to dance.

"People will laugh," they said.

He said, "I don't care."

"You'll be the only boy."

"That doesn't matter to me."

"Don't you want to play soccer or football with your friends?"

"I want to dance alone until my feet ache and bleed."

So many times, people had tried to set this child's rhythm, and each time, he subverted that rhythm. Even when he wished he could be like everyone else, he found himself unable to escape the call of his passion. They didn't understand, his parents, his teachers, his peers. It wasn't *just* dancing. It was his heart given legs. All he wanted was for them to see him, to acknowledge that this was who he was. Al had known all along that, despite his best efforts, he could never be anything other than a dancer.

As Al moved with perfect elegance across the stage, the tulpa joined him. Something so large and horrifying should never have been able to dance, and yet it did with a dangerous grace. When Al reached into empty darkness, the tulpa took his hand and held it as he spun. It held his hips straight, helped bend his back to impossible poses. Behind him, the smiling toddler taking his first steps became a boy with a tight-lipped smile. Then a teenager with dark eyes who never smiled. A shell of a person barely alive unless he was on stage. The dance itself slowed, having fewer jumps and intricate spins as the song wound down.

With the final bar, Al returned to his former position, lying on the stage, except this time he held his hands crossed over his chest in imitation of death. Had his chest not been rising and falling with heavy breaths of effort, even I would have believed it.

The song ended and the auditorium thundered with applause. I planted my cane against the mildly sloped floor and tried to rise. Jade had to help me to my feet. She held my arm as I applauded. More people rose. Jade turned away. She didn't want me to see her push away the tear that fell, but I did.

Al rose from the dead with a wide smile and bowed deeply before practically floating off stage.

My heart sank with the realization that he was at an all-time high. Asking him to cast off his only friend in the world would destroy him for sure now, if he was even amiable to the idea. In Al's mind, he had no reason to get rid of the tulpa that had just helped him dance his way into his dream.

Rather than sit back down, Jade and I shuffled down the row of seats and made our way to the auditorium exit. We pushed through the doors just as the next pair of dancers readied to begin their performance. Outside, it was eerily quiet and empty. Everyone was in the auditorium except for a few kids who must've finished their performances before we ever got there. They huddled in twos and threes, whispering to each other and running their thumbs over phone keyboards.

A sign directed our way backstage. To get there, we had to go down a ramp that ran alongside the auditorium and up a short set of stairs. A paper sign taped to the door announced no visitors were allowed. I pulled the door open anyway.

We stepped into chaos. Half-dressed kids ran back and forth in a small area, yanking clothes down from rolling racks or applying last-minute streaks of makeup. An emergency outfit repair stand had been set up near the door and a girl in pink stood there while someone hastily sewed up a hole in her pink dress.

Only two adults were backstage beyond Jade and I. One was an older lady with a clipboard standing near the stage entrance. She was too busy watching the performance and counting steps to pay attention to us. The other was a tall, thin man with short curly hair the color of dry ash. He stepped in our way.

"You can't be in here," he said, putting a hand to my chest to stop me. "You must go." He had an accent that placed his home country somewhere in Eastern Europe.

Jade put a hand gently on my shoulder. It was the only thing that kept me from swinging my cane at the guy. "We need to speak with Allen Miller."

"Then you can wait outside. No visitors. Didn't you see the sign?" He pointed emphatically back at the door we'd just come through.

"It's okay." Al appeared behind the man. He'd shed his shirt since the dance, but still had glitter on his cheeks. "We can talk in the hall." Al led us back into the hallway. "I know Felix, but who are you?"

"Jade Haneda," said Jade.

"So, you're my alibi." He pulled open the door and held it for us.

Jade glared at me.

I cringed. "I can explain later."

We stepped into the hallway and Al followed us, carefully closing the door behind him as quietly as he could. He folded his arms over his skinny, white chest. "What is it? What do you want?"

"We found out what the creature is," I said.

Al's expression didn't change. He glanced from me to Jade and back. "You know, I didn't expect you to come back. I thought if I gave you some of my mom's medicine, you'd fuck off and stay gone. I never actually expected you to help me. It would've been better if you didn't."

I shook my head. "What do you mean? I promised to help you. Look, it doesn't matter. That thing is a tulpa. You created it, Al."

"I know."

My heart skipped a beat and could've sworn I felt an icy breath on the back of my neck. I turned my head and found the tulpa there, staring me down from behind. Its nostrils flared and the cold breath struck me again.

"What do you mean you know?" Jade pushed.

Al kept his arms crossed. "Tulpamancy is intentional. I had to have intent when I created him."

"Was any of this an accident?" I slowly

turned back to the kid.

He shrugged. "You were. I never could have counted on you breaking into the house to steal. And you staged the robbery gone wrong so perfectly. There's even footage of you bothering my mom at the hospital. It's not even a half-truth for me to tell the police you broke into my house to steal my mother's Vicodin." He uncrossed his arms and circled like a lion stalking his prey. The tulpa circled opposite. "But when we came home, we surprised you. I didn't see the hunting knife. It happened so fast."

"You know that's not true." Jade turned to follow him as he moved.

I kept my eyes locked on the tulpa.

"The truth doesn't matter. It only matters what version of the truth a traumatized kid tells the cops. I was so stunned, I didn't know what to do. He threatened me, said if I told anyone he'd kill me too. Even showed up at my dance recital to drive the point home." Al reached his original spot with his back to the wall and paused.

"You wanted your tulpa to kill your father," I said.

Al didn't show a thread of remorse. "He didn't want me to dance. He didn't want me to do anything! I could never be the person he wanted me to be!"

"So, you killed him?" Jade shook her head. "Allen…"

His head snapped to her. "Don't call me

that. Don't call me anything. In fact, you should be running. I'm going to go home soon and see the body lying in blood and have a panic attack as everything comes rushing back to me. You won't have long before the police find you after that."

The muscles of Jade's delicate throat moved as she considered fleeing like Al suggested. I knew it wouldn't matter. There was nowhere we could run, no place we'd be safe. Even if we evaded the police, he would send his tulpa to finish the job. Jade and I were essential witnesses to a crime, and we couldn't be allowed to live after what we'd seen and heard.

CHAPTER TWENTY-SIX

NOW

I woke with a terrible headache and the worst dry mouth I had ever experienced, but that wasn't my biggest problem. My skin prickled with electricity that made the tiny hairs stand on end. Goosebumps rose on my arms, legs, and chest as something invisible tugged at my psyche even before I opened my eyes.

There was a sound in the room like thunder and the feeling intensified.

I flinched and opened my eyes.

The white ceiling from before was gone. Above me hung my own reflection strapped to a table. I wore electrodes on my head and chest with colored wires running to the floor and flowing away in a rainbow river. Fireflies danced in the space between me and my reflection. No, not fireflies, sparks of raw power.

I blinked, staring. Was I seeing…magic? I didn't know what else to call it. Yes, it was undeniably powerful, but it wasn't electricity or any other form of familiar energy. This was something new, something ethereal and terrifying.

But where was it coming from?

Thunder boomed again through the room. The magic fireflies danced faster, moving in hypnotizing waves. A horrible ache rose from my stomach and spread in an agonizing wave through the rest of me, building to a crescendo of pain. I opened my mouth to scream. A handful of new, brighter lights fluttered out of me to dance in the air with the rest.

"Beautiful," cooed Dr. Bellamy.

The machinery of my table whirred as he lifted me again to mimic a standing posture. The doctor sat next to a machine that had not been in the room before, his hand on a large lever. It didn't look like any machine I had ever seen, but one that might have come out of a children's storybook with its mismatched parts and salvaged pieces. I recognized parts of vacuum cleaners, several fan blades, and what might have been a disassembled EKG machine. The wires connected to me ran straight into the machine while another set flowed out the other side to electrodes attached to Connor's chest and head. Dr. Bellamy had completed his transplant if the fresh stitches on Connor's chest were anything to judge by.

Dr. Bellamy removed his hand from the lever. "I had thought to just let you sleep until I was ready for the lobotomy, but then I realized the importance of this moment. I thought someone should be here to witness as we conquer death." He pulled the lever down ever so slightly.

Pain wracked my body in waves, ripples of electrical signal working their way through my muscles and forcing contractions. The glowing power filled my vision, blocking out all sight for a moment. I jerked forward, or as far forward as the restraints would allow, and heaved from an empty stomach.

"Yes, I'm sorry about the pain," said the doctor. "It's unfortunate, but any numbing agent I would give you would have to be at dangerous dosages, especially given your tolerance level. It's important that you retain cognitive function."

The pain finally stopped. I fell limp against the restraints, choking on pained sobs. "You're killing me..."

"Oh, Felix. Don't be so dramatic." He rose from his seat, pushing through the wall of dancing lights, sliding a stethoscope into his ears. The end he pressed to my chest was so cold, I flinched. "I'm not going to kill you. You're going to survive this. That's why we have to do the lobotomy. I can't have you telling people my secrets."

"Why?" The quiet, broken voice that came out didn't sound like mine.

"Why let you live?" He retracted the stethoscope and lowered it to rest around his neck, his lips turning down into a frown. "If only I could tell you everything I knew. I wish I could. So many half-truths you must believe! So many lies." He gripped the side of my face and leaned in to rest his forehead against mine in a strange gesture of solidarity. "Whatever happens, don't stop looking for Sean. The truth of what happened is out there, Felix. I want you to find it."

"Then tell me. Who were those men in black? Are they part of it? Just tell me!"

He closed his eyes. For a moment, I thought maybe he would tell me what I needed to know. Instead, he let me go and took a step back, shaking his head. "I can't. Not when I've worked so hard to come so far. If I tell you what I know, I put everything at risk. I've built a life for me and Connor when he comes back, and I can't put that on the line. You will have to find the truth for yourself."

"How am I supposed to do that if you lobotomize me?" I watched the fireflies of power dancing between us, waiting for him to rationalize the irrational.

Dr. Bellamy turned away. "I'm sorry. I'm doing what I can, but no arrangement is perfect." He gripped the lever and yanked it down.

If I thought I had felt pain before, I was wrong. Whatever Bellamy's machine was doing, it felt like it was sucking the life straight out of me. Maybe it was. I couldn't pretend to understand the science or the magic, whichever it was. Could've been both for all I knew. The how didn't matter, nor the why. All that mattered was it hurt.

My vision blacked out, but I didn't lose consciousness. The pain was enough on its own to keep that from happening. Somewhere deep in my brain, I was working on finding a way to cope with the pain, but I couldn't quite form a complete thought. There was a wall of agony between my words and concepts. I forgot how to breathe.

I wasn't aware of the pain subsiding, but when it died to a tolerable level, I opened my eyes again and the room was awash in green. My forehead pounded with the reminder that I hadn't taken enough breaths recently and sparks danced in my vision, a sure sign of low oxygen in my blood. Mixed with the furious dance of the fireflies, the room glowed with the promise of life from death. Bellamy's exact words...

I panted through a few shaky breaths. My muscles twitched, remembering the electric agony that had just been flowing through them.

Bellamy left his switch behind and rushed to Connor's bedside, fists clenched so tight his knuckles were white. He held his breath, watching the monitors hooked up to the dead man.

Nothing happened.

And then, the monitors beeped. Lines rose into steep peaks and fell into sudden cliffs. Zeroes became double-digit numbers. Connor, who had been dead for more than a decade, took his first shaky breaths right along with me.

Bellamy laughed, but it wasn't the dark, terrifying laugh of a villain. It was the joyous relief of a man in love whose love had come back to him. Tears sparkled in his eyes, spilled over in small, uneven streams. His hands trembled as he lowered his stethoscope to Connor's chest, listening to Reuben's heart beating within.

"He lives," Bellamy whispered and wiped away tears. "My wonderful, perfect Connor has come back to me!" He took Connor's face in his hands and placed a small kiss on his lips.

For a moment, I let myself slip into a familiar fantasy in which I played the role of Dr. Bellamy, and I successfully retrieved Sean from wherever he had gone. In it, we held onto each other with so much to say and no words to say it. I tried to tell him all I had gone through and done to get him back, but part of me was ashamed at all the horrible things it had taken. Sean didn't care. It didn't matter. All that would be sorted out. What mattered was that we had each other. The rest of the world could wait.

Would I go as far as Dr. Bellamy? Could I kill six people that trusted me? Six innocents. Could I forsake every oath given to God and man to save the man I loved? Could I become the wolf where once I had been the shepherd?

Bellamy planted another kiss on Connor's forehead, but it wasn't Connor he was kissing.

Connor's ghost stood beside the table between his body and the machine, no more a part of the living, breathing dead man than he had been before. Dr. Bellamy hadn't brought Connor back. Yes, he had made a heart beat and blood flow. He had forcefully reawakened electrical activity within a dead brain, but the body was still an empty shell.

He stared at me with his sad green eyes and waifish face. *Don't forget me.*

"Bellamy..." My voice was raspy, my throat raw and sore.

The doctor stood and wiped his eyes. He cleared his throat. "Yes, of course. There will be time for sentimentality when he wakes up. That will take some time. In the meantime..." He went to a drawer in the corner where he retrieved a sealed package containing two metal tools. The first was a simple stainless steel hammer. The other, an oversized ice pick.

"No," I shook my head violently. "You don't understand. It didn't work, Bellamy. That's not Connor!"

His face was stone as he came to my bedside and struck the lever to lower the gurney back into its original position. "I know you're afraid, but you mustn't be, Felix. Thousands of people have had this procedure and they were much happier afterward. Don't you want to be happy?"

"You're not listening to me!" I squirmed

against my restraints. "Whatever you've done, you have to realize you haven't brought back the man you think you did. Even if the body is alive, it's not him!"

He pushed my head against the back of the gurney and drew another strap over my forehead, tightening it so I had to lie still. "Just what I'd expect a man of the cloth to say. I don't believe in God or the Devil, Felix. Nor Heaven or Hell. Connor is alive. That's enough for me." He leaned over me, assessing. "Now, normally you'd be unconscious for this part of the procedure, but that's a formality we can do without. I feel it's important to judge a patient's condition in progress. Don't you? Please hold still."

My breaths came quickly and my heart pounded in my chest. I curled my fingers into tight fists as Dr. Bellamy attached clips to my eyelids, holding them in place.

He turned away a moment and came back with eyedrops that stung when he squeezed them into my eyes. I never realized what torture it would be not to blink away a burning irritant in my eyes until I couldn't do it.

"Please don't," I pleaded, though I knew it wouldn't matter.

Dr. Bellamy leaned in, the metal pick in hand, his face fixed in a look of pure concentration. "You'll thank me after," he said simply. "You'll be cured."

The pick slowly lowered toward my eye

and went out of focus. Sudden pressure stung the top of my eye as he slid the delicate metal between my eyeball and the eyelid, carefully wedging it in behind the top of my eyeball.

I tried to blink, but between the clips and the pick, my eyelid wouldn't even twitch.

After what I had just been through, the mild pain was nothing. It felt like I'd gotten a small bit of debris stuck in my eye and was grating on the lens like sandpaper. Uncomfortable, a mild sting, but not the deep agonizing ache of what the machine had done.

Once he had the pick wedged in where he wanted, he picked up the small hammer. "The transorbital bone is very thin," he said. "Two or three good taps and I'll be through. Don't worry. There are no nerve endings that register pain in the brain. You'll have two black eyes after, but it'll feel no worse than getting into a fight in the schoolyard. I'm sure you had your fair share of those. This is safer. Very few people have died from this particular procedure. It did a lot of good before it was foolishly banned. One shouldn't have to feel negative emotions like grief and loss if they don't want to."

He held the pick firmly with his left hand and struck the flat top of it once with the hammer. The sound of metal chiseling against bone was something like tapping on a thick pane of glass with a screwdriver. There was a fragility in the sound that made it clear the bone there was incredibly thin and delicate. Just a bit more pressure and he would be through, free to swirl the metal pick around in my brain where he would destroy healthy tissue.

Tap. Tap.

I took in a sharp breath with each sound, afraid it would be my last. Bellamy had promised he wouldn't kill me, but this was far worse. Like the horrible creature he had turned Connor into, I would be alive but not living. To live, a human needed to be able to feel pain, to know fear, to understand loss. I'd never find Sean if I didn't embrace my rage and guilt, both of which drove me to search for him in the first place. Dr. Bellamy was about to take more than just my emotion from me. He was going to take away everything that made me *me.*

The monitors hooked up to Connor suddenly went crazy. Dr. Bellamy pulled the chisel out of my eye and turned around. "Connor? No, you mustn't…" It was all he got out before Connor struck him and sent him flying into the wall.

The soulless Connor let out an inhuman cry from the back of his throat and ripped the sensors from his skin. He rose from the operating table and smashed a fist into the center of it, nearly breaking it in half. He flung his arms out and knocked over a tray containing surgical equipment, then lumbered over to a metal supply cabinet, walking like a drunken toddler. Connor crashed into the cabinet before grunting in rage, grabbing it and tearing it from where it hung on the wall. Packaged sterile supplies spilled like guts from the cabinet as he lifted it over his head and threw it at the machine.

"No!" Dr. Bellamy staggered away from the broken wall he'd crashed into, a hand raised in Connor's direction, but he was too late.

The cabinet crashed into the machine and both broke apart. Sparks flew. The lights flickered. Metal groaned and crashed as pieces broke off the machine and tumbled onto Bellamy's unwilling organ donors still strapped to their beds.

One of the larger parts of the machine that looked like the back end of an air conditioning unit smashed into someone's head, crushing it in an instant. I hoped he was already dead.

Once Connor saw blood and human meat dripping from the gurney, he wandered over to the body and pushed the air conditioner off the crushed man. His limp hand splashed in the broken remains of the dead man's crushed skull the same way a child might play in a puddle.

"Connor?" Bellamy advanced again toward him, a cautious hand out. "Connor, it's me, Thomas. Look! Don't you recognize me?"

Connor quit playing in the remains and looked at Bellamy over his shoulder, gnashing his teeth.

"Don't be afraid," Bellamy said, coming closer. "I know it must be confusing."

Connor turned away, but when he moved, he caught sight of his reflection in a part of the ceiling mirror that extended onto the wall. He tilted his head right and left, watching his reflection move along with him. Then he looked down at the broken body he had his fists in and made a small, scared sound. That small sound became an anguished cry as he lifted his bloody hands and panicked as he tried to wipe the blood away.

"It's okay, Connor." Bellamy made the mistake of putting his hand on Connor's arm.

Connor screeched and struck him. Bellamy slammed into the nearby patient bed with a loud snap, his eyes wide. With an inhuman grunt, Connor tackled Bellamy to the ground. They slid out of sight between two patient beds under flickering lights

"No, Connor! No! What are you doing?" The scream that followed was visceral, pure terror. I had heard screams like that before in the basement of the Hemlock mansion as Belial ripped apart John and Laura Hemlock.

Slowly, Bellamy's terrified screams faded to barely audible grunts.

When Connor stood again, he was so blood-soaked, his skin looked nearly black from the nose down. Strips of human viscera hung from his teeth as he ground them together in a macabre bloody smile. Connor tilted his head back and roared at the ceiling.

I watched Dr. Bellamy's shoes twitch as blood flowed in a small river underneath the patient beds, torn between the urge to struggle free and the knowledge that I would look like prey if I did. Maybe if I stayed still, he would ignore me and leave the room in search of easier kills.

Connor stomped over to stand in front of me, nostrils flaring. I stayed frozen, playing dead. Belatedly, I realized that might be just as dangerous as moving. After all, he'd just been playing in a smashed skull. He didn't seem able to differentiate between live humans and dead ones, or maybe it just didn't matter to a sentient man without a soul.

Connor leaned forward, glassy dead eyes staring straight through me, so close I had to fight not to gag on the rotten smell of him. He sniffed the air around me in a loud, raspy pull of breath through bloody nostrils. With a gagging sound in the back of his throat, he grabbed the side of the bed I was strapped to and gave it a hard push. It rocked to the right off balance for a moment before falling back into place. He pushed it again, harder this time. It fell back another time. With the third push, he knocked the bed off balance. I crashed hard to the floor, striking something on my way down. A familiar burst of pain exploded in my right temple and blackness clouded my vision.

In the threatening dark, I watched Connor's bare feet shuffle to the next bed in line, upending it with a metallic crash. The sound of him tearing apart the room followed me into my unconscious dreaming.

CHAPTER TWENTY-SEVEN

THEN

I followed Jade to the parking lot. She left in a hurry after Al laid out his intention to frame us. Her gait told me she was pissed, but I still didn't know what she wanted to do. We couldn't just leave Al to frame us for murder, and we couldn't leave the tulpa on the loose either. It'd just keep killing people. Anytime it thought Al was in danger, it would destroy the danger. That's what Al had created it to do.

I grabbed her wrist as she reached to open the car door. "Jade, wait."

She had me in a hold against the side of the car faster than I could react, my arm twisted back into a painful position and my cheek pressed to the side of the door. "Touch me again without my permission and I'll break your arm. Got it?"

"Got it."

She released me.

I shook out my arm and rolled my shoulders back. "We can't just leave him."

"I'm not. I'm going to call my lawyer." She hesitated and crossed her arms, frowning. "You should probably call someone too, although any story you spin isn't going to look good, Felix. It's your word against his."

"If this goes to court, I'm going down," I said, pulling my coat closed and buttoning it. "I know that. I'm less concerned about Al's story and more about his tulpa. They're just a thoughtform, right? So, it's like a child. It doesn't know right from wrong. He's abusing it and it's going to lash out again."

"What do you want me to do, Felix?" She leaned in so the few people in the parking lot around us wouldn't hear her. "I'm not going to lie for you. It's already bad enough that you dragged me into this!"

"Me? You're the one who dropped this in my lap in the first place!"

She stepped back, all the anger draining from her face. "I did. You're right. I thought having something to do would help you. You'd lost your purpose in this world, Felix. When I first found you, you'd given up. You needed something to live for, and you needed to see that you can still do some good in the world."

"So, let's do it." I gestured back to the school we'd just left. "Let's help this kid."

Her jaw muscles flexed. "You can't save someone who doesn't want to be saved, Felix."

"Fine," I spat and turned to plant my cane

on the asphalt behind me.

"Where are you going?" Jade shouted.

"To do what you said I can't."

I pulled myself across the parking lot, carefully avoiding anything that shimmered like black ice in the moonlight. More people were coming out of the school's auditorium doors: couples holding hands and laughing, parents with younger children, a few of the dancers. The program must've just ended. No sign of Al or his mother.

With so many people pouring through the doors, I couldn't go back in the way I'd come. Someone was bound to bump into me and knock me over, especially as weak and sore as I was feeling. I decided it would be best if I went around the side of the school to the back entrance. That would put me closer to the stage door anyway.

It was dark on the side of the school, and devoid of people despite the noise of many voices nearby. A strange feeling, to be so close to so many happy people but to carry an unwavering sense of dread in my belly.

"What are you going to do?" Sean asked. He was beside me, so real I swore I could see the clouds of his breath floating into the air above our heads.

"I'm going to try to talk some sense into the kid. He has to see the tulpa is dangerous."

"And if he doesn't?"

I didn't answer. I'd reached the edge of the

brick wall. Around the corner, there was a ramp for deliveries. Through the door at the top of the ramp, I could access the same hallway we'd been in earlier, but I didn't need to go that far. Al was outside, sitting on the side of the ramp with his legs dangling over the side. He held his head in his hands, sobbing into them.

A fresh chill ran through my bones, rattling my spine to straighten. Without asking, I already knew what had happened. He would only be outside wracked with grief for one reason. Al didn't get his scholarship, despite putting everything on the line.

I shuffled over to the edge of the ramp.

Al's head shot up when he heard me, but that wasn't all. His arm shot out. In his hand, a silver revolver that caught a glint of moonlight. "Don't come any closer!"

"Easy." I put my hands up and stayed where I was. The tulpa was beside him, and I had the strange sense that it was on alert. "I just want to talk."

"Why?" He sniffled and used his free hand to wipe his nose. "You want to gloat? Is that it? Go on. I deserve it. I killed my dad for no reason."

"No, Al." I shook my head. "I'm not here to gloat. Where did you get that gun?"

He hesitated, then let out a bitter explosion of laughter. "It's my dad's. He kept it in the car. He was supposed to be the good guy with the gun. Didn't help him much when my tulpa tore him apart. Funny how he thought this could save him from anything."

"Al, just put the gun down and we can talk."

"We can talk now." The gun, which he'd lowered slightly, snapped back up, still pointed at me. "Let's talk about how you lied to me. You and everybody else. You said I was good. The best they'd ever seen."

"That wasn't a lie."

"Shut up!" Tears streamed down his face. "If I was good, why didn't I get the scholarship offer, huh? Instead, it went to someone who didn't even need it! She's not half as good as me! It's not fair, dammit!"

"It isn't," I agreed, daring to inch closer. If I could just get close enough, maybe I could get the gun away from him. Then what? Then his tulpa would rip off my arms and stuff them down my throat, that's what, but I couldn't just do nothing.

"Stop!" he shouted again, but this time he put the gun to his temple. "I said fucking stop!"

I stopped where I was, raising my hands higher. "I know it hurts right now. It feels like the end of the world. Bad shit is closing in from all sides and you don't have anywhere left to run. I know it doesn't look like it, but there's a way out if you'd just let me show you."

He sobbed. "What's the point? I killed my dad and it wasn't enough. Nothing's ever going to be enough. All I wanted was to dance. Why can't I just dance? Don't I deserve to have my dreams come true too?"

"Of course you do. We all deserve the chance to be happy and love what we do. You can still have that chance. But not if you pull that trigger."

The tulpa leaned in, suddenly more interested in what was happening as Al thumbed back the hammer. I saw what would happen in a flash of insight before the tulpa even moved. Al had made a mistake, pressing the gun to his head. One he wouldn't survive.

The tulpa's arm-like appendage thrust through Al's, severing it. The arm clutching the gun tumbled from Al's body and crimson sprayed against the door behind him. Al screamed in terror as he watched his arm fall to the snowy patch of pavement at his feet. His tulpa reacted with knee-jerk grace, swiping claws across the front of Al's throat. Three distinct lines of crimson appeared. Al, suddenly silenced, grabbed for his neck, but even the strongest pressure wouldn't stymie the bleeding.

I forgot all about the tulpa and rushed forward to grab Al before he could fall, but I misjudged and wound up landing on my ass. He fell into my lap, gripping his throat with his one remaining hand, trying to contain the spray.

He died in my lap with terror in his eyes,

behind a school, in the snow. But he didn't die alone. I held his hand until the blood stopped pumping, as a crowd gathered and people snapped photos with their phones.

His blood was cold and freezing into slick puddles of crimson when Jade appeared and pulled me from a numb stupor. They took the body away with his mother sobbing over it. She didn't even know she'd lost her husband and son in the same day. Perhaps it was kinder to lose them both at once.

As for the tulpa, it waited at Al's side until the paramedics officially declared him dead. Then it looked at me with sad eyes and faded to nothing but smoke in the icy December wind.

"What happened?" Jade asked me.

I was still wearing Al's blood, sitting in the front seat of her car. My fingers trembled as I struggled to strike a light on my cigarette. X had said we'd all find a way to cope with the pain of the world. The car stank of death. "He threatened himself with a gun. The tulpa did what he had taught it to do. It removed the threat."

"His tulpa killed him?" She frowned at me. "Do you think it knew that it was destroying itself in the process?"

"Maybe it knew." I blew out a mouthful of smoke and stared at the blood drying on the back of my hands. "Love is destructive by nature, isn't it? Al made the tulpa because he wanted someone to love and accept him unconditionally. I guess he got what he wanted in the end."

"It's not your fault, Felix." She reached over to grip my knee. A comforting gesture.

"Not this time," I agreed. "But if I'd seen it sooner, maybe..." I tipped my head back, resting it against the headrest. "This would all be simpler if things were like they were before. If I hadn't been able to see the tulpa."

"But you could. You did."

"I don't know if I can help people, Jade. I'm broken. At least as broken as Al was. Whatever this power is I have, I don't know if I want to know more about it. I'm afraid of it."

She drove a while before she asked, "Are you afraid of what the power will do, or what you'll do?"

I puffed on the cigarette. "Both."

"Good," she said. "Fear means you're alive. It means you haven't gone too far. Hold onto that fear, Felix. It will keep you human when there's nothing else left."

"Odd advice coming from a psychologist." I rolled my head to the side to look at her.

"You know, I was thinking of quitting, but there's a part of me that likes being bitchy to assholes like you." Jade plucked the cigarette from my fingers and took a long drag before tossing it out the window. "But being responsible for your mental health is what got me into this mess."

"What else would you do?"

"I don't know," she replied with a small smile. "But I've always wanted to try being a dominatrix."

CHAPTER TWENTY-EIGHT

NOW

"Felix, wake up."

"Sean?" My eyes fluttered open, but I didn't understand what I was seeing at first. I was face-down on a cold floor, my cheek stuck there by some unknown adhesive, still wet. Everything ached the way it had my first day free from the hospital after my broken back. Something heavy pressed into my back. A buzzing alarm bleated out in steady beats somewhere outside the room.

My hands crawled along the cool floor through cold puddles of thick paint. No, not paint. Blood. I knew the smell, even if I couldn't see the color. It was too dark.

I tried to push myself up, but something held my legs in place. When I looked down, I saw they were still strapped to the bed, though my head and arms had come free. My fingers trembled as I unbuckled my legs. The bed was too heavy for me to push it off of me in that position, especially as weak as I was, so I pulled myself forward through spilled supplies and drying puddles of my blood.

Once I was free, I collapsed against the floor to catch my breath and checked myself over. There was a gash on the side of my head that must've bled like a son of a bitch. It probably needed stitches, but it wasn't serious enough to be life-threatening.

I touched my right eye and winced. It was bruised, swollen closed. It definitely felt like someone had just been chiseling away at my skull with an ice pick. Even when I tried to force my eye open, all I could see through it was a shadowy red blur.

A moment of panic struck me. What if he'd messed up my eye and blinded me? I still had one good eye, but I'd be debilitated for life.

"At least you're alive," said Sean. "Now get up. It's not safe here."

I searched through the scattered supplies on the floor and found a roll of gauze and some medical tape. It was good enough to cover the open wounds. I wished I had an ice pack for my eye or some pain medication, but I couldn't risk it.

My wounds seen to, I pushed up onto my feet and surveyed the room. Connor had wrecked it. Everything that had been hanging from the wall, he'd torn down and smashed. Bellamy's patients had been torn apart or crushed. I didn't even need to check for a pulse.

No one could survive what had been done to them. I'd lived only because of the way the table fell, and because he hadn't thrown anything too heavy on top of me.

The mirrors on the ceiling had been smashed. Glass littered the floor like crystals of ice. There was no way to walk anywhere without stepping on it. All I could do was move carefully and try to brush what I could aside. Blades cut into my feet, slicing them raw. I left bloody footprints behind me on my way to the door. It had been pushed out of its frame and lay in a bent heap on the hallway floor. The alarm was coming from out there too. The normal lights weren't on, but instead, some orange emergency lighting flickered from small, caged bulbs on the wall.

"You won't be able to get out." Dr. Bellamy's voice startled me.

I turned around. He was sitting with his back to the wall between two mangled hospital beds. Blood splattered the wall on either side of him and gathered in a dark pool under where he sat. The whole front of him was bloody, though his hands were the worst of it. He clutched his stomach, holding in whatever Connor hadn't chewed out of him.

I put a hand out, propping myself up in the doorway so I wouldn't fall over. "I should kill you."

He closed his eyes. "I'm already dead. Connor made sure of that. My body just hasn't caught up."

"Serves you right. Destroyed by your own creation."

"Perhaps." His eyes opened again, half-lidded. "It feels like fate. Like I was meant to go this way. I wouldn't have wanted anyone other than Connor to do it."

"That's not Connor." I limped forward and dropped to my knees. That hurt too much, so I fell back on my ass and sat there, trying to will myself to move. I couldn't, so I sat there, studying the dying man. "What does it feel like? Dying?"

Bellamy's throat worked. "Dry. Apparently, dying is thirsty work. There's bottled water in the cabinet."

"Connor tore the cabinet apart."

"Ah, I see." He closed his eyes again.

I twisted and scanned the floor near where the cabinet's insides had spilled out. There were two bottles, badly dented, sitting near one of the dead patients' feet. With a grunt, I stretched to grab one. The cap twisted off easily. Too easily. I watched my hand make the motions but felt nothing.

I held the bottle to Bellamy's lips while he took a sip. "You can't bring back the dead and expect them to be the same."

His voice was strained as he smiled and said, "I know."

I sighed and turned my head, searching for Sean. He'd been there a moment ago. I knew I had heard his voice. "Maybe I should take my own advice. Sean's gone. He's not coming back. Sean Yeats is dead."

"He's not."

I narrowed my eyes at the doctor. "Don't lie to me. Not now. Don't try to fuck with my head."

"I'm not." He rolled his head back and forth against the wall. "Listen to me...I told you before I wished I could tell you everything. That wasn't a lie either. I was just so...consumed by my work. I thought I could escape this. Now I see what I should have seen all along. These people, they destroy every life they touch. This was meant to be."

"What people. The Men in Black?"

Bellamy nodded. "More water?"

I helped him take another drink.

He smiled after. "Never knew water could taste so good."

"The Men in Black, Bellamy. Who are they?"

He leaned his head back, closed his eyes, and let out a raspy sigh. "They're everyone and no one. To some, they're simply The Organization or The People, or just the Men in Black. They're agents without an agency, spies without a home country, assassins without loyalty. They have no name for themselves, but they are everywhere, orchestrating everything. When smoke rises from the Sistine Chapel, it's because they have willed it. When a world power falls, it's because they have toppled it. And when a good man with a strange power becomes interesting, it's because they've taken an interest."

"I don't understand what you're saying. You're talking conspiracy theories. Like the Illuminati?" Maybe Bellamy was insane. I couldn't believe a word that came out of his mouth. He had tried to lobotomize me, so why should I? But this was the closest I had been to answers. Even if the answers I wanted were the ramblings of a madman, I had to hear them.

He laughed, then coughed, then winced and clutched his gut tighter. "They've gone by that name."

"What does the Illuminati want with someone like Sean? He wasn't anyone important to anyone but me."

"Neither was Joseph and yet he was chosen to be Christ's guardian and teacher." He offered a tight smile. "They are rather fond of raising insignificants from obscurity to greatness. But if you think my methods abhorrent, then you will be shocked at theirs." He took in a sharp, shuddering breath, eyes wide. The doctor's bloody hand shot out to grip my shoulder. "You! You were once a priest?"

"I was almost a priest," I corrected. "I can't give you Last Rites. I wouldn't if you asked."

The corners of his mouth twitched into a half-smile. "Just as well. I understand the sacrament of confession is required, and one must show contrition for his wrongdoings for forgiveness. I die with no regrets for the men I've killed. I won't ask to be forgiven for that which I do not regret. But you would pray with me, hear the truth of what brought me here? And if you would, perhaps it would help you find what I could not."

"What's that?"

"Peace," he answered simply. "Companionship. Happiness. Joy. Life, Felix. Isn't that what we all want?"

I clenched my jaw to keep it from trembling, answering him in a whisper. "Yes."

"Then you must listen to a dying old man who failed at finding all of those things."

CHAPTER TWENTY-NINE

THEN-Bellamy

Bless me, Father, for I have sinned. It's been at least twenty-five years since my last confession. I used to be a good Catholic, despite my attractions of the flesh.

I was born the only son of an upper-middle-class family from Buffalo, but my story doesn't begin until September of my freshman year at Columbia. That was when I met Connor Williams. He wanted to be a writer; I wanted to be a psychiatrist. Connor was fascinated with the fantastic and I had always been drawn to the fanatic. The one place where our interests intersected was in our love of the written word. He read Chaucer and Shakespeare while I struggled to make sense of either.

He became my tutor. I fell in love and he lost his mind, descending into madness and death for which I will always bear some level of responsibility. That's the long and short of the technical aspects. But no story is so simply told. We are more than characters, plot, and setting.

This, Connor taught me most of all, how complicated people can be.

His eyes drew me to him. I had never seen irises that color, a deep and polished jade that practically glowed in the dark. I took months to work up the courage to ask if they were naturally so brilliant or if he wore contacts. He laughed at me when I asked and I thought to myself, "How will I ever face him again?"

But love finds courage in strange places, and I was motivated to pass my medieval literature class, if for no other reason than to see him again.

We had our first kiss under a full moon in October. The stairway smelled of leaves and mud, but he always smelled of cinnamon and granny smith apples with a touch of smoke. It was dark because it had to be. Though we never spoke of it, we knew no one could see us. Not on the Columbia campus, not in 1982, not if we wanted to have professional careers. Things were changing then, exciting things, especially in New York, but everything was still very underground.

Later that year, as winter semester droned on, I lay awake in my bed, staring at an empty ceiling as I agonized over the decision I knew I would soon have to make. Connor and I had just had our first big argument, you see. He wanted to date openly, but I couldn't. While he could still write regardless of what his peers thought of him, if I came out then I knew I would never be allowed to practice. Our whirlwind romance felt like it was already coming to an end after just a few short months. I knew I would have to choose between Connor and pursuing my passion for psychology.

And then I got the phone call that changed everything.

I turned over in my bed, staring at the phone ringing on the wall. Next to it sat a desk clock, ticking away the early hours of the morning. It was three o'clock, far past time when any sensible person would call. Somehow, even before I reached for the phone, I knew it was Connor on the other end. Dread filled my being, a terrible sense that something had gone horribly wrong. My mouth was dry, my voice hoarse. "Connor?"

"Thomas?" He sounded as scared as I felt. "Oh, Jesus, Thomas, it's good to hear your voice!"

"Do you know what time it is?" I rubbed my eyes and sat up.

"I don't know where I am," he said, "or how I got here and there's a man that's following me. Thomas, I'm scared."

If it was anyone else, I would have told him to call the police, but this was Connor. Hearing his voice, the raw terror in it, had me on my feet, grabbing my coat from the back of the chair where I'd left it. "Where are you?"

"I don't know." He was near tears. "I don't

know!"

"Connor, take a deep breath. Now, look around. Describe your surroundings. What do you see?"

"An empty street. It's dark. I'm using a public phone booth. There are people in the alleys, Thomas! They're following me and I don't know what to do! Just tell me what to do! I think they want to kill me."

"Are you still in the city? Near the water? Do you hear anything?"

Connor made the same sound a small wounded animal would make. There was a dull thump and the call ended.

I cursed and put the phone down to rush out the door. New York was a big city in an even bigger state. It'd been six hours since I'd last seen Connor. He could've gone anywhere in that time, or been taken anywhere. He'd seemed so confused and disoriented on the phone, convinced he was in danger. I *had* to find him.

All night, I drove up and down the streets around the university searching for any sign of him, but without more information, there was no way I'd ever find him. In those days, there was no GPS, no cell phones, no internet. Finding one man in a sea of millions was a hopeless endeavor, but I was unwilling to return to campus until I found something. At least, that was what I told myself.

By noon, I was too exhausted to be on the

road. I resolved to skip my classes for the rest of the day and went back to my dorm room to get a quick nap.

Another telephone call woke me less than an hour later. I grabbed the phone so quickly that I nearly fell out of bed. "Hello? Connor?"

"Is this Thomas Bellamy?" said a stranger's voice on the other end.

"Yes." I held my breath, waiting to hear that something terrible had happened. In my mind, I imagined him dead in that phone booth, and me driving by without seeing.

"This is Darla Williams. I'm Connor's mom."

She knows. I clenched my teeth and waited for the angry accusations, the tears, the blame to be laid at my feet for whatever she thought I'd done to her son.

"I…they said Connor's in the hospital." She sounded close to tears.

I sat up. "The hospital? Is he okay?"

"They don't know." Her voice was so tight I could barely understand. "I'm on my way soon, but…well, he said you were his friend. I know it's a lot to ask, but could you…"

"I'll go and sit with him until you arrive."

"Thank you. Thank you so much. I'll be there as soon as I can."

We hung up and I raced to the emergency room hoping to see him. The patient they brought me back to see was barely recognizable.

He had Connor's eyes, his face, his body, but all the refined grace I had come to know and love was gone. He lay on a bed, restrained and muttering to himself, bloodshot eyes darting back and forth. He'd bitten his lip so hard it bled and scratched his arms.

"Thomas!" He surged against the restraints as hard as he could when he saw me. "What are you doing here?"

I frowned and turned to the nurse who'd shown me back to his room. "Are those restraints really necessary?"

She glared at me. "Yes," she said and went to the other side of the curtain. "Call if you need anything."

Not knowing what else to do or say, I turned back to Connor. "Connor, what happened?"

"I told you last night. Those people in the alley. They're a cult, Bellamy, and they want to kill me. They followed me across the border."

"The border? What border?"

"Come on, Thomas. You know. The border crossing? Into Canada? How did you get here so fast?"

"Connor..." I gripped the only chair in the room and pulled it up to the bed. "We're in New York. At Mount Sinai Hospital?"

"No," he said, drawing out the vowel. "That's not right. Last night, I was in Buffalo. And then this song came on the radio. The one with the phone number in it." He started singing the chorus from Tommy Tutone's song. It seemed that stupid song wouldn't go away. "Anyway, it was halfway over when it hit me. That number, it's not a phone number. It's a code. I had to pull over and decode it. And that's when they showed up. One of them knocked on my window with a gun, Connor. I ran out of there as fast as I could!"

"You called me last night from a pay-phone," I said. "Don't you remember?"

He blinked and scrunched up his face. "No, I couldn't have. I didn't...I don't..." His expression went blank before he turned his head away, jaw quivering. "I'm not crazy, Thomas. I heard it. I know I heard it. I know what I saw!"

I took his hand in mine, a numb feeling churning in my gut. "It's okay, Connor. We'll get to the bottom of all this."

For three days, they kept him and ran a battery of tests. He was fine for hours at a time and then he would fall back into insisting he was in Canada, but he didn't hurt anyone so they finally removed the restraints. After his mother and sister arrived, he only seemed more convinced of where he was.

His sister Vera was a young woman, just a few years behind him. They could've been twins as similar as they looked. Those similarities ended with their appearance, however. Where Connor had been quiet and reserved, introverted even, Vera was extroverted and pushy. She largely dealt with the doctors once she arrived. It was a good thing, too, because his mother didn't have the heart to fight for his care.

"Oh, honey," said his mother one afternoon, taking his hand as I had. "You're just confused."

"I'm not confused!" Connor jerked his hand away and ground his teeth together. "Why are you lying to me? Why are all of you lying to me? God, you're with them, aren't you?" He looked straight at me, his eyes watering. "You too, Thomas? What did they promise you to betray me?"

He would have hurt me less if he had stabbed me in the heart. "I'm on your side, Connor!"

"Why would you lie to me?" he sobbed. "Why you?"

"I'm not lying to you!" I rushed to his other side to put a hand on his shoulder.

Connor's face jerked up out of where he kept it hidden in his folded arms. Teeth snapped first at me and then at his mother. I was quick enough to get out of the way. She wasn't so lucky. Connor closed his teeth on her pinky finger and wrenched his head to the side. His mother screamed as her finger broke with a loud snap. The bone tore through delicate flesh, sending a waterfall of blood cascading over Connor's face. Nurses rushed into the room to whisk her away and restrain him. I was pushed into the hall, helpless to stop what Connor had set in motion.

Even then, I knew enough about mental illness to guess at the gargantuan disease Connor was grappling with. Still, I told myself it was a dozen other things. It could've been a tumor, or encephalitis, or perhaps Connor had just taken drugs. If that were the case, all we had to do was wait for them to wear off.

Yet as time marched on and on, Connor got no better. He became more distant, refused to see me, refused to cooperate with the doctors. I watched a mild-mannered student of literature fall apart over the coming days and could do nothing to stop it.

It was a week before Mount Sinai decided that what was wrong with him was mental and not physical. They wanted to move him to the inpatient psychiatric ward upstairs, but that wouldn't do. There, I knew he would be forgotten. Medicated, made tolerable, and kept out of sight. That was what state-run hospitals did. Even if he got better, Connor would never live down the shame of having been hospitalized. No, he needed the best care. Care I would pay for myself for as long as needed. I had money in a trust, and I would empty it if required.

His sister agreed and we spent the next twenty-four hours poring over lists of the finest private hospitals in New York, searching for one that would be just the right fit for Connor.

When we found Saint Dymphna's, it felt like a miracle. Private, secluded, faith-based approaches to care at the cutting edge of psychiatric science...I was so enthralled, I wanted to go there myself. Our visit to the facility and the grounds only served to make the place more enticing. Not only would Connor get all the best care money could buy at Saint Dymphna's, but he could rest his weary mind away from the city. He could transition gradually back into the world when he was ready.

I had no idea I was sending him to live in a nightmare.

In 1982, homosexuality still had an entry in the DSM-R, the handbook for diagnosing mental disorders and conversion therapy had begun to pick up steam in private psychiatric circles. Barbaric treatments were touted as cures for homosexual urges from electroshock therapy to what they called sex therapy. Today, we would view it as sexual assault. The whole point of such therapies was to create strong negative associations in the patient's mind with their sexuality. And Saint Dymphna's was far more interested in curing Connor of his gayness than his schizophrenia.

Had I only known it at the time...

They drugged him while I practiced my Latin.

They raped him and called it therapy

while I mastered abnormal psychology.

While I joined the debate team and studied philosophy, they castrated Connor without permission from his family and called him cured.

"Now that his body is no longer a threat," they said when I came to visit him the week after it happened, "we can heal his mind."

He was pale as a corpse, barely responsive. I sat across from him, wracked by guilt over what I had allowed to transpire, and saw death in his glassy eyes. His heart beat, and breath rattled in his chest, but the monsters...they had killed his passion for life.

I held his clammy, thin hands in mine. "I'm going to talk to Vera and we're going to get you out of here," I promised.

"It's all right." Connor's voice was calm but empty. He tried to smile, but it sat crooked on his face. "I forgive you, Thomas Bellamy."

Those were the last words he said to me before he shuffled away.

That night, yet another phone call woke me from a sound sleep. Before I could even say hello, Vera was sobbing on the other end.

"He's dead," she wailed. "Connor's dead. They killed him, Thomas! My baby brother is dead!"

I made the three-hour drive out to Saint Dymphna's that same night and demanded to see the body. He looked so lifelike even as his skin grayed and his lips changed color to match an eggplant. I looked at the bruises on his neck from where he had tied the bedsheet and wound it tight enough to cut off air.

"He died quickly," said the nurse on staff.

A lie. I knew how long it would take to strangle to death in a bedsheet.

"Suicide," she added and studied my face.

Another lie. Connor may have died by his own hand, but this place, this awful, terrible asylum, and the disgusting people in it, they had killed him as much as I had.

I placed my hat on my head. "You should expect a call from some lawyers very soon. If I were you, I would be in touch with legal counsel," I said and left the hospital.

They were waiting for me outside, the first of the Men in Black. He sat on the edge of the fountain, which didn't run after hours, staring at his reflection in the shallow pool. He wore a black suit with a black tie, black shoes and a black hat, the sort that had gone out of fashion years ago. A man from another time and place.

Strange, I thought, for someone else to be waiting outside the asylum at such an early hour. Maybe he was an employee on break. I started down the sidewalk for the car.

The man turned his head and watched me. "You're just going to walk away?"

I slowed to a stop several paces past the man and turned around. "Excuse me?"

The man approached me, the heels of his polished shoes clicking against the pavement. He stood in front of me, features plain, unremarkable. The most average looking man I had ever met. But the way the moonlight struck the hardened edges of his features told me all I needed to know. This man was dangerous, a killer with no remorse.

Muscle for the hospital, then? Sent to threaten me into silence?

"I won't be intimidated into doing nothing." I clenched my fists. "This hospital murdered Connor Williams. I intend to sue the whole place out of business."

"Is that all?" He tilted his head to the side, emotionless. A cat attentive to a bird in the bush. "Such small ambitions."

"What else am I supposed to do?"

I tensed as the man opened his jacket, expecting a weapon. Instead, he brought out a book. I frowned at the title. "The Modern Prometheus? You want to give me a fairy tale?"

"Not a fairy tale, Bellamy. A future."

I snatched the book from his hands. I'd read it before, just as every educated young man did. The story of how Doctor Victor Frankenstein sought to become God and defeat death. It was a fiction, a dream. In my anguished state, I also forgot it was a cautionary tale.

I flipped open the book and shifted it so I could read in the moonlight and the distant hue of the asylum's lamps. At first, I thought the book was just an annotated version of the same fictional tale. Connor had liked to make notes in the margins of his books. My throat felt tight at the memory of that. But as my eyes adjusted to the dim light and I began to read, I realized that what I held in my hands was not a fictional tale, but a scientific treatise, an in-depth study on death and methods by which it may be reversed. Death, the text argued, was held in supernatural regard only because we didn't understand its processes. Yet it was just another pattern of behavior, a series of predictable events, and any pattern can be reversed, if only one knows how.

"Impossible." I snapped the book closed and held it back out to the man. "It would take science that is far beyond our current capabilities to even begin to deconstruct where life ends and death begins. Bringing someone back is wishful thinking."

"For some small-minded men, perhaps." He took the book and held out a card with his other hand. "But if you find yourself curious, be at the address on that card tomorrow at noon. Alone."

I frowned down at the card. "I have class."

"You have a destiny that is far greater than what will achieve attending a traditional classroom," he promised and placed the card in my hand. "But it's your destiny. I can't force you to accept it any more than you can go back to undo what you've done." He smiled, tucked the book back into his jacket, lifted his hat, and walked away in complete silence.

I drove back to campus with the dawn all around me, but still shrouded in night. My heart was numb to the loss. It didn't feel real. Any minute now, I would wake up from the terrible nightmare and find us back together, Connor and me. He would laugh at how seriously I took the dream and assure me that the world had become too modern for such tortures.

"Things are changing," he would say as we sat together at the breakfast table. "The world is getting better for men like us."

That was Connor for you, always blind to the darker, more brutal possibilities. He was the sort of soul who never understood the hatred harbored in the hearts of men. A good man, a believer that justice, truth, and love would always prevail over evil.

A dead man.

I didn't recall reaching my dorm, parking the car, or even finding my way back to my room. It happened in a numb blur as if my body had moved without me. My mind was still stuck back that the asylum, unwilling to leave until I was certain it was real and irreversible.

The bed squeaked as I sat down on the edge. Cold sunlight came through the window, warming as it slid seamlessly through the glass. It fell in a pool on my desk where a book waited.

A book that wasn't mine. The Modern Prometheus. How had the stranger in black gotten to my room before me? Maybe a better question was to ask why he was so insistent on giving me a copy of this book to read.

The manipulation may seem obvious looking back, but living in the moment, drenched in grief and dressed up in my private anguish, I couldn't see it. A great curiosity seized me, and I picked up the book against my better judgment. With the first few pages, my doubts waned. Death was a simple physiological process already well understood by medical science, the book argued. It outlined everything with an intense degree of understanding, both the biology of death and the psychology of it, citing expert papers I had read in my academic studies.

Moreover, the book argued that death had already been defied many times over. The Ancient Greeks understood the process of mouth-to-mouth ventilation. Direct heart massage dates back to the late 1800s. More recently, CPR had been introduced and simplified so that even a layperson could administer the life-giving technique. Dead hearts were resuscitated all the time.

If death was the result of a still heart and starved brain, then there must exist certain processes by which both problems could be solved and life restored to the dead provided decay had been limited. That meant no embalming. No burial. No internment. If I was to have a chance at bringing Connor back, I had to act quickly and prevent his body from ever getting into his family's hands.

Am I a mad man? I thought, looking up from the book. This should be impossible.

I suddenly recalled something I had heard in a recent lecture about the impossible: "The only way of discovering the limits of the possible is to venture a little way past them into the impossible." Everything that was now possible had once been impossible. Why, some had even said it was impossible to put a man on the moon, but Kennedy did it.

With trembling fingers, I withdrew the card from my pocket that the man in black had given me to look at the address. It was almost noon and I had read the book cover to cover. The impossible seemed possible, but did I dare to challenge God?

What else is the purpose of man if not to defy the will of God? This, I told myself, was why we were given free will. No creator wishing obedience creates a provision for insubordination. We were made to sin, and sins of pride were perhaps the most enticing of all.

I met the man on a park bench which sat on a small rise overlooking a playground. He was dressed as before, conspicuous but unremarkable in his conspicuousness. When I approached, he didn't move or get up, but just sat there, looking at me from behind his sunglasses. My reflection stared back at me, hair disheveled and eyes dark from the lack of sleep.

"I read your book," I said.

He was silent.

"What is it you want from me?"

"I don't want anything," said the man in black. "But the people I represent are very interested in you, Thomas Bellamy."

I put my hands deep in my pockets and glanced around. No one was watching us. At least, no one I could see. "And who are they?"

He smiled in answer.

"I'm no fool," I said. "I know what you want me to do, but I don't have the resources. I don't have the money or time. A project like this would cost billions and take years, maybe decades. The expense would be astronomical."

"You have benefactors willing to finance whatever you need. No price is too big," promised the man in black.

"I assume there's a quid pro quo in there somewhere. What is it these wealthy benefactors expect me to do in return?"

"Now that I can't tell you until you sign on. I can tell you it's not much. Just a little more research on the side. Some...creative problem-solving. Beyond that, your benefactors are prepared to finance the rest of your education at an institution of your choosing. You'll be provided with a private laboratory and resources without a spending cap. You can use it for whatever you like so long as you're producing results."

That was a hard bargain to turn down. My own private research fund and endless resources? Who else would offer such a thing? And I could be on the cutting edge of breakthrough science. One day, it could be me the students at Columbia were reading about in their textbooks.

"Why me?" I shook my head. "I'm not even a medical doctor. I'm not any sort of doctor. I'm training to be a psychiatrist for Christ's sake. I'm no one special."

The man leaned back against the bench and folded his hands in his lap. "Does it matter? When greatness calls, you don't get to ask why."

I glanced behind me at the playset occupied by a few children who had chosen to brave the cold and their worried mothers. What would they say if the man in black made them the same offer? You can have everything you want for free, but you have to agree to work for people you've never met on projects you can know nothing about in advance. I knew I didn't have long to decide. Connor's body would be released to his family that evening.

I turned back to the man in black. "I will need his body brought to this lab. Tonight. It will have to be preserved in an air-tight chamber free of bacteria and foreign particles. If they begin the embalming process, I won't be able to reverse it."

The man smiled and stood, adjusting his suit jacket. "We'll be in touch, Bellamy."

"That's it?"

"For now," replied the man and walked away.

For three long days and nights, I agonized over my decision. I skipped classes. I refused to eat. When Connor's sister called me, fraught with distress over the disappearance of her brother's body, I could scarcely listen or feign sympathy. When I slept, I dreamed of Connor's body, bloated and rotten, his perfect ivory skin a putrid shade of green.

And then, on the fourth morning, more men in identical suits and hats showed up to escort me to a van. They placed a black bag over my head and drove me somewhere in the country to show me my new lab. There, I found Connor's body in a glass coffin like some fairytale prince, perfectly preserved. He looked almost alive. It was the first time I wept since I'd heard he died, but those were tears of joy. I knew then I could save him and got to work immediately.

Those first few months were bliss other than the awkward way in which I had to be brought back and forth from the lab. Always under armed guard. Always with a black hood obscuring my vision. Progress was painfully slow, but there was no need to rush. Connor showed no signs of decay, no matter how much time went on. I couldn't find a reason for his state, but there was also a part of me that was afraid to ask. Even when I had to miss my classes, or missed turning in homework assignments because I was so engrossed in my work, I somehow passed with flying colors. The rudimentary coursework was boring and college lectures felt wasted on me.

Eventually, I dropped out altogether to focus on my work. Somehow, I still would come into the lab on a June afternoon every few years and find a diploma with my name on it waiting in an envelope on my desk. I never questioned the source. Never asked how or why. Nothing mattered but finishing my work.

One spring morning two years into my work, I came into the lab and found another man in black hovering over Connor's coffin. He held a file out to me. "The time has come for you to repay some of your debts, Bellamy."

I took the file and flipped it open, annoyed that I would have to deal with him instead of getting straight to my research. My interest piqued when I saw what was inside, but not in a good way. I looked up at the man in black's sunglasses. "The names on these dossiers have been blacked out. What am I supposed to do with these?"

"They're not real people." He shrugged. "But the organization is running an exercise. The

CIA experimented some time ago with prisoners, dosing them with LSD and other drugs in hopes of producing superpowers."

"I've heard the rumors. What does that have to do with me?"

"The organization is curious," said the man, "if something like that is really possible."

I closed the folder and held it out to him. "I'm a scientist. Superpowers are fiction."

"Are they?" The man lifted his hand. Little red sparks appeared on his fingertips a moment before disappearing. He lowered his hand, putting it behind his back. "Let's assume some unexplained abilities are, in fact, real. Psychics, for example. Maybe the ability to be in two places at once. If you believed such things were possible, how would you go about amplifying those abilities?"

"Well, it would depend." I crossed my arms. "LSD apparently doesn't work."

"Or maybe it was only part of the package." He shrugged and paced around the room. "Some of the organization's other scientists have suggested that combining an altered state with physical pain might amplify these abilities."

"Physical torture has been shown to be ineffective in nearly every study," I countered.

"For the purposes of interrogation, maybe." He picked up a beaker full of red liquid.

I walked over and took it carefully away

from him, placing it gingerly back into its stand. "There have been cases of hysterical strength recorded, but those are few and far between. That's probably the closest thing in reality to what you're talking about. Usually, the stimulus is a traumatic event, a life-or-death situation, say a loved one pinned beneath a car. A mother who might normally not be able to lift her own weight might be able to move an entire car to free her trapped child. Theoretically, the release of adrenaline might be responsible, but the time it would take for it to be released into venous circulation is problematic. It simply isn't stored in sympathetic nerve terminals in sufficient quantity."

"But a person could be prompted to do the impossible if it meant saving a loved one in dire circumstances?"

I shrugged. "Of course. Explaining why and how and then replicating that process is another matter."

"Then I'd get to work if I were you." He placed the file on my desk and left.

That's how it started, working through theories. But each answer I found led to more questions. The scenarios they presented me with got even more ridiculous until even I couldn't take it. I had to discover what was going on. Not an easy task when my every move was watched by those men in black. I had to wait for the right night.

One fall evening, heavy winds knocked out the power to my lab, plunging everything into darkness. I seized the opportunity to crawl through a service hatch and found my way to a small closet with a window I was able to fit through. Pelted by rain, I walked backward through an overgrown yard, trying to glimpse the building that housed my laboratory. Thunder boomed and lightning tore open the sky, illuminating a great black box of a building. The tall pines bowed as the wind howled. In the darkness, I searched around me for some sign of where I was, but there was nothing. Just me, the storm, the building, and the bent pine trees.

A hand came down on my shoulder suddenly and I nearly jumped out of my shoes. I turned around to find myself face to face with one of the Men in Black, but he wasn't alone. Someone stood with him, another man in black. They were the same except this second man wore a bright band of white around his neck.

A priest? What was a priest doing out there?

"You shouldn't be out here, Dr. Bellamy," said the priest.

"I...my lab. The power went out." I tried to stammer through a decent lie, but I knew it was already too late. I would pay for my arrogance.

CHAPTER THIRTY

NOW

"Who was he?" It took all my self-restraint to keep from grabbing the dying doctor and shaking the answer out of him.

Bellamy shook his head. "I don't know. No one ever used names at the facility."

"The facility?" A chill ran down my spine.

He swallowed more dryness in his throat and licked his lips. "They closed that one down shortly after, of course, and moved me here, but there must be more."

"What does any of this have to do with Sean Yeats?"

"Don't you see?" He took two heavy, hoarse breaths. "They had me developing and testing these ridiculous theories. Only I was never really testing them at all. They were. On their prisoners. This organization—whatever it is—they're collecting people like you and your friend. But they're not killing them. No, they want something from the special people. They want to make you into their Men in Black. They want...to *use* you."

My gut instinct finally won out. I grabbed

him by his bloodstained white coat. "Why should I believe anything you say?"

He opened his eyes half-lidded. "You shouldn't. The proof...my laptop. My office. I was going to...expose them. They wanted to shut me down. Tried already. It's why I turned to using patients. I was out of time to play with theories and tests. Had to be now or I would lose him forever."

"Looks like you lost him anyway." I let him slump back against the wall and stood under the flickering light.

Bellamy nodded, exhausted, and then laughed, despite the pain it must've caused him. "It's funny, isn't it? That I who sought to conquer death will instead...be defeated...by it."

He was still. I thought he was dead until I turned my back and heard him call my name.

"Felix...ask the man you call Bishop X. He knows."

I spun around, but I was too slow. Bellamy let out a final rasping breath and his hands fell limp into his lap.

Maybe I should move him into a more dignified position, I thought, and quickly dismissed the idea. Doctor Thomas Bellamy had murdered six people, spent his life developing torture methods for some secret organization, and damaged countless others. That was to say nothing of the horrible thing he'd created that was now wandering the halls of Saint Dymphna's. He didn't deserve to die as painlessly as he did after what he'd done to Reuben, Mickey, Connor, and the others.

I pushed through the door, limping into a narrow basement hallway. Orange emergency lights flashed with the intermittent buzzing of the asylum alarm. The place would be on lockdown with the alarm going off, meaning it wouldn't be easy to get out. Maybe someone had discovered the bodies up on the ward I'd come from, or maybe someone had run into Connor.

I put a hand on the wall and used it as leverage to pull myself down the hallway. The first door on the right had been smashed in and hung on twisted hinges, creaking as it shifted back and forth slightly in some invisible breeze. It groaned as I pushed it open the rest of the way.

Inside, several gray fuse boxes had once been on the wall. Connor must've taken offense to their blandness and ripped them off. The ones he couldn't pull down, he smashed with a fist. Sparks flew from some of the boxes, lighting up the darkened room. So much for the lockdown. The asylum would be running on whatever backup generators they had, and those would fail eventually too.

How long would it be before someone came out there to lock the place down? Hours? Days? Weeks? If those men in black Bellamy had killed on the unit really were from some shadow government organization, someone would show up sooner rather than later, but it wouldn't be to lock the hospital down. It would be easier for such an organization to clean up the mess if some sort of accident killed everyone inside. They'd pass it off as a gas leak or a fire. Everyone would die, and any evidence of Bellamy's story and his crimes along with them.

I need to get into his office before that happens. I turned away from the electrical room and took in a sharp breath.

I wasn't alone in the hallway. A dozen ghosts had appeared, staring at me with their thin, emaciated faces. Their black eyes focused on me with an intensity that left me chilled to the bone. To make any sort of escape, I would have to get past them.

The one closest to me was a young woman with sharp cheekbones. She ran a pale tongue over her dry, dead lips. I pressed myself against the wall opposite her and slid by. She turned to follow me. The ghost of an old man stood in my way. He raised his head, opened his mouth, and showed me a mouthful of serrated teeth. The fat woman behind him burst into a fit of barking laughter that made me jump. She surged toward me, clicking her teeth. I flinched away and shuffled my aching feet a little faster.

Most ghosts weren't dangerous, but then most ghosts I'd encountered weren't in an insane asylum with a history like Saint Dymphna's. These ghosts hadn't been here before Bellamy turned on his machine either. With as much energy as he'd needed to power it, it must've been a beacon to hungry ghosts everywhere.

I didn't want to be eaten.

With more ghosts floating into the basement hallway behind me, I hurried my pace. The hallway felt endless, but it wasn't. Everything ended. Eventually, I would end too. It could've been that day, the next, or any other. One wrong move and I could wind up just like the hungry ghosts nipping at my heels.

The ghost of the old man from before suddenly grabbed my arm. I looked back into black eyes. Ghostly saliva dropped in thick strings from his teeth.

"So...hungry," he whispered.

I pulled my arm free and ran. Or, I tried to. With a bad back and Bellamy's drugs still working their way out of my system, the best I could do was limp faster. The ghosts, however, weren't impeded by physical pain. They rushed after me in a mass, arms reaching, teeth snapping and lips smacking.

"He's mine!" hissed one.

"I saw him first."

"There's plenty to go around!"

"Back off, bitch. I called dibs."

I kicked over a ceiling tile that had fallen, knowing it would do nothing to slow them down. There was nowhere I could go that they wouldn't follow.

A spectral form flew up from the floor in front of me. I threw my hands up to shield my face, but there was no need.

"This way," Poe said and darted to the right.

I rushed to catch up as he turned a corner. At the far end of the hallway, an open elevator car waited. It was made mostly of steel, a material which ghosts seemed to have an aversion to. I almost let out a relieved sigh, but I couldn't afford to slow down enough to enjoy my good fortune. I rushed for the elevator with the ghosts close behind.

A door opened just as I passed it and a hand reached out from it to grab my collar. I tried to pull away, but whoever—or whatever—had grabbed me had too good a hold. They yanked me through the door and slammed it shut behind me before I could react.

I spun around to see Sister Mary Sabina spread her fingers. An invisible shockwave of power shook the air and rattled the door in its frame. I waited for the ghosts to force their way through the door and the wall that stood between us, but everything had gone silent.

"S-Sister Mary Sabina?" I stammered. "What the hell was that?"

She turned away from the door, her expression hard. "We don't have time for long explanations, Felix. That will only hold them temporarily. We must get off this floor as soon as

317

possible." She marched past me and picked up a straw broom sitting in the corner, using the handle to move aside an access panel in the ceiling.

I finally got myself together enough to move. "You have powers."

"And so do you. So do many of us, though mine are quite weak." She got the panel open and tossed aside the broom in favor of a rickety metal step ladder. She moved the ladder under the opening and held it. "Up you go."

"Ladies first."

"I'm a nun, not a lady. Now get your rear up the ladder, Felix."

"Yes, ma'am." I knew better than to argue with her, and I wanted out as bad as she did, so up the ladder I went. There was still a decent-sized gap between where I stood on the ladder and the entrance to the access shaft. The only way to get up into it was to grip the sides and pull myself up. I didn't think I was strong enough, especially not as exhausted as I was. My arms still ached from whatever Dr. Bellamy had done to me, but I had to try. With a grunt, I lifted my body an inch. Two.

"Oh, for Heaven's sake." Sister Mary Sabina climbed up onto the first step and bent over, putting her back beneath my feet. It gave me the leverage I needed to get the last few inches.

The space above looked like a maintenance shaft. It was just barely wide enough to allow me to turn around and offer her my hand.

She took it and, between both of us, I managed to help her up into the tiny space.

"Thanks," she said, curling up slightly, trying to catch her breath.

I winced and put a hand on my aching lower back. "I should be thanking you."

"You should." She nodded. "The elevator you were running for is out. Went out with the primary power just like most of the rest of the doors in the facility." She gestured to me. "What happened to your eye?"

I put my fingers gingerly to the swollen eyelid and winced. "Dr. Bellamy happened. Tried for a lobotomy."

"I'm sorry. I didn't know."

"Can we just get out of here?"

The sister pointed behind me. "That way. Keep your head down."

I turned myself around and we crawled through the vents. Metal creaked beneath our combined weight and I was certain a panel somewhere would give out, but they held. "What happened?"

"I didn't see everything," she said. "I think I missed most of it. When I reported for my shift, the power was already out. I came down to investigate and..."

"Bellamy's little project succeeded. Sort of."

The vents behind me quit creaking as Sister Mary Sabina stopped moving. "He brought

Connor back?"

So, she had known what he was up to all this time. "Oh, he brought something back, but it wasn't Connor. That thing wrecked his lab, killed the patients that Bellamy hadn't managed to murder yet, and then eviscerated Bellamy. Would've killed me too if I hadn't been lucky enough to get knocked over behind some equipment."

She let out a long, deep sigh. "I'm sorry all of this happened to you, Felix, and I'm sorry for the small part I played. You were right. I forgot my purpose."

I reached a small crossroads in the vent system and paused, turning around and pulling my legs up so we could face one another. "I understand. I don't forgive you, but I understand your position. You lost a son and you blamed God. If you can't beat 'em, join 'em, right? Except you and Bellamy thought you could beat God at His own game."

She pressed her lips together in thought. "I believed in the work Bellamy was doing. If he had succeeded as he planned, imagine the world he would've made. A world where no one needed to fear losing the people they love. A world without the pain and suffering of loss."

"A world where you wouldn't have to bury someone else." I moved my forearms onto my knees and rolled my shoulders to take some of the pressure off my back.

Sister Mary Sabina lowered her eyes to where her palms lay flat against the bottom of the vent. "I was too weak."

"You were human. You made a mistake. A child died. Nothing you can ever do will change that, just like there's nothing I can do to change what happened to Sean." We sat in silence for a long moment before I said, "Dr. Bellamy told me a wild story about some shadow government and their torture facilities funding this place and his work. Is that true?"

She met my eyes and held them. "Of all the demoniacs you've helped, how many showed supernatural abilities?"

"All."

She tilted her head to the side, raising her eyebrows as she waited for me to draw my own conclusion.

"No. That's insane. Why?"

"Think about how the world works, Felix. What if someone with your abilities worked for the CIA instead of the Church? A well-placed operative can learn state secrets with a touch." She raised a hand as if to demonstrate. "There are some who can kill with their minds. Others who can be in two places at once. Some, like me, have minor telekinetic powers."

"They did this to you?"

She finally reached where I sat and pointed to the right branch. I hesitated, but slowly got back onto my hands and knees to progress. Staying in one place for too long would be dangerous with Connor on the loose and those ghosts looking for me.

"It happened while I was pregnant," Sister Mary said. "I let it in just like I let poison into my veins. I was easy prey, and I wasn't lucky enough to run into someone like you. After I lost my child, these men came to visit me in the hospital. Said they could help me get out. I was supposed to be admitted, you see. They thought I was insane. I don't remember the facility they took me to, but I bear its scars still."

"Why help Bellamy then? Wasn't he doing their work?"

She let out a bitter laugh. "Oh, he hated them as much as I did. I helped Bellamy because I believed in his work, and because I believed in him. He wanted to expose them. We had dedicated our lives to collecting the evidence we'd need to do that. It's all likely to be destroyed now, if it hasn't been already."

I grunted. "Helping him murder his patients is a funny way of getting there."

"Ahead, on the bottom. There's a panel like the one we used to get in here."

I stopped crawling forward and slid my palms over the cool metal, searching for seams. I found one a few inches ahead and slammed a fist into it. The trap door popped open, clattering to the floor. Beyond waited another hallway almost exactly like the one we'd just left behind, except this one ended in stairs, not an elevator.

I hopped down and reached up to help lower Sister Mary Sabina down as quietly as possible. Once she was down, she adjusted her clothing and I started for the stairs.

"Now all we have to do to get out is make it up one floor," I said, grabbing the banister.

"The front door will be locked."

I stopped on the first stair and turned around to frown at her. "But you said most of the locks failed when the power went out."

"Some, not all. The front doors and the exit doors to the CD unit are on a separate system that should hold, provided they're not directly damaged."

I shook my head. "CD unit?"

"Stands for criminally disturbed. It houses those with mental health diagnoses deemed unfit to stand trial, or with a sentence to serve." She lifted a key on a plastic chain from her pocket. "I have the master key, but…"

My stomach dropped. "But you want something in return."

Sister Mary Sabina stepped up to stand toe-to-toe with me. I was taller, but she was meaner. Ruthless, even. I harbored no doubts about her. "If there's any proof at all about the organization, it'll be on Bellamy's laptop. I can't make it to Bellamy's office on my own, not with all the patients running amok. I need someone to help me break into the place. I'd have preferred one of the orderlies, but you're what I've got. If you want me to unlock the front door, you have to help me get to his office to retrieve the laptop first."

With his dying breaths, Bellamy had told me the proof was there. Maybe what I needed to find Sean was there too. He seemed to think Sean might still alive, and if what Sister Mary Sabina said was true, maybe he was right. After ten years of searching, I couldn't walk away from an answer just a few floors above me.

CHAPTER THIRTY-ONE

We took the stairs two at a time. I paused on the ground floor landing, considering. I had promised the sister that I'd go up to the sixth floor with her, which was where Bellamy's office was. That was also where I'd find something, anything, that might point me to Sean...if there was any evidence at all. I still couldn't be sure this wasn't some elaborate lie by Bellamy and Sister Mary Sabina. They'd lied to me before, leaving me with no reason to trust them.

I could take the key from her, I thought, casting a glance behind me at her as she came up the last few. *I'm bigger, stronger, more powerful. It would take nothing for me to overwhelm her now that she's not surrounded by orderlies and armed with sedatives.*

She gripped the handrail and paused looking up to me, through me, as if she could hear what I was thinking. Her hand went to the key around her neck, closing it in a fist.

I turned away from the ground floor doors and started up the stairs. "What are you going to do after this?"

She dropped her hand to her side with a

sigh of relief. "Penance, I imagine, in one form or another, though I don't imagine they'll let me see the inside of a jail cell. I'd be dead long before sentencing."

Our footsteps echoed through the empty stairway. "Nothing you do will ever make up for the lives you helped destroy."

"Penance isn't an act of equal exchange, Felix. Didn't they teach you that in seminary?"

I shrugged. "I was never a very good student."

A door squeaked open somewhere above and both of us froze in place, turning our gazes upward. Bare feet padded across the floor followed by a guttural scream. A shape flipped over the banister of one of the upper floors. At first, I thought it might be a dummy. It didn't look like a real person. Not until he hit the floor at the bottom of the stairs. Empty eyes stared up at us, face twitching as a halo of blood spread behind his head.

Sister Mary Sabina and I exchanged a look.

"There's nothing you can do for him," she said and pushed past.

As we climbed, more noise rose above us. The murmur of voices became constant. Looking up, we could see a dozen patients or more had shuffled through the door into the stairway. Some leaned over the banister, staring at the dead man or us. Others paced back and forth, hugging themselves, whispering.

We slowed as we reached the landing where most of them were. I curled my fingers into fists, ready to defend myself if any of them attacked me. "Which floor is the CD unit on?"

"Fifth floor."

I nodded but kept my guard up. Just because they weren't criminals didn't mean they weren't dangerous.

Another door below us swung open violently. I rushed to the banister, shoving aside a skinny young man. One floor below, two men stumbled into the stairway. The first man was older and balding with scraggly strings of graying hair hanging down in uneven patches. The top of his head was bright red and beaded with sweat.

The other man wore the bloodstained scrubs of an orderly. Tears streamed down his face. He held his hands up, blubbering something incomprehensible.

"Shut up," growled the patient. He pulled his hand back and slammed his fist into the orderly's back several times, crimson blossoming wherever he struck. It wasn't until the third stab that my brain made sense of what I was seeing. He had some small, improvised weapon in his fist, one he was using to stab the orderly to death.

After a few stabs, he simply gave the orderly a push and he went screaming over the side to land atop the dead man below.

The killer looked up, straight at us, and flashed a yellow smile.

"Run." Sister Mary Sabina pushed me toward the next set of stairs. "Run, Felix!"

I turned and pushed my way through the small crowd that had gathered around us. Some of them didn't want to move and had to be physically shoved aside. Others suddenly became fascinated with our presence and reached out to grab us, giggling. I pushed their hands away and raced for the stairs.

After just two steps, something in my knee snapped like a rubber band with a resounding pop. I let out a surprised gasp of pain and fell. Dammit! Too much movement too fast. The sister stopped to pull me to my feet again, staring behind us.

The killer patient had reached the third-floor landing and shoved three others aside. One of the same patients that had been trying to grab us latched onto his arm. He turned and jammed his weapon into the other man's stomach, dragging it across in a jagged, bloody line before continuing toward us. Behind him, the dying man fell against the wall, trying desperately to contain the insides falling through the slit the other man had made.

The dazed patients latched onto the dying man, some out of shock. Others busied themselves pushing his hands away to get at his wound. One of them grabbed hold of a fat string of intestine pushing its way through the slit in his stomach. He threaded it out of the dying man like rope from a spool.

Maybe it was the sight of blood or the smell. Maybe man is just a predator by nature with the natural-born urge to kill, but once one started, they all jumped in on it, tearing the dying man apart.

I finally scrambled to my feet with Sister Mary Sabina's help and leverage from the banister, but there was no chance I was running anywhere. My knee screamed in pain with every step. I gritted my teeth and forced my way up the stairs, leaning heavily on the banister.

The killer closed in, just a few feet away. He paused once he realized he was going to catch us and showed off his bloody knife, drawing a finger over the small, thin blade.

I pulled myself up another stair. Another. I could practically feel him breathing on my neck.

The sister had already reached the fourth-floor landing. She waved for me to move faster, but there was no point. I wouldn't make it.

I turned around to face the killer.

Sister Mary Sabina's hand closed on my shoulder and jerked me back. She threw out her hand and released a concussive blast that sent the killer flying back into the crowd of dazed patients. They grabbed him, pulled him to the floor, and, still in their blood frenzy, started taking chunks from his body in handfuls and mouthfuls.

The sister turned away and practically dragged me up the last few steps to drop me near the door. She lifted the master key from around her neck and thrust it into the knob to unlock the door with all the force the killer had used to eviscerate his fellow man.

I found my feet. "This is the wrong floor."

"If you want to risk going past the CD unit unarmed, then be my guest. I'm stopping here for supplies." She cast a glance upward before shoving the door open.

I looked back at the bloody crowd on the third-floor landing and decided I'd better follow.

The fourth-floor ward was an empty shell of concrete pillars and hanging plastic. Wooden carts full of construction supplies sat around at uneven intervals. Pyramids of steel beams waited next to stacks of drywall panels. Wires hung loosely from the walls on small hooks. Several ladders leaned against one of the nearby pillars along with a rack of welding equipment and a circular saw. Moonlight came through naked windows in strips and slits.

Sister Mary Sabina went straight to one of the carts, searching through it for something suitable to swing at any other dangerous patients we encountered. The first cart she went to contained only a few nuts, bolts, and fasteners, plus broken bits of drywall and empty paint tins. She moved them all aside before she determined there wasn't anything of interest and walked deeper into the ward to access another cart. I decided that I'd better get a weapon of my own and limped over to dig in a toolbox near the circular saw.

As we were searching, we heard something rattle behind us. Both of us looked over our shoulders, watching as the doorknob slowly turned. Sister Mary Sabina patted herself down and lifted the key. She'd forgotten to lock the ward from the inside. Our eyes met for a beat. The doorknob clicked. We scattered to hiding places.

The sister pressed her back to a metal filing cabinet and slid into the shadow, barely visible. I found a place behind the saw and the cart. It wouldn't shield me from view if someone came too far forward, but as long as they didn't come past the door, they wouldn't see me. I hoped whoever was on the other side of that door just peeked in and went on their way.

The door gave a stuttering creak as it came open. I squatted in my hiding place, leaning all my weight to my good knee. Through the narrow space between shelves on the cart, I watched the killer from before step onto the fourth-floor ward. Dark, arterial blood streaked his face in glistening ribbons. It soaked his clothes, gluing them to his body. He swung the door closed behind him with a loud slam. With his arm outstretched, there were fresh bite marks visible in the exposed skin. Whole chunks of his flesh were missing, torn away nearly to the bone. I didn't know how he could still be up and moving and not curled up screaming in agony.

He lumbered forward, breathing heavy, eyes wild. "I know you're in here," he croaked out in a raspy voice. "I can smell you. Smells like..." Big nostrils flared with loud, slow sniffs. Teeth turned pink with blood flashed. "Fear."

I held my breath as he wandered forward, pushing over the closest cart. Nuts and bolts spilled onto the floor, flowing across it like water. One bolt rolled over to where I hid and bumped against my shoe.

"You know," said the killer, nudging the overturned cart with his bare, bloody foot, "I always wondered about you nuns. What you looked like underneath your modest little frocks. You call yourselves brides of God." He put his foot on the cart to steady it and gripped one of the wheeled legs. The wood groaned as he bent it. Nails protruded. Layers snapped into jagged edges. He hoisted the broken cart leg over his shoulder like a bat and closed on my hiding place. "I'm gonna fuck you with this knife, Sister, and then I'm gonna cut new holes in you and fuck those too until you stop moving. I'm your god now." He moved closer, sniffing the air like a hunting dog. Four more steps and he'd see me. No, three. Two.

I looked over at Sister Mary Sabina. She

pressed a finger to her lips and shook her head, a signal she didn't want me to break cover. But if I was quick, I could jump up, push the cart I was leaning against into him, maybe buy enough time for her to run for the door. With my sore knee and bad back, I'd never make it, but maybe I could knock him over, push him into those big windows, and pin him there.

I almost fell over as the circular saw near my head started up. The killer's profile was clear now. He stood so close, I could smell the blood and sweat on him. All he had to do to see me was take a half step forward and look down. I envisioned myself shrinking back into the shadows, becoming a part of them where he'd never see me, even if he looked straight at me.

He lifted his right foot to step forward.

Sister Mary Sabina threw herself from behind the cabinet with a war cry. A screwdriver raised above her head, she charged at the killer and jabbed it into his chest. His hand closed around her arm, twisted it, and yanked it down toward the saw blade. Blood sprayed the side of my face. The blood-spattered screwdriver clattered to the floor right in front of me while the blade sawed right through the first bone of her forearm. It wasn't strong enough to get through the second. Sparks flew and smoke rose. Sister Mary Sabina screamed bloody murder as the killer held her arm in place.

My fingers closed around the screwdriver.

I picked it up and jammed it into the killer's foot, finally thankful that it was Saint Dymphna's policy to take away patients' shoes. He let out a weak grunt of pain and released his hold on Sister Mary Sabina. She fell to the floor while I rose.

The last expression I saw on his face was surprise before I grabbed him by the hair and forced his face down on the saw. It smoked but it kept spinning so I held his head against it, putting as much downward pressure as I could. Blood flowed freely. He opened his mouth to scream and the saw caught on teeth, ripping them out by the roots and flinging them like bullets into the walls. I shifted my hands to the back of his head, pushing down harder. Chunks of flesh tore away. The smell of cooking meat filled the room. Still, I pushed. I pushed until I heard the crack of bone and the whole head shifted down as the saw entered his brain, bent but still spinning on a wobbly axis.

I let him go and stumbled back a step before my foot went down in a thick wet puddle and slid. My knee buckled and I went down to the floor next to Sister Mary Sabina. Her arm hung half off, spurting blood everywhere. Somehow, she was still awake and aware, holding her arm over the wound as if pressure alone would stop the bleeding.

In a panic, I searched the area for something, anything I could use to tie off her arm. The best option I could come up with was an extension cord.

"Don't trouble yourself. It's over for me," she said, rolling her head back and forth.

"Why would you do that?" My hands quaked as I wrapped it tightly around her arm above the elbow and tied it as tight as I could. Blood still wept from the wound with the steady pace of a heartbeat. "I can stop it," I promised. "I just need to get it tighter."

She hissed in pain as I tightened it further. "Leave it!" She pushed my hands away. "I deserve my fate. Take the keys."

I swallowed and shakily lifted the key from around her neck. "I can't take a confession, Sister, but I can pray with you if you'd like."

Her pale lips stretched into a small smile. She gripped my hand with the one she had left. "I'd like that very much."

And so, I held her hand and spoke words I hadn't in years to a God who, until that moment, had seemed so distant. Yet as I reached into my memory for prayers and verses, I could swear we weren't alone in the room.

Sean's hand closed on my shoulder. "She's gone."

"I know." I touched her cheek. She looked like she'd fallen asleep. "Do you think she's with her son?"

"What do you believe?"

I thought for a moment. "And Jesus answered him, 'Truly, I tell you, today you will be with me in paradise.' Christ forgave the sinner crucified next to him. Promised him Heaven even as they were dying. Maybe it wasn't too late for her."

I stood and turned around, but I was still alone in the room.

CHAPTER THIRTY-TWO

I moved Sister Mary Sabina's body out of sight from the door and covered it with plastic just in case Connor came by. He'd already proved he wasn't afraid of sticking his hands in corpses. I didn't want him to desecrate hers if he got the urge again.

Once she was out of the way, I resumed my search of the ward under construction, hoping I'd find a more practical weapon than the bent blade of the table saw. The screwdriver was still in the killer's foot. I wedged it free and cleaned the blood off using some paper towels I found wedged in a corner.

Armed and ready, I left the construction ward and carefully made my way back to the stairs. Two more floors up, I'd find Bellamy's office and the ward full of patients I'd been with. Between where I was and where I wanted to be stood the criminal unit. From the fourth-floor landing, I could already see the door up there had been knocked aside. It lay in two pieces resting against the banister. Maybe that was where the killer had come from.

I carefully crept up the stairs, keeping

low. The sounds coming from above and below weren't encouraging. Distant screams and slams echoed through the stairway. It was impossible to tell if the screams were from Connor eviscerating more patients, other dangerous criminals hurting them, or if what I was hearing were the normal sounds of the asylum. Whatever the case, the stairway smelled of blood.

I tried not to look down at what had happened to the crowd on the third-floor landing, but I couldn't help myself. A few were still alive, but they weren't in good shape. I locked eyes with a man who'd had his jaw torn from his skull. He was crawling away from a bloody scene, his tongue hanging freely as blood poured. The poor man wouldn't make it far, but there was nothing I could do for him. I couldn't help anyone down there. All I could do was get the information off of Bellamy's laptop and maybe help a few people from my ward find their way out.

I reached the fifth-floor landing and stepped gingerly around the broken door. Dark shapes shuffled around in the flickering hallway lights beyond. The inpatient ward door —which should have been locked, hung open and crooked on its hinges. One of the patients scraped his fingernails across the metal surface of it. When the light flashed on briefly, I saw the door streaked with red lines from his fingertips.

I shuddered and rushed past the door as quickly as I could.

My footsteps echoed in my ears as I rushed up the last flight of stairs. I kept turning around to see if the man with the bloody fingers had followed me, but the stairway was empty, despite all the sounds. Shaking, I slid Sister Mary Sabina's key into the door and turned it in the lock. I twisted the door handle and pushed but the door didn't move more than a fraction of an inch. I tried again, this time slamming my shoulder against it, but it wouldn't budge.

Dammit, something must be blocking it on the other side, I thought, shaking out my arm. But this is the only way into the ward. I flexed my fingers, thinking. No, there was another way. A back way. The way we came in from arts and crafts. I'd only been to the arts and crafts room two times during my stay, so I'd almost forgotten about it.

I didn't know how to get there from where I was though, which meant I needed to find a map of the building.

I turned around, hands on my hips. If I were a building map, where would I be? In the pamphlets probably, which meant admissions. That was on the bottom floor. My heart sank as I realized I'd fought my way up those stairs for nothing. I had killed a man and watched Sister Mary die, and for what? To find the door blocked with no way around but to go back the way I came? It was almost enough to break my spirit. Part of me wanted to sit down right where I was and wait for something else to happen. Yet I knew if I waited, it wouldn't be the police coming to deal with what had happened there.

I turned around and started back down the stairs.

When I reached the open door to the CD ward, I glanced inside again. The man with the bloody fingers was gone. All that remained of him were the red streaks he'd left on the inner door. For a moment, I wondered if I could cut through one of the wards and find a stairway on the other side. I had a general sense of where the door was, and it shouldn't be that hard to find it a few floors below. All the wards were replicas of each other. Hospitals were built on the whole concept of sameness. They weren't exactly architectural marvels.

I limped past the CD ward and the empty ward where Sister Mary's body was, down to the third-floor landing covered in blood. A woman who hadn't been there before stood near the open door but darted away when she saw me. I took a step and slid an inch or two in the blood before I caught myself against the doorframe. My lower back sent a jolt of pain up the left side of my body, letting me know it wasn't happy about the sudden stop. I grimaced and had to stand there a minute, waiting for the pain to subside before I could continue.

The hallway beyond was a replica of the sixth-floor hallway I'd been in a dozen times, except this one didn't hold Dr. Bellamy's office. The little room off to the side was a nurse's lounge. A handful of patients had already made their way in there. They stood in front of the open refrigerator, food and drink spilling out of it as they tore through the contents, gorging themselves on the sandwiches and sodas the nurses had brought for their lunches. One woman looked up at me, her eyes catching light from somewhere as she scooped melting ice cream out of a container and sucked it from her fingers. After a moment, she rushed forward to close the door.

I supposed if I were her, I wouldn't trust me either. There was no telling what kinds of criminals had gotten out of the ward upstairs, or where they might be. To her, I was just another dangerous patient, looking for someone to hurt.

I shuffled into the hallway, headed for the broken ward doors. I'd always wondered how sturdy they were. As it turns out, they were just doors like any others. Enough force and determination could break them down. Once the power went out, things must've gone downhill quickly. Patients attacking the staff, staff going after the patients. The remnants of the fighting littered the entry to the ward, a story told in blood. Two nuns sat by the door covered in blood. The eyes had been gouged out of one while the other nun's head was on the wrong way. Someone had snapped her neck like a twig.

A third sister hid, shivering under the desk with her knees drawn up.

"Sister?" I leaned down so she could see me more clearly.

When I reached for her, she screamed, pulled herself out from under the desk, and fled past me, nearly knocking me over in the process. She wouldn't be any help.

Once she was gone, I wandered further into the ward, searching for the door, but this ward was arranged slightly differently from the one I was familiar with. Some sort of exam room had been put in next to where the door was. I went to the stairway door first, but paused when I heard muffled grunts coming from the exam room next to it.

I put my hand on the stairway door. I should just go. Whatever's happening in there, it's none of my business. I can't help everyone. My fingers closed one by one, forming a fist before I pushed back from the door. *But I can help this one.*

I cracked open the exam room door just wide enough that I could see into it. It was dark on the other side, and since the room had no windows, it was darker than the rest of the ward. Shadows upon shadows. It took a moment for my eyes to adjust enough to see the two women inside. One of them was a nun that must have been on the unit when the power went out. She was face-down on the exam table, her head turned to the side facing me, her habit thrown up over her shoulders. Blood dripped from her mouth over a dried trail and her glassy, unblinking eyes told me she'd been dead a while, probably since the fighting broke out.

The other woman was shoving medication bottles into the nun, muttering something about taking some of her own medicine.

I turned away from the door, realizing there was nothing I could do.

"Wait!" Feet padded over the floor. The exam room door jerked open and a brown-eyed woman with messy hair peeked out. The same one who'd just been violating the nun's corpse. She smiled, then laughed and reached to touch my face. "Holy shit, you're real! You're fucking real!"

"You should get out of here." I eyed the door that led to my alternate route.

She moved between me and the door, stepping uncomfortably close and grinning too wide. "What's the hurry?"

"My hurry?" I looked back to the entry area where the dead nuns were. "There are dangerous people here. You could get hurt. People are dying. Don't you want to leave and go somewhere safe?"

"It's safe right here." She shrugged one shoulder while grabbing the bottom hem of my shirt.

I pushed her hands away and stepped back. "Quit that."

Her smile faded a moment. "Don't worry. We can still have fun even if it doesn't work." She leaned forward and whispered into my ear. "The nurses around here like to give people medications that don't make it work, but I know a special trick."

I took several steps back, but she advanced toward me, closing the distance with every step. My hip hit the edge of a table. I reached back to steady myself and almost dropped the screwdriver. "Please leave me alone."

"Don't be silly." Her wicked smile returned. She grabbed the waistband of my pants.

I brought the screwdriver out in front of me. "I don't want to hurt you."

"Oh, kinky." She pushed her neck up against the metal end while her fingers unbuttoned my pants.

I kicked her back and ran for the door.

She was faster. Fingers tangled in my hair and yanked backward. My feet went up and I slammed to the floor, back first. Pain exploded in my spine and in the back of my head, leaving me dazed. I forgot how to breathe.

While I was trying to remember, she climbed on top of me. "Now, where were we?"

I tried to roll to one side, but my back spasmed and wouldn't cooperate. When I tried to grab her by the shoulders and physically shove her aside, she pushed my hands back down. I wouldn't have believed a woman could be strong enough to snap someone's neck or hold a grown man down with one hand when I first came onto that ward, but after encountering her, I believed it. She was strong, stronger than I was, especially with my back in spasms. She only let me go because I quit fighting, which she responded to with the cooing, encouraging praise teachers gave kindergarteners when they colored inside the lines.

Flashes of Laura Hemlock came to mind, the way she'd used and abused me. At least she'd had the decency not to put her hands on me. I couldn't excuse Laura by rationalizing she was insane, just like I couldn't blame the woman trying to take advantage of me in that darkened hospital ward. It wasn't her fault her brain was messed up.

But I wasn't going to lie there and take it either.

She started to pull my pants down, still muttering praises.

I swung the screwdriver at her head. I'd intended to hit her hard enough to stun her, maybe knock her out. That would've been enough for me to get away. Instead, the blade slid through her skull with barely any effort and sank in to the handle. A surprisingly small amount of blood dripped down her face. Her eyes fluttered and her head shook until I pulled the screwdriver out. She slumped to the floor beside me, twitching.

I scrambled away from her, almost forgetting to pull my pants up and button them again. "I'm sorry! I'm sorry! I didn't mean..." I didn't think she could hear me. She wouldn't hear anything else ever again.

There's nothing you can do. It was an accident, I thought. At the same time, I couldn't stop quoting the sixth commandment in the back of my head. She wasn't the first person I had killed, or even the most brutal death at my hands, but she was the first person to die that I hadn't intended to kill. She didn't have to die, and yet she had. It was just a matter of being in the wrong place at the wrong time. I should never have looked into that exam room.

I blinked and found my cheeks wet. Though I was crying, I felt nothing. Not even guilt. Just shock at how easy she'd been to kill. So damn easy, it was almost automatic. What if I'd meant to do it all along? I had to have known I wouldn't just stun her with a strike like that. I should have felt something other than surprise and relief.

I scooted further away and put my hand upon another table to find some leverage to rise to my feet. The table tipped and I fell over. Another hand grabbed mine keeping me from falling over completely. I turned my head and found Poe standing there.

"They're coming," he said and pulled me

behind the tables.

Before I could scream, the crowd of hungry ghosts burst into the ward and swarmed the dead woman, swirling around her like a hive of angry bees. They bit into the dead woman's flesh, tearing away chunks of flesh one mouthful at a time. The dead consuming the dead.

Poe let me go but rushed in front of me, a finger to his lips.

I thought about the killer that had chased us into the ward under construction. He'd had bite marks all over him. Maybe the ghosts could eat the living too. I stayed hidden behind the table, listening to the sound of ripping flesh while Poe peered pensively out at the feasting ghosts.

Why was he different from the rest of them? The other ghosts were violent, hungry, starved. They weren't interested in interacting with me or anyone else except to devour them. Poe had tried in his own way to warn me from the beginning, even if his ability to communicate was hampered by how his mental health had suffered in life. He'd shown me what he wanted in every vision. He wanted to rest without being forgotten. Perhaps that's what made him different. Poe still had a very clear vision of what he wanted. These other ghosts only wanted to feed. They'd lost their humanity. No, they'd forgotten it, just as the outside world had forgotten him. Bellamy held onto the memory of who Poe—Connor—used to be, keeping it alive even after the body had died.

When the sounds died down, Poe guided me cautiously out from behind the table. There wasn't much left of the dead woman. They'd taken her face, broken off her fingers and pulled out her teeth. The only way to identify her body now would be through DNA.

I hugged myself and turned away from the carnage. "Why are they doing this?"

"They don't remember who they were," Poe said quietly. "Sometimes, we all forget."

"But you remember?"

He nodded solemnly. A long beat of silence followed.

"Why didn't you go back into your body when Bellamy turned on the machine?" I asked.

"That's not who I am anymore," said Poe.

I looked around as if I would spot Sean standing nearby. What about him? He wouldn't be the same person I'd known, not after ten years of whatever hell this organization had put him through. Not after spending all that time in his head with that demon. I'd had it in me for a few weeks and it nearly killed me. Was it possible he'd survived ten years? Sean would have to be the strongest, most willful son of a bitch on Earth to survive that and have any shred of humanity left.

I went to the door and unlocked it before pulling it open slowly. The hallway on the other side was bare but clear. A service elevator waited at the far end but just to the right of it was the door to a stairway.

"Your body is still walking around here somewhere. It's hurting people." I turned around to face the ghost. "How do I stop it?"

He shook his head and shrugged. "It's just a body. Kill it."

"I've killed a lot of people, Connor." I swallowed and tightened my grip on the door handle. "It's getting too easy to do." When he didn't respond, I glanced over my shoulder, but he was gone.

I sighed and stepped into the stairway, peering up. Two floors. That was all that stood between me and Bellamy's office. I was almost there.

CHAPTER THIRTY-THREE

The hallway where Bellamy's office waited was empty, the ward doors still closed. Maybe no one had come up to that floor. I tried to imagine the patients inside and how they might handle a sudden blackout. Not only that, but the murders that had taken place on the floor. They'd all been in their rooms on lockdown. It was possible they were still there. How long had it been? Surely long enough some of them had started to realize something was wrong, especially with the power out.

I imagined the rockers huddled in the corners of their rooms, their knees drawn up while they shook and rocked back and forth. Some of them covered their ears and wept. Others probably just curled up on their beds and fell asleep. There were at least a few on the unit that had probably started to pound on their doors and scream, but I couldn't hear them from the hall.

I should help them, I thought, and closed the stairway door tight behind me. To get to

Bellamy's office, I'd have to go through the unit. There was probably another way, but I didn't know it. I couldn't have them with me when I went into the office though, and I didn't know how I'd manage to escort fifteen or sixteen mental patients down to the exit, especially as much trouble as I'd had getting there. Perhaps the best thing I could do was leave them there and let someone else come help them.

I found the unit door and slid Sister Mary Sabina's key into the lock. It squeaked noisily when I pushed the door open. It was dark inside, just as the rest of the hospital was. The curtains had been pulled open to allow natural light through. Outside, fluffy gray clouds marched beside a nearly full moon, which gave the unit enough light that I could see my way around. There weren't any patients in the main area. Strange, but not unexpected if everyone was still in lockdown. But where were the nurses? The orderlies? The sisters who tended to the patients?

I stepped into the unit and the door closed slowly behind me with a click. The unit was quiet. No, not quiet. Silent. No murmurs from patients talking to people who weren't there. No pounding on the doors. No shouts for help, and perhaps most disturbing of all, no nuns or orderlies rushing up to me, demanding to know what I was doing there.

It was clear why when I arrived at the

nurse's station. Sisters Agatha and Glorianna had been on duty earlier. They occupied the chairs at the desk, or rather, their bodies did. Sister Agatha lay face-down on the desk in a congealing puddle of blood. Glorianna slumped backward in the chair, her glassy eyes fixed on the ceiling. The wall behind her head bore dark splatter marks. She had a single hole in the middle of her forehead. A bullet entry wound.

Who the hell had a gun in Saint Dymphna's? None of the patients, that was for sure. I didn't even think the security was allowed to carry firearms onto the property. I recalled seeing signs coming into the building that all firearms were prohibited on the premises. It wasn't impossible that some particularly ingenious patient had figured out how to create a gun, but not one that would fire multiple rounds. Plus, there was no sign of a break-in to the ward. The door I'd come through had been locked up tight. I checked the main door. It too was closed and locked.

Fearing the worst, I left the nurse's station and went back to the patient rooms. Silence rang in my ears as I pushed open the first door. There, I found the Chessman lying curled up on the floor, a single bullet wound to the back of his head. The way he was lying made me think he'd been made to kneel and shot in the back of the head execution-style.

I reached to turn him over.

When my hand closed on his arm, a wave of nauseating cold passed over me, taking with it all my fear, uncertainty, anxiety...everything I felt on a normal day vanished along with everything I'd been feeling since I walked onto the ward. The disconnected numbness I had felt earlier after killing the woman downstairs returned, but stronger this time. It was as if I had walked into a bubble devoid of emotion, where every sensation had been reduced to background data.

The room was sixty-eight Fahrenheit. The body's limbs were flexible, pupils dilated, and eyelids relaxed, placing death within the last hour. Pallor mortis wasn't yet pronounced, and the body's skin was slightly waxy, but not yet cool. It held a near-lifelike temperature. Given his proximity to the front of the ward, he must have been one of the first to die, but not so long ago.

It was both sensible and necessary to kill the sisters at the desk first, as they would have done whatever they could to stop the killer from completing his task. He approached quickly, drew his gun quicker, and fired off the first shot, hitting Sister Agatha first. Sister Glorianna had tried to reach for the phone, which earned her a shot in the forehead.

Even with a silencer, some of the patients must have heard the shots, maybe even recognized them. He had to move quickly. The patients had been trained to obey orders from the orderlies, so he used it against them, knocking on each door and pretending to be one, he ordered the people inside to their knees, facing away from the door. For their own safety, he claimed. Then, it was a simple matter of opening the door, putting the gun to their heads and pulling the trigger.

Fish in a barrel.

I pulled my hand away and gasped out a painful breath, nearly falling over as my own emotions flooded back into the icy void the vision had left. I stared at my clammy palm. Whoever had killed the patients on this ward wasn't some psychopath or random killer with a gun. He was cold, calculating. A professional. The organization was already trying to clean up their mess.

Bellamy's laptop! The evidence! I staggered back from the Chessman's body and rushed through the ward for the front door. My fingers shook so hard trying to put the key in the lock that I had to use both hands. I threw myself into the hallway, leaning heavily on the wall. My back and knees felt as if they'd give out at any moment, but I had to get to the office, had to get the laptop and get out of there. If I ran into the assassin, I stood no chance. Connor, too, was still somewhere in the hospital. It was only a matter of time before I ran into one of them.

I unlocked Bellamy's office and went inside, closing the door and locking it behind me. It wouldn't stop any assassins from following me, but at least I'd hear them if they came in. At least, I hoped I would.

I need a weapon, I thought, scanning the office. I'd left my screwdriver in the ward below, too shocked by what had happened to remember to pick it back up after it rolled out of my hands.

There wasn't much at the secretary's desk that would be useful. No staplers, no paperclips, no scissors. It was all probably locked up somewhere, which meant there had to be a supply cabinet somewhere in the office. I didn't see one out in the waiting area, so I went back to where Bellamy and I had eaten hot dogs together not so long ago. It felt like a lifetime ago, but it couldn't have been more than twenty-four hours. How much had changed since then, and quickly too. Now, he and Sister Mary Sabina were dead. I was running from some unknown assassin and an undead body without a soul with no one but a ghost for help, and I hadn't seen him for a while. He was unreliable at best, a figment of my over-stressed imagination at worst.

The supply cabinet wasn't in there, but I did find a set of fountain pens in Bellamy's desk. The metal nibs were sharp enough to pierce human flesh, especially in vulnerable spots like the eyes or the neck. If I ran into Connor, I didn't want to get close enough to try for one of those spots, so I searched for a backup weapon. The best I could do was the laptop charging cord which I found in the bottom drawer of Bellamy's desk along with the laptop.

I placed the laptop on his desk and opened it. The screen prompted me for a password. Dammit, Bellamy hadn't given me a password, and I didn't know where to begin guessing at what it might be.

Yes, I do. I leaned over the laptop keyboard and typed in Connor. The computer informed me that wasn't the correct password, so I tried another: Connor1982. Bingo. The login screen disappeared, and the desktop loaded. Now all I had to do was find the files he'd been talking about. For all I knew they were buried some-where, and it'd take a technical genius to pull them out. I was about as far from an expert on technology as one could get, but it was worth a try.

I didn't even know what I was looking for. It could be notes in a password-protected docu-ment, facts and figures in a spreadsheet, or com-plex diagrams. When I stumbled across the first video, it was by accident. I meant to click on the documents folder and accidentally opened the media player sitting next to it. It immediately replayed the last file that'd been opened.

The image on camera was of me sitting in front of Bellamy's desk the night we'd had our hot dogs. I had the dumbest-looking smile on my face. Bellamy was out of frame, but in the room. His voice asked, "And you've been in contact with this ghost since your arrival?"

"Poe?" I shrugged. "Sure, though he's not the only ghost here. There are tons. Tons, Doctor." I snickered as if it were the punchline of a joke.

"Study the picture. Are you sure it's the same person?"

I looked down at the photo I held in my hands as if I hadn't realized it was there before that moment. "They look a little different. Poe is skinnier. More scraggly looking."

"But they could be the same person?" Bellamy pressed.

"They probably are. Who is he?"

"Never mind that." Bellamy moved into the frame and took the photo away from me. The video cut off briefly after that but picked back up again after some time had passed. This time, the camera was focused on Bellamy who sat behind his desk, eyes sparkling with excitement. "This is it. I've found the catalyst I need. F.C. can communicate with the ghosts and spirits around the asylum, and he's almost certainly been in contact with Connor, which means it's highly likely that by connecting him to the machine, I can draw Connor's soul back to his body. This eliminates the fear that bringing Connor back after so many years dead will leave him fundamentally changed. I believe that the soul is the key ingredient that my previous experiments have been missing."

I stopped the video because listening to it was making me sick to my stomach. I didn't have to watch Bellamy's notes because I already knew what he'd done and why. That video didn't tell me anything I didn't already know.

I used the file information to track down the folder where the video log was stored and found more of the same organized by date. After scrolling through a few dozen, I picked one at random and clicked for it to play.

Bellamy sat down in his chair with a sigh and removed his glasses. He pinched his nose and sat in silence for a long moment. When he lowered his hand to address the camera, I saw the man in the video wasn't the Bellamy I knew, but a slightly younger version. I checked the date on the video. It was five years old.

"Torture," he spat. "That's what they've had me working on all this time. I knew…I knew when they came to me and still, I hoped. I prayed that the good I was doing would outweigh the bad. I thought to myself, 'Thomas, if they're torturing prisoners, what's it to you? They're bad people and you're saving lives.' But they're not. They're…" He trailed off and took a minute to compose himself. "I went to church. I listened to the sermons and took my communion. I thought I believed in God and the Devil. But demons?" He shook his head. "What I just saw changes *every-*

thing. Demons are real. Hell is real, and these people, they think they can control it?"

Bellamy leaned forward, gripping either side of whatever he'd used to record the video, adjusting its tilt. Satisfied, he continued. "The organization funding my research is kidnapping people who have had encounters with demons. In some cases, before their exorcisms are complete. No, kidnapping isn't right. They're buying these people. They have a budget for this, for buying the possessed from the Church. They take them to these...facilities where they subject them to physical and psychological distress in hopes of manifesting superhuman abilities. They're torturing them using methods I've been developing." He pointed emphatically to his chest as his voice rose and his face reddened with anger.

After an explosion of frustration, he rose from his desk. Somewhere off camera, something crashed and Bellamy shouted a string of curses. It was a long two minutes before he returned to his seat in front of the camera. "I can't stop. If I stop developing these techniques, they'll stop funding my research. Worse, I believe they'll expose me. No, they'll throw me to the wolves and pin everything on me. I refuse to go down for them. But once this is done, once I have Connor back, I'm going to tell the world everything. Over the next few weeks, I'm going to document everything. If they decide to kill me to keep me quiet, at least I'll have that. Someone will find it. The world deserves to know."

A click-bang sound made me look up from the computer screen. Was that a gunshot? Maybe with a silencer. I'd never heard one before, so I couldn't be sure. Whatever it was, it meant someone else was on the floor with me. Someone living. I snapped the laptop closed and tucked it under my arm. Whatever else was in those videos, I could watch it once I was safely out of the asylum.

With the laptop in one hand, the charger wrapped in a circle along with it and a fountain pen in the other, I carefully pushed open the door to Bellamy's office. Connor stood at the end of the hall near the ward doors, peering in. As soon as I saw him, I shrank back into the office, trying to decide what to do. His back was still to me. If I hurried, and if I was absolutely silent, he might not even know I was there. I could slip into the stairway and be long gone.

With my bad back and knee, what were the chances of that? No, I had to deal with him if I wanted to get past.

I carefully lowered the laptop to the floor. After Connor was dealt with, I could retrieve it and get the hell out of there before something else went wrong.

I wrapped the electrical cord around my knuckles, gripped the fountain pen, and stepped into the hall. Connor turned away from the ward when the office door clicked closed behind me. His nostrils flared, sniffing the air. He must've recognized my scent because his eyes widened, reflecting something like recognition.

"Connor, we don't have to fight." I raised my hand. "Nobody else has to die here."

If he understood me, he gave no sign. With a loud bellow that rattled the doors in their frames, he lowered his head and charged at me.

CHAPTER THIRTY-FOUR

If I had stood my ground, he would've broken me in half, so I dove for the other side of the hallway.

Unfortunately, I miscalculated how well I could move. My knee gave out halfway through the jump, which meant I threw myself into a belly flop flat on the floor. Connor's foot caught on me and he fell to the floor. I tried to push myself up. He grabbed my ankle. I fell face-first back to the floor. Connor grunted and climbed on top of me. Thin fingers wrapped around my chin and pulled back, bending my spine into a painful curve.

I gritted my teeth and clawed at his bare arms, tearing through skin and muscle. He let out a deep, guttural cry and let me go, but he was still on top of my legs. My fingers curled, digging into the tile floor. With everything I had, I pulled my body forward, desperate to be free, to get away.

Connor's fist came down in the center of my back with enough force to knock all the air out of my lungs. I tried to gulp air into them, but it felt like they'd never fill again. I blinked and tears fell. The sound that crawled out of my throat sounded more animal than human.

His hand closed around the back of my neck. I rolled to the side and wound up on my back. Good enough. On automatic, my foot shot out and connected with his chin. Pain shot through my foot and up to my shin even as he fell back in shock. I didn't have time for pain. I swung the pen at his neck, but Connor shifted at the last second and it went into the meat of his upper arm.

He batted me away, backhanding me hard enough it nearly knocked me out cold. I was still trying to work out what'd happened to me when he yanked the pen out of his arm and threw it at the wall. Connor's fist closed around my neck and he lifted me from the floor, squeezing. My pulse raced in my temples, the pressure increasing with every passing second. I thought my head would explode. I didn't know which hurt worse: my inability to draw a breath or the pounding in my head.

Somewhere deep in my mind, it registered that he was squeezing the life out of me. Just a little more pressure and he'd crush my windpipe. A little more and my cervical spine would crack. At least then the pain would stop. Then he'd snap my head to the side, maybe rip my head off. Connor didn't look like much, but he was abnormally strong. Whether that was because of something Bellamy had done, or his lack of humanity didn't matter. All I knew was that I was fucked.

Survival instinct kicked in and I clawed at his hands, peeling skin away with jagged fingernails. Still, he held me tight. I kicked and found only air. My eyeballs felt like they'd rupture any second. Bright lights danced in my vision like fireflies. Saltwater tears flowed in small rivers from the corners of my eyes.

The ward doors opened and a man in a black suit stepped into the hallway. I wasn't sure he was real at first because he looked too out of place, as if he was in the wrong time. A time traveler from the forties or fifties. Other than the impeccable neatness in his appearance, the only thing that stood out about the guy was how normal he would've looked anywhere other than a hospital on lockdown. I had the strange sense that I'd seen him on every busy Manhattan street, riding every subway, standing in line at every airport I'd been.

With all the casualness I'd use to get out my wallet, the man in black reached into his suit jacket and produced a nine-millimeter handgun with a silencer attached. "Hold still, please," he said, placing the gun to the back of Connor's head.

Connor froze in place, eyes dilating.
"Thank you."

There was a loud, airy sound, and chunks of Connor's brain and skull splattered over my face. His hands released me and we fell together, Connor with a hole the size of a bottlecap where his eye used to be. The bullet had bored straight through him and slammed dully into the wall behind me, just inches from my face.

I stayed on my knees, gasping in desperate breaths while the man in black tucked his pistol back into his jacket.

"Who the fuck are you? Why'd you kill him?" My voice was raspy and it hurt to talk.

"Who I am is of little importance. I killed him because I was ordered to." His tone was even, emotionless. The same voice a normal person would use to explain addition to a kid.

It finally struck me who and what I was dealing with. Bellamy's secret organization. The men in black that had wanted to shut him down. "You're one of them, aren't you?"

He stared down at me. "Where is Dr. Bellamy's laptop?"

I spat blood onto the floor, gripped the wall and pulled myself shakily to my feet. "I'm not telling you shit."

He sighed. "Then we can do this the hard way. *Where is Bellamy's laptop?*"

A tidal wave of nauseating power struck me as he spoke the last sentence. I doubled over, thinking I would vomit but nothing came up. I'd missed my last few meals. He tried to make me obey, just as he did to Connor, I realized. This was his power, his ability. Just as Sister Mary Sabina could push invisible waves of concussive force through the air, this man could order people to do anything he wanted, and they'd be compelled to obey. That's why most of the patients had just knelt and let him shoot them in the head. He must've ordered them to. So why wasn't I spilling the location of Bellamy's laptop? Maybe his powers didn't work on me.

I forced myself to stand up straight.

The man in black tilted his head to the side, confusion knitting his eyebrows together. In one swift move, he stepped over Connor's corpse, passing me by. I stood still as he pushed open the door to Bellamy's office and eyed the laptop sitting right there in plain sight. It would be a lie to say I didn't think about killing him. I still had the electrical cord wrapped around my fist. With his back to me, I thought maybe I could manage it. Maybe. But he had a gun, and I couldn't die, not now that I was finally on the verge of finding the truth.

"Tell me," I said as he retrieved the laptop, "is it true? Everything Bellamy said? Do you work for some secret shadow organization? Are there torture facilities out there trying to produce super spies using demoniacs? Is the Church in on it? Is Sean still out there somewhere? Or am I just a paranoid nutcase?"

"Yes." The man in black gave me a flat

smile, tipped his hat, and walked to the stairs.

I thought about following him. Wherever he went, that was where I'd find more answers. Then I looked down at Connor's lifeless body and thought about all the patients he'd executed, all to clean up Bellamy's mess.

Why had he left me alive?

The stairway door opened. The man in black held it. "Are you coming?"

"Where to?"

He gestured vaguely. "Outside."

I didn't know what else to do so I followed him to the stairs. "Is everyone dead?" I asked as we navigated the flight of stairs.

"If they aren't yet, they will be."

"Why didn't you kill me?" I paused on the bottom stair.

He turned around on the landing, expression blank. "I was specifically told you were off-limits. My secondary objective was to ensure your survival and escape. You do, of course, understand that you're not to speak of what happened here. If you make allegations, they'll be denied, your committal to a psychiatric hospital made common knowledge. I would think long and hard about the few people you love before you tell anyone what you know, Mr. Cross." He started down the stairs.

So, this organization didn't want me dead, but they'd taken Sean and they were torturing him somewhere. Why? Why had they singled me out? How had I even gotten on their radar? Before I was possessed, I was nobody.

Before you assisted X with his exorcism, you mean. I clenched my fingers into fists. Bellamy had suggested X knew. He'd singled Sean and me out that day in the classroom. Maybe it was for more than just the exorcism. We'd been marked somehow, and everything that had happened since was because he'd chosen us.

We reached the bottom floor without speaking to each other again. The man in black opened the front door and held it for me. Outside, the first signs of dawn had begun to color the black horizon in hues of crimson and indigo.

I hesitated in the doorway and looked to the man in black. "Where am I supposed to go now?"

"Wherever you like." He dangled a key fob in front of me. "You're free to pursue whatever you like."

"As free as Bellamy was?"

The corner of his mouth turned up. "Don't look a gift horse in the mouth, Mr. Cross. You have your life and your freedom, which is more than you had this time yesterday. Be thankful the only price you had to pay was your eye." He tossed the keys to me. I caught them on instinct. "Drive carefully, Mr. Cross."

I walked out into the parking lot with my thumb over the button, pointing it at random cars until an unassuming white Ford truck beeped. Whatever the organization wanted from me, they weren't going to get it. I would drive straight to Chicago, corner Bishop X, and find out what he knew. Bellamy wasn't the only one who could be creative when it came to torture.

I got into the truck and turned the key. The engine purred to life and the dashboard lit up, a glowing GPS display flashing in the center console. I typed in my destination. With luck and a prayer, I could be in Chicago by nightfall.

EPILOGUE

Bishop Xavier ducked under the line of yellow police tape and lifted a silk handkerchief to his nose. The motel—if it could be called that —reeked of sulfur and blood. After so many years of dealing with the possessed, he should've been used to the smell, but his nose never seemed to fully adjust.

Father Michael was standing just inside the door, chatting with one of the local officers the Church had on their payroll. Buying the police was easy enough, even if it was troublesome. There was always one holdout that still believed in justice and mercy. The officer standing with Father Michael, however, wasn't one of them. He raised his coffee cup to Bishop X in a toast.

"How bad?" X asked Father Michael.

Michael's lips sagged, his expression grim. "Bad. Does His Holiness know?"

"Not yet and not if I can help it." He hesitated, cringing beneath the handkerchief. "I'll need to see the bodies to be sure."

Michael nodded and gestured for him to go in.

Carpet squelched beneath his shoes. For

once, X was glad he'd picked out the old pair to wear for the day.

There were two bodies, a male and a female, unidentifiable at first glance, but X already knew who they were. No one from The Order went anywhere or did anything without someone else knowing. Even when they thought they weren't being watched, they were. He glanced over his shoulder to where the dirty cop watched him, but quickly turned away.

They had been skinned like rabbits. That must have made it difficult for the killer to get their bodies up on the hooks. X wondered if they'd been hoisted them into the neon light before or after their killer boiled their brains inside their skulls. A rosary with wooden beads hung from between the woman's hands. Fishing line tied them together as if she were praying. The man had been suspended in much the same way, which must have taken some doing. The only difference was his body was frozen with one hand outstretched as if he were blessing someone unseen.

Bishop X stared at the dead priest and the dead nun, friends both. Now, they were just meat upon which a message had been carved. Just in case everyone missed the clear message, their killer had written it on the walls in blood for them to find.

"I looked up the verse," said Father Michael, suddenly beside him.

X didn't need to look it up. It was one he knew from memory. "Vengeance is Mine, I will repay. The Lord will judge His people."

Father Michael frowned. "Is it one of yours? I thought they were programmed, X. They *can't* go rogue."

X's phone rang. "Apparently," he said as he fished it out of his pocket, "they can. X. Who is this?"

"You should get your affairs in order, Bishop," said a voice on the other end. "Mr. Cross is on his way to Chicago now. He'll be there within the day. Father Leon wants to know what you plan to do."

X looked up at the bodies whose heads were missing from the ears up, splattered in drying chunks on the bed where they'd been murdered. "Tell Leon we have a bigger problem. One of his psychic assassins has gone rogue."

Thank you for reading and reviewing Whispers in the Walls! Felix returns to hunt down an assassin in book three, Blood of the Lamb, coming in early 2021.

FROM THE AUTHOR

A year ago, a good friend and fellow author warned me about burnout and obsession. I've been going through a hard time in my life for a variety of reasons, which somehow makes it easier to throw myself into my work. When I started writing this book, it had been 18 months since my last true day off. Even when I wasn't writing, I was thinking about all the work I had to do, planning how it would go in my head. Otherwise, I was formatting, advertising, attending endless meetings and sending emails to contractors who help me make a book into a reality.

I kept telling myself that I was so close. One more book and I could afford to take time off. Just one more.

And then, on July 24th of 2020, as I was sitting in my bedroom, working on this very book, I got the news that my eleven-year-old dog had died. While I've never been much of a dog person, the news rocked me. I couldn't help but feel I hadn't spent enough time with her. In fact, I hadn't been spending time with hardly anyone. For eighteen months, I'd been locked in my office, writing book after book and failing to connect with people and pets alike.

Not only had I been working non-stop, but I was having physical symptoms of burnout: frequent stress headaches, exhaustion, insomnia, stomach aches. You name it, I had it. I almost didn't want to write at all anymore. All the enjoyment had gone out of the job.

It was at this point that I realized I was writing myself a cautionary tale. Whispers in the Walls is a tale about the abuses that one can undergo as an inpatient in the mental health system. (I myself experienced some abuse while seeking help.) But it's also a sort of fable outlining the dangers of defining yourself only through your talent or your work. Bellamy becomes obsessed with saving a lost loved one. Al dies because he's unable to fathom a world beyond the right now, and his failure to connect with people. Both are destroyed by their own creations. In a way, I felt as if my creations were destroying me too.

It's easy to forget some days that I'm supposed to like my job. Yes, there will always be aspects that I don't enjoy. I'll never love formatting paperbacks, for example, or endless email chains between editors, audio narrators, and cover designers. Those are just part of the job. The act of creating, of putting words down, however, is supposed to be something I enjoy. It was fun once. It can be again.

This has been a tough year for everyone, but for creative people especially. To create, we absorb the world around us and process it through a series of what-ifs. To make fiction, we still have to be aware of what's going on in the world and how our modern audiences will receive what we write. I also happen to be living in a county with a very high number of coronavirus cases and a large number of people who don't take it seriously enough to wear a mask or stay home. I'm frustrated by my fellow humans and their disregard for the lives of my husband and child who both have compromised immune systems. That frustration has worn me thin.

That's not to say I didn't enjoy writing this book. There were parts I loved. Parts that tugged at my heartstrings or gave me a little more hope that tomorrow could be better. Those parts reminded me why I do this and what I love about writing.

As much as I don't want to do it, I think I'm going to take some well-earned time off after this book to rediscover my passion for writing. If you feel yourself worn out, burned out, and losing faith, I hope you're able to take some time to focus on you and what you love. I sincerely hope that you find your passion, and you're able to hold onto it, especially in these dark times.

~E.A.

THE FELIX CROSS SERIES

Shadows Over Hemlock

Whispers In The Walls

Blood Of The Lamb

Sins Of The Father